A Fr

CW01513253

Adventures of a
Jump Space Accountant

Book 8

Andrew Moriarty

Andew Moriarty

This is a work of fiction.

Names, characters, businesses, places, events and incidents are either the products of the author's imagination or used in a fictitious manner. Any resemblance to actual persons, living or dead, or actual events is purely coincidental.

Special thanks to my dedicated team of beta readers – A J, Adam G, Aleeta, Alex, Barbara M, Bryan, Christopher G, Chuck B, Daniel C, Danny H, Dave M#1, Dave W, David H, Djuro D, Elizabeth S, Gary L, Greg D, Haydn H, J Anderson, Jim C, John E, John K, John S, Jolayne W, Justin H, Keith C, Kent P, Lorna, Mark H, Michael G, Michael R, Nathan T, Penny L, Peter B, Ralph J, Robin C, Ross C, Ryan P, Sally S, Scott, Scott M, Simon, Skip C, Susan G, Terry H, Tigui R, Vince P, VJL, Wolfgang R, and to my editor Beth Lynne.

Chapter 1

Accounting Error slid silently past Delta's jump limit en route for Rim-37's orbit. Jake had jumped them in beyond any of the orbital stations, even outside of the Dragon's magnetosphere, counting on *Accounting Error*'s better shielding to protect them from the hard radiation beyond the jump limit. He'd minimized their comm traffic, sending only directed messages.

"Good thing we have our shields. The radiation out here is deadly," Jake tapped his screen. "If we were on a Militia cutter or a regular freighter, we'd be in trouble. We're getting bombarded with billions of energetic particles every second. The *Flandre* wouldn't have lasted an hour this far out."

The *Flandre* was their jump freighter, left behind with the rest of their crew in the last system. It was a hundred times more massive than *Accounting Error*, one quarter as fast, stuffed full of trading goods, and refueling it was like using a hand laser to melt an asteroid. They'd tethered it to an icy comet, but without a proper fuel processing system, it would be weeks slurping ice before it could jump again.

"Why is it so dark, Jake?" Nadine gestured at his console. "I can barely read that."

"I was trying to figure out loading options for trading packages. I had all the screens running. The dark is quiet. It helps me think." *And I don't understand the coded transmission I got from Dashi. Transfer of assets? An inheritance? Read Roi's report closely? Why is he transferring assets to me? Why should I check out Roi's reports? And why isn't he answering my comms? Did something happen to him?* "I forgot to turn them up when you came on watch." He pushed the slider. "Better?"

Nadine nodded. "Thank you, temporary admiral and high muckety-muck Mr. Stewart, for lowering yourself to take into account your humble crew's requests." Jake had led a diplomatic mission to the planet Magyar and had been made a temporary admiral for the duration.

"That was temporary, Nadine. Once we get back, I'm just Jake. And you're never humble."

"Why should I be humble? I'm awesome!" Nadine grinned. "But I'm always more cheerful in the light. Darkness is depressing. The less time we spend out here, the better. Let's get out of this radiation bath."

"Not until we have more info on the current situation, Nadine. And it was your idea to get information first. Sneak in. Make sure nobody beats us back. To be safe."

Nadine sighed. "Yes, but I forgot how boring safe is. Stewart, we haven't seen any pirates since we left Magyar. That was a month ago."

"There was that one reading—"

"It was a ghost. They would have caught up by now. They're gone. We chased them away. And we're not even sure the ship was a pirate."

Accounting Error and her crew had bluffed a hostile ship away from the planet Magyar four jumps ago without identifying it.

"I don't know that they weren't." Jake took another sip of basic. *Could have been pirates. Could have been an armed Free Trader. Could have been part of what's left of the Imperial Navy. We can't gamble either way. If they followed us back here, things could get bad.*

Nadine slurped up the last of her food tray's contents, grimaced, and tossed the empty tray in the recycler. "That was awful. I think you Belters had your taste buds removed surgically at birth. Can we at least sneak in closer to somewhere we can get a decent meal?"

"We've got plenty of trays. And basic." Jake gestured at the cloudy liquid filling their cups.

"This Basic is sooo vile." Nadine slurped up some liquid from her cup, then spat it back. "You'd think space trader types as rich as us could afford a better quality of drink powder." Basic was recycled water mixed with powder. The powder had sugars, salts, vitamins, minerals, half a day's worth of calories, and a horrible taste. "Smells like a thruster control line popped and leaked propellant into the main cabin." She scanned the repeater system display over the aft hatch. "No fuel leak, so what I'm smelling is what this is supposed to taste like."

Jake didn't respond. He brought another spreadsheet up on his screen and examined it.

Nadine gulped the last of the basic, grimaced, and tried another tack. "This is stupid, Jakey, we're too far out to do any trading. We're in the middle of nowhere. The butt end of the rings. Only things out this far are the dregs of humanity, thieves, degenerates, and people who marry their cousins."

"This is my old neighborhood. We could rendezvous with my old station, Rim-37, and visit if you were bored."

Nadine rolled her eyes. "That's exactly what I mean. The one time I was on your station, whenever I shook hands, I checked for webbed feet."

"How would you check for webbed feet if you were shaking hands?"

"Because for you Rim people, they're probably the same appendage."

Now it was Jake's turn to roll his eyes. "We're not all freaks, Nadine." He turned back to his console. *We're poor, uneducated, unsophisticated, and some of us are lazy. But that's no reason for the corps to take advantage of us like they did. Well, now it's my turn. The mag-boot is on the other foot.*

"Can't prove it by you. Weird math-loving person. You spend more time looking at spreadsheets than you do looking at girls."

Jake kept his mouth shut. There had been an embarrassing incident earlier, when Nadine said she 'wanted to teach him a new trick'. *Just because I wanted to pause to write down something doesn't mean I wasn't interested in what we were doing. I didn't want to forget her instructions, that's all.*

"In fact, I even raided the cargo and get us an extra jar of soy sauce, since we used up the whole last one, but—"

"I had to write something down, that was all. Changing the subject, the news is bothering me," Jake said. "Or the lack of news. There's this new Senate elected while we were gone, there's no news about Dashi, and there're fewer Free Trader ships than before."

"You counted the Free Trader ships?"

"I counted every ship in the system." Jake played with his display. "And categorized them, plotted their courses, and tried to get an idea of their cargo."

"Of course you did."

"Dashi hasn't answered my comm. I've got a private code for him, and he isn't responding. What did the admiral say when you called him?"

"I never called the admiral."

"Of course you did."

"You told me not to."

"When do you ever listen to me? Tell me what he said."

Nadine frowned. "We don't need the admiral. We've got the best trader in the galaxy right here, according to you. And all I need is to keep an eye on you to make sure nobody shoots you. Need to guard my investment."

Jake locked his board. "He hasn't answered you either?"

Nadine shook her head and pursed her lips. The admiral was the former head of the Delta Militia. Also, her grandfather. "We don't need him."

"We need somebody."

"You've got your friend, Dinner?"

"Skimmer," Jake said.

"He's helping us. Rounded up a tug, you said."

"He did that. Or he'll do it."

"Would he be able to do that during some sort of system problem? Some sort of political problem?"

Jake frowned. "He's so out of it most of the time, he wouldn't notice if the station was on fire. He can't even spell political. And Rim-37 isn't exactly in the mainstream of anything."

"Well, he got us a tug, right?"

"He said he did," Jake said. "One problem."

"Which is?"

"It's supposed to be here now." Jake checked his board. "And there's nothing nearby. He stood us up."

Nadine stood and stretched, then shook the bottle of soy sauce. "Well, if it's just the two of us, I know what we can do while we wait."

Skimmer arrived four hours late, parked his tug next to *Accounting Error*, and free-jumped over. He gave Jake a bear hug when he cleared the airlock. "Sorry I'm late. I had to stop to take a smoke break, Jake."

"Skimmer…" Skimmer was a childhood friend of Jake's. He was short, stout, and often forgot to wash. He didn't like math, and his reading skills didn't extend beyond the label of a whiskey bottle. But he was tough, loyal, and he and Jake had been piloting tugs and barges together since grade school. Sometimes even with the owner's permission.

"Cargo ship came running into port. Free Trader, from one of the drop stations. Needed fuel badly. They traded hard for it. I got me three cartons of the good stuff."

Jake and Nadine had drifted on an un-powered orbit, waiting, pretending to be a hole in space. A silent hole. One orbit later than expected, Skimmer had shown up with his tug. "Knew I'd missed you, so didn't bother to chase," Skimmer said. "I knew the orbit would circle back."

"Glad you didn't broadcast your delay to the whole system."

"No problem, Jake," Skimmer shrugged. "Silence is Goldman, right? And my long-range comm is broken, so I couldn't do that."

"Silence is golden, you mean," Nadine said.

Skimmer shook his head. "Golden? No, Goldman. Dave Goldman. Works at the caf at the station. Never talks, quiet guy. When you want to be quiet, you don't talk, like Goldman."

"Show me your hands. Spread your fingers. I want to see—"

"Not now, Nadine," Jake said. "Glad you made it, Skimmer."

"What you want to do with these containers?"

Jake split his cargo across four containers. His plan was to offer one each to the two largest corporations, one to a Free Trader's ship, and one to a crooked Militia officer—it wouldn't be hard to find one. Skimmer would take care of the delivery. Rim-37 wasn't much of a station, but they'd been spiraling cargo into the inner belt for fifty years. They knew how to launch a container into orbit to intersect somebody. Jake explained his plan.

"And I'm getting my money?" Skimmer asked.

"Half now, half when all the containers are popped," Jake said. "As agreed."

"Always knew I could count on you, Jake," Skimmer said. "You're pretty cheerful, considering."

"Considering what?"

"Considering what happened to your friend."

"Which friend?"

"Your friend Dashi," Skimmer said. "Didn't you know? He's dead."

"We'll be at the dock soon, Jake," Nadine said. Jake had been so shaken, she'd had to pilot them to Skimmer's rendezvous. He'd questioned Skimmer over and over, but the story hadn't wavered. Dashi was dead. He'd heard it on the news. No other details.

"It can't be true." Jake slumped in his chair. "He should still be alive." He tapped his screen. Then again.

He kept banging it until Nadine grabbed his hand. "Let me." She shut down his screen. He'd started a dozen new spreadsheets since the news, but abandoned them all. "Skimmer says he's dead. And now that we know what to look for, we found the news."

"He was like a father to me." Jake blinked back tears. "Like a father." *Better than a father. He gave me a chance when nobody else would.*

"Better than some real fathers," Nadine said. "And I guess you didn't get the rest of the news."

"What rest?"

"Dashi wasn't the only one who died in the fighting. Lots of Free Traders, including our friend Marianne, Jose's girlfriend."

"Marianne?" Jake tilted his head. "The Free Trader? No loss, not compared to Dashi."

"And one other person died."

"Who?"

"The admiral."

"Admiral Edmunds? your…." Jake knew Nadine didn't like to talk about him. "Your grandfather? How?"

Nadine slapped the controls, but her voice was level. "I'm still trying to find out more. He was poisoned, same time as Dashi."

"The news said Dashi died. Didn't say anything about poison."

"Well, I've read some other news. I have other friends who kept an eye out for me. It could have been Jose who killed him. He was in the room with Dashi and the admiral when they died."

"He was? Who else was there?"

Nadine slapped another control. "Marianne. And Shutt."

"All three? Do they…?"

"News says officially they don't know. Unofficially, Jose blamed Marianne. She's dead. Justice served."

"Do you believe him?"

"Nope." Nadine shook her head. "This is too convenient for Jose. His boss, dead. His biggest rival, dead. The head of the Militia, who hated him, dead."

"Well, who…"

"We'll find out." Nadine snarled. "We'll find out. But one more thing, Stewart."

"What's that?"

Nadine slid a knife from its forearm sheath, spun it across her fingers and rammed it back in. "Until we find out exactly what happened, we're keeping to ourselves, and we're not going anywhere near the inner system. We don't want to make it any easier for Jose. With Dashi gone, there're two people who could run TGI- his assistant, Jose, or his number one troubleshooter, Jake Stewart. And I don't want to get too close to Jose, cause he may decide he wants to up his chances."

Chapter 2

"Jake, this course sucks." Nadine hammered her board. "Stupid universe."

"Yes," Jake said, "it does. It's the wrong course."

Nadine glared over her shoulder. "No, I mean seriously, it sucks. We're going to the wrong spot." They sat side-by-side at *Accounting Error's* control station. Skimmer and Jake had loaded up four containers of mixed goods and hid them in Rim-37's floating junk farm. Jake kept small quantities of samples, but dumped all the other containers in an orbit known only to Skimmer and him. Now they were creeping in-system for their first clandestine sales meeting.

"Remember, our database is out of date by 50 years?"

"But you updated that at Magyar."

"I did. Which only brought it up to the last time they got something from the Empire—which was 50 years ago, when Imperial ships moved through. We're up to date for the rest of the galaxy, at least the Imperial Galaxy, but we don't have the latest mappings from here."

"You made me drive this course. This out-of-date course? Anything could have happened. We could have run into a comet."

"You said you're an amazing pilot, so I'm counting on your amazing piloting skills to amazingly pilot us where we need to go. And comets are easy to avoid."

"Fine." Nadine slapped the board. She'd done a lot of slapping since she'd heard the admiral had died. "As simple as changing the jewelry on an outfit. A slight adjustment, but a big effect."

"Why were you complaining?"

"Because I wanted to yell at somebody. I'm angry."

Nadine and Jake exchanged looks. Their reactions to the deaths—of Dashi and the admiral—had been varied. Nadine exhibited screaming anger, followed by a smoldering fury. Jake had initially been disbelieving, and then had quieted to an icy calm.

"I don't want to be out here," Nadine said. "I'm going to go in and stab whoever killed my grandfather." Her hand strayed to a sheath, then drifted back.

"Fine with me," Jake said. He brought up another spreadsheet, his seventh in the last hour, and turned the cabin lights down. "Who did it?"

She closed her mouth. "I don't know. Probably Jose."

"Prove it."

"I don't need to." Nadine reached for her board and pulsed the cabin lights to max. "I just know."

Jake shaded his eyes from the glare. "What if it wasn't Jose? Don't you want to stab the right person?"

"Don't you want to do something about Dashi?"

"Yes," Jake said. "I want whoever killed him to die."

"See? So we should go to Landing."

"And do what?" Jake spread his hands wide. "You don't know who killed your grandfather. I don't know who's responsible for Dashi's death. We need to find out what's going on first, and do some trading."

"Trading. Don't you have any emotions? Don't you have any feelings? Aren't you angry?"

"I'm angry, Nadine," Jake said. "But I don't run and scream and yell and shoot people. That's not my way. As soon as I have enough information, I'll let you know who to shoot. Or stab, whatever you want."

"You promise?"

"I promise." *Dashi would want me to ignore who killed him and get on with saving the empire. I'll do that. But that doesn't mean I can't let Nadine have some fun first...* "Have I ever let you down before?"

"Many, many times."

"Let me rephrase that," Jake said. "Have I ever failed to execute my plans before?"

"You always execute your plans, but they never work for me."

"And inevitably, whose fault is that?"

"Usually mine." Nadine grimaced and pulsed one thruster. "Fine. Figure out who these people are, track them down, and I'll stab them."

"You don't have to kill them, Nadine. Not directly. It's enough that they are punished."

"I want to do the punishing personally."

"It's not necessary."

"It is for me. This is non-negotiable, Jake. Either I'm willing to wait for you to hunt them down, or I'm the one who gets them. You don't promise me that, I'm going to go on my own."

Jake looked at her. "What would you do?"

"I'd spin this ship on its Y-axis, head straight for Delta orbit, dock at one of the stations, and take the first shuttle down. Then start shooting people until somebody answered my questions."

"A better order of operations," Jake said, "would be to ask the questions first and shoot later."

"You've got your methods, I've got mine. I'm willing to wait for your super brain and smarts to sort this out, but I want my revenge."

"Served cold?

"What?"

"Never mind. Classical reference. But we have to account for unforeseen circumstances. I might not be able to give you exactly what you want."

"Not good enough, Jake," Nadine said. "You always get exactly what you want, eventually. I don't know how you do it. You organize it, you plan it, you change things, you manipulate things, but you always get what you want. This time, I get what I want. I want you to promise."

"What sort of promise will you accept?"

"On the soul of your dead friend, Dashi."

Jake blinked at her. Except it wasn't a blink, it was a tear. He took a moment to control his voice. "All right, I promise on Dashi's soul—you'll get what you want." *I wasn't here for him when he needed me. This time I won't let him down.*

"Good." Nadine slapped her board again. "Now, where are these Free Traders?"

Jake organized a meeting with the Free Traders. He'd given Skimmer briefcases of samples—linen, denim, cotton, wool— all the different things that came from Magyar. He told Skimmer who he wanted contacted, and to have the sample cases sent coreward. Skimmer knew a cook on a Free Trader that was passing through. He arranged to have her send one to a contact at a drop station. One of the station tugs owed him a favor and was willing to dock with a passing corporate ship and transfer one. The others went similar routes, hand to hand. It took two days, but delivering contraband from rim stations was a lucrative sideline for ship crews. And they knew better than to ask questions.

Jake expected a bidding war, so he included a message that he had these goods to sell in "considerable quantities", and he expected payment in mixed metals.

"If anybody asks, I want a little of everything," Jake told Skimmer. "All sorts of things—copper, zinc, selenium."

"Got it," Skimmer said, and went off to arrange the meetings.

"Do you trust him?" Nadine asked after Skimmer had left. "He's got all our best samples."

"Trust him? I mean, you know, generally. He's one of my oldest friends. He'll stop for smoke breaks, but it'll get done eventually. You have to be patient."

"He's going to get those boxes delivered to the people you asked? Without anyone else finding out?"

"Oh no," Jake said. "He's already screwing that up. The Free Traders will know all this in a day. The Corps in two days. Jose in three at the latest. They'll know exactly what type of things are on offer, know exactly where those shipments came from, and they'll have a good idea of what I want in return."

"So why hire him?"

"Because they have to find us. One thing Skimmer won't tell them is where to find us."

"He's reliable under torture?"

"What? No, he has horrible math skills. He has to navigate by sight. The only way he got to that meeting was to go and rendezvous at an old station we used to prospect from. He knew how to get there—he had the course written down somewhere. Complete rote piloting. Without the course already calculated in, he'd have no idea how to get anywhere, and he has no idea where we came from." Jake brought up another spreadsheet. "And in the meantime, we gather information on what happened here."

Chapter 3

"There's a hit out on you." Chaudhari pushed the wooden stud into place. "You know, a contract?"

"All I know," Sergeant Russell said, speaking through the nails he held in his teeth, "is that if you move that brace again, the one getting hit will be you, with this hammer." Chaudhari and Russell stood on a dock where the Landing River ran into the ocean, or at least an estuary. They took turns holding wooden beams upright and hammering them together into a frame.

"A hit. A contract. The Free Traders have spread the word, they'll be happy if you die."

Russell hammered a nail in and reached for another. "What have I ever done to them?" He sniffed. "It smells like a thousand troopers crapped in that water."

"Tidal flats." Chaudhari gestured at the river, where the rapidly draining tide was exposing large swaths of muddy bottom. "The mud stinks."

"The shore stinks too. You stink too, for that matter."

"That's the rotting seaweed. What haven't you done to them? You supported the rebel Militia during the uprising, occupied TGI main, and imprisoned their members. Then you fought around the Shuttle landing, attacked and boarded occupied ships, oh, and killed their number one Senator girl, Marianne."

"But other than that…"

"They're out to get you."

"That all was by accident," Russell said. He hammered a nail.

"They don't think so. They think you did it on purpose."

"If I did, it was just work, it wasn't personal." Russell grunted. "Not that she didn't deserve to be killed, but I only do that when I'm told."

"They think you enjoyed it too much."

"Did not." *Did too. I enjoyed it a lot.* "Besides, it was Senator Jose's fault. He gave me the fake bullets." Russell hammered another nail. This one bent. He cursed and pulled it out.

"They don't believe that either, they think you planned it."

"Chad, I'm a grunt. A foot soldier. I run squads and smoke too much. Do I look like the type to arrange a political assassination?"

"Doesn't make any difference to them." Chaudhari stepped back and wiped sweat from his face. "These wooden beams are heavy."

"No, you're a wuss." Russell helped him shove another into place, then tacked it up with four small nails. The beam was pre-drilled for through-bolts. Russell fished in a bag at his feet, brought out a long bolt, slid it through and threaded a nut and washer. After hand tightening the nut, he produced a wrench and ratcheted it in harder. "Have to be heavy to handle the cargo." Russell strained on the bolt.

Chaudhari sneezed, then wiped the snot running down his face onto his arm. "I'm hot, I'm bothered, and I'm allergic to seaweed stink. This is no job for a Senator."

"Here you're just a corporal." Russell wiped the sweat from his own face. "Hotter than my old girlfriend after three drinks." Delta was in the warm part of its two month seasonal cycle. That meant higher tides and stronger currents, which let the ships they used move faster when they could take advantage of them. But it also means hotter weather and frequent, draining, humidity.

"Can't we use power tools?"

Russell gestured at the wooden dock. The rickety pier that extended into the river was used by small shippers and smugglers who sailed up the river with the tidal bore. This was as close to Landing as you could get. Unless you wanted to climb up a waterfall at low tide, or get battered to pieces on the rocks by the onrushing tidal bores. "You see any power here?"

"Batteries."

"Batteries don't last forever. Where would we recharge them?"

"Take them into town—right, can't do that. They all have corporate markings." Russell and his troops had 'liberated' piles of corporate equipment from stations cutoff when the monorail was damaged. The corporations had retreated to Landing because keeping them open without the monorail operating was uneconomic. Russell and his crew had marched in, occupied the empty factories and kept them running. They now brought in supplies and took out goods on a schooner captained by their friend Balthazar. He arranged with his friend, Senator Vincent Pletcher, the purchase and exchange of necessary supplies. They used their 'liberated' tools and equipment as necessary.

It wasn't illegal. Not entirely.

"The less the corps know about what we're doing out east, the better." Russell twisted the wrench, pulling the bolt tight. "Right you lot, supports are up, get that wheel in here."

Members of Russell's squad swarmed over the framework, and rolled an eight foot tall wooden wheel with metal axle down off the ship and onto the dock. After a dozen heaves, the wheel clicked into place onto the frame, and the squad snapped steel caps down to hold it steady. Then they brought shaped wooden beams along and fitted them onto guides on the front.

"Where are the squirrels?" A voice behind them asked. Vincent Pletcher, a Senator and their smuggling contact, walked onto the dock with Balthazar, the captain of their schooner. From Balthazar's smug smile, Russell surmised that he'd been paid. From Pletcher's smug smile, Russell figured that even after the inflated payment, he was still making bank. "You put the squirrels in the wheel and have them run?"

"Squirrels are too smart for this," Russell said. "I need something stupider. I use Militia troopers."

Russell's new factory produced food trays, sawed lumber, and small consumer items for trade in Landing. Also custom built forged metal items, and large quantities of small arms ammunition. Balthazar, the schooner captain, was an expert in landing questionable cargos on dark nights in out of the way beaches. Pletcher provided necessary parts and precursors. His people staffed this rickety, out of the way pier, and arranged to market any dubious products.

"They walk inside the wheel, and lift the cargo? How does that work?"

Russell explained while his crew finished assembling it. The core was a wooden wheel, like an old school water wheel. It was large enough that a person could walk upright inside. Their weight pushed the wheel down, and the mechanical advantage of a big wheel turning a small axle gave them the power to hoist heavy loads up to the top of a wooden frame. The frame extended from behind the wheel over a pivot. Once the weight had been hoisted high above the ground, the whole frame could be pivoted.

Pletcher inspected the rear of the frame, "One man can lift the cargo, but you'll need six or more to pivot this frame."

"Four will do it," Russell said. "We'd only need one if you put in a permanent metal base, and a geared winch. Then one guy to walk it upright, another to winch it out of the boat. Less friction that way. But right now we need all four of them to deal with the weight issue, counterbalance the cargo at the end of the crane arm."

"Who designed this?"

"One of our Mules did," Russell said. "And they used their cosmic connection with a squad member to explain it to us."

Pletcher and Balthazar exchanged glances. "A cosmic connection with a Mule?"

Russell nodded. *Might as well be a cosmic connection. When Kim One came to me with this idea, she said she'd discussed it with her Mule, Sweet Pea. She's a nutcase, but she's a smart nutcase, and if she comes up with more smart ideas like this after talking to her mule, then I'm going to invite the smelly thing over for dinner and drinks twice a week.* "Works, doesn't it?"

Pletcher nodded. "It does." He studied the crane. "Why didn't you build the base first?"

"Lots of work to build a base," Russell said. "And it's heavy, and we have to bolt it to the dock. The dock timbers have to be able to handle the torque. But with a pivot, the crane sits there like a lump."

"Tip over if the weight is too high."

"That's why the four guys," Russell said.

"Lot of work to move trays of food. Easy to unload them by hand."

"Not so easy when you have single items that are two, three hundred pounds a box. Like metal ingots, or machine parts."

Pletcher nodded. "I forgot, you have a forge out there?"

"We do some metalworking," Russell said. *And no, I'm not going to tell you what equipment I found or what I can make. Ask me for something and I'll tell you if I can deliver. But I don't trust you.* "We could do more with some more supplies. Send me more metal ingots and I can make all sorts of things with my printers." Metal came from the sky—orbital distilleries boiled it off asteroids in the belt, then brought it down in shuttles. *And I'm sure Pletcher has a guy in the shuttle service.*

"What would it take you to build a bigger crane?"

"A bigger dock," Russell said. "Stronger beams and footings. But if I attach the crane directly to the dock, it's part of the dock. Which means it belongs to the dock owner. This one is removable, so it belongs to me. If it were permanent, you'd have to pay me to install it."

"Building a new dock is expensive," Pletcher said. "But It would be nice to be able to handle heavier cargo, and more of it with less people. But that's a lot of money for one or two shipments a month."

"I know a ship captain." Russell pointed at Balthazar. "He's got a couple of brothers. Some cousins too, I hear. Bet they could captain a ship each. Then there would be one or two shipments a week, rather than once a month."

Balthazar looked to his ship. "I'd need to hire more crew…"

"Lots of people out of work, all the problems in the City," Russell said. "Militia knows some people need work."

"I can find you some more people." Pletcher pointed at the end of the pier. "I can get this dock extended in a couple, three weeks."

"Then I can build you a new crane," Russell said. "We can start moving serious volume. Cut your, and my, dependence on the corps."

"Cool your jets, guys," Balthazar said. "That's great, and I can get some more crew. But what do I put the crew on? There aren't more than a half dozen of these trading ships on this moon, and most of them are owned by the corps. They won't sell to the likes of me, and we don't want to bring corporate types into this."

"Build your own ship," Russell said.

"I know how to sail ships," Balthazar said. "Not how to build them. Pletcher, can you build a ship?"

"Nope. I'm a land guy. Russell, you know how to build a ship."

"I do not." Russell grinned. "But I know somebody who does."

"Who's that?"

"A disgraced, banned Militia officer. One who's been exiled away from shore, and who would jump at the chance to get involved in something like this."

"Roi," Pletcher and Balthazar said together.

"But, isn't he dead?"

"Not yet. But we can make him wish he was."

Roi, a former Militia Colonel had been on the wrong side of the last revolt. In a complicated turn of events had been first captured by Russell, then released, then tried to shoot down a shuttle, then captured, then convicted, then exiled. The late Emperor Dashi had been behind the exile, sending Roi out to do mapping of the oceans, and requiring him to report back on his discoveries from time to time. And Dashi had sent all that information to Jake Stewart, along with contact codes.

Chaudhari stood with Russell while the last of the cargo they'd traded with Pletcher was loaded on their schooner. "Did you hear Jake Stewart is back?"

"The trading guy? Dashi's troubleshooter?"

"Back in town. In the system at least, that's the word. With a ship stuffed with rare silks, and woolen shirts, and leather, and exotic food."

"He's a rich troubleshooter then."

"More of a troublemaker."

"Wonder if he needs ammunition?"

"You promised Shutt she'd get all the ammunition you made."

"I did, didn't I." Russell watched the crew hand carry the boxes of food to Pletcher's truck. After assembling the crane, they swung a pallet of a dozen boxes up and out of the hold, then swiveled it down the dock.

"Still have to hand carry the boxes into the trucks," Chaudhari said.

"On this dock." Russell pointed. "Look at Pletcher. He's already designing a new dock in his head. One with a permanent crane that can lift directly from a schooner to one of his trucks."

Pletcher paced down the dock, counting, then made a note on his comm. He dropped down and checked the piers holding things up. "

"Give him a week," Russell said, "He'll have a new dock built and ready."

"Then pay you to install the crane?"

"He might buy the lumber from me, but if he's smart, he'll not want to depend on me. He can build it himself if he wants. Wonder which way he'll choose?"

"You'll know in two weeks."

"Yep. But either way he needs me to make the metal fittings, so I win." Russell climbed back on board the schooner. "I want to meet this Stewart guy. Set it up. I'll be back here in two weeks."

Chaudhari tapped his chest. "What am I, your messenger?"

"Exactly that. You're a senator-messenger. That's why I pay you."

"You don't, oh right, you do." Russell regularly gave Chaudhari cash.

"He'll know somebody in the Senate. You can get a message to him that way. Tell him I want to meet him in person."

"Got another cigarette?" Chaudhari asked.

"No, it's my last." Russell grunted. "When did you start smoking?"

"I didn't. But I want all this stuff out of here, and I wanted to know how much longer I'll stress while you stand here smoking. If that's your last one we're nearly done." Chaudhari coughed. "The Major finds out you're talking to Jake Stewart, she'll want more than ammunition. The corps won't like the Militia talking to him either."

"We're fine."

"It only takes one suspicious corp person to blow the lid off this. And if the Free Traders get wind of it, they'll shoot you."

"They're welcome to try," Russell said. "Didn't work so well last time. I need you to get on the monorail and head to point-west. Roi comes in for supplies once a month, he can only stay one tide, terms of his exile, while he collects supplies. Give him the co-ordinates of our plant, tell him to come there. I'll give him food and suchlike, hide him. He just has to build us a ship."

"What if he can't build a ship?"

"He'll lie and say he can. Doesn't matter. We've got lots of wood, tools, a sawmill, metal fabrication and everything he needs. We'll try one. Might take a couple of tries to get it right, but he'll speed up the process."

"I thought the idea," Chaudhari said, "Shutt's idea, was for you to head out east and be quiet. Build up a little Militia factory for her, keep you out of the limelight. Be her secret weapon."

"I'm doing that. But I won't tell her about this project. She doesn't need to know. She still gets her shipment of ammunition from me, so she's not beholden to the corps for it. But no reason we can't make more things, and make some other deals."

"Getting greedy now, are we?"

"I'm not greedy at all. I'm in the Militia. I take orders from Shutt, same as I used to take orders from the admiral. But the admiral is dead now. Who knows what might happen to Shutt? I've got troops to look after, and a factory workforce, and a bunch of people. The more stuff we have, the better I can look after them if something happens."

"You still on Shutt's side?"

"If she's still on my side." Russell sucked in the last of his cigarette. "But whether she's on my side or not, from now on I know what side I'm on first."

"Whose? Jose's? Jake Stewart's?"

"Mine." Russell tossed the cigarette into the river and watched the red tip fizzle out. "I'm on my side from now on."

Chapter 4

The first rendezvous was a Free Trader ship.

"Bonjour," said the voice on the comm. "You are Jake Stewart?"

"I am. Who are you?"

"I am a Captain who understands you have goods to sell."

"Good enough," Jake said. "I do."

"We will want to inspect them for quality."

"No," Jake said. "You won't. You've already seen the quality. You're going to buy them sight unseen or not buy them at all."

"That is not the way we do business."

"That's fine," said Jake. "That's the way I'm doing business. Are we done here?" Jake leaned back in his chair and put his hands behind his head while he waited for the response. Transmission delays were a fact of life in high orbit.

The delay was longer than necessary. "Perhaps it would be best if we did this in person."

"Perhaps it would," Jake said. "Why don't we go over there? I have no problem hopping out an airlock and jumping over."

The unnamed captain gave course coordinates. Two hours later, the two ships floated beside each other in the void.

"Right, off we go." Jake locked his helmet and pulled on his gauntlets.

Nadine sealed her suit, inspected her knives, and holstered two revolvers. "Jake, isn't this dangerous? I mean, they could capture us and keep us prisoner on their ship."

"They certainly could," Jake said, "but they're not going to do that."

"Why not?"

"Because if they do that, you're going to kill them."

"What?" Nadine blinked. "Jake, normally that's me going all 'let's kill them', but you usually have a plan…"

Jake pointed a finger at her. "Here's the plan. We're going to go over there, we're going to talk to them. If they get angry at us or try to steal the samples, you're going to shoot them. We'll agree on price, collect the money, and leave. If they try to short us on payment, you'll shoot them. They sneeze in a way you don't like, you shoot them. That's the plan, got it?"

"Got it." Nadine nodded. "Wow you're…"

"Angry? Yes. I'm tired of all of this. I'm tired of what happened to Dashi, and the others. People are going to pay attention and treat us fairly, or they're going to deal with the consequences." *And if I seem angrier than you, there's less chance you'll blow your top and start shooting when I don't want it. I still don't know what's going on. Dashi wouldn't want me to go in shooting. He'd want me to have a plan. And I'll make one, I promise.* "And then we'll give them the course coordinates of the container that Skimmer sends."

"They said they want to inspect the container."

"That's not how Jake Stewart does business now. If they want this, they have to pay in advance. Let's go."

"Jake, wow, you're. Wow. I wish…"

"Wish what?"

"That we weren't already in these suits." She grinned. "You being so masterful is making me hot."

Jake and Nadine both had custom skin suits from before, including customized tool and weapons attachments. Jake added gear—hard boots, hard helmet, gauntlets, a complete Belter kit. Nadine contented herself with a belt festooned with revolvers. He'd tried to convince Nadine to wear a hard suit herself, but she refused, said it was a fashion crime. Jake didn't complain too much, he liked the way she filled out the regular suit. Safety isn't everything.

They popped open the airlock and shoved off. Both of them were experienced in zero-g, they latched on next to the airlock of the target ship. Sixty seconds later, Jake had the door open, closed, and was inside, his vision dimming as the in-rushing air clouded it. He waited until the green light came on, spun the wheel, and pushed the inner door open. Like all airlocks, it opened against the flow of air out of the ship. In an emergency, it would slam shut to keep the atmo in.

"Good morning," Jake said to the man inside. "I'm Jake Stewart. You have money for me."

The man facing them said, "If you have goods for me."

"I recognize you. You're on the Free Traders Council, aren't you? Captain LaFerme?"

"Yes."

"What happened to your friend Marianne?"

"Dead," LaFerme said. "She was killed in the fighting, as were many others, including the Emperor Dashi and Admiral Edmunds."

"They were not exactly killed in the fighting, at least that's what I heard."

LaFerme shrugged, then related what he knew—the poisoning of Dashi, Edmunds dying of his wounds at the hospital.

"Sounds suspicious," Jake said. But it matched up with what he'd heard elsewhere.

"It is suspicious. It is also irrelevant to trading. Tell us where this container is, and we will inspect the goods, and then we will pay you and be on our way."

"No," Jake said. "We'll take full payment ahead of time. There'll be no inspections. I don't have time for this. You know who I am. The Free Traders have done business with me before. You know my reputation."

"You're coming from another system, I'm told. Did you discover the Empire?"

"I'm not prepared to share those details with you yet," Jake said. "I have discovered some trading sources for commodities, that's all I'll give up."

"It was difficult to collect all the materials you demanded. We cannot collect them all in one place. There have been confiscations."

"Confiscations?"

"The current government is having some problems funding themselves. Fines for…questionable activity have increased. As have seizures."

"Doesn't matter to me," Jake said. "Pay up, or I'll move on to the next person."

"Surely you would accept substitutions in different kinds of metals?"

"Nope," Jake said. "I want the whole variety. Gold, some silver, some copper, some zinc, some boron, and the rare earths as well. I sent you the proportions. It's not open for negotiation," Jake sealed his suit back up. "If you're not prepared to pay, we'll go now. Thanks for your time."

"Wait here one moment. I need to confer with my colleagues." LaFerme floated down the corridor to the next pod.

Nadine waited until he left. "Why are you being such an ass? I know this much—one piece of metal is as good as another. I mean, why not take more of the things that are in short supply on Magyar?"

"Because then they'll know what's in short supply on Magyar, and then they'll know what to raise or lower the prices on. This way they're guessing. They don't know which one we need and which ones are camouflage. We can always trade the others back to somebody else later. It obscures the source."

"Sneaky," Nadine said. "Well done, Stewart."

"I have my skills."

Nadine sniffed. "Do you smell beefalo? And spices."

"I'm not sure."

She sniffed again. "Free Trader ships always smell of great cooking. We should smell like that."

Jake shrugged. "All it takes is you learning to cook. And maybe showering more regularly."

"Shower more often?" Nadine rounded on him. "Let me tell you—" she detailed Jakes' failures in cooking, cleaning and showering, until LaFerme returned with two other silent men. He didn't introduce them. "We are prepared to dicker."

They argued back and forth for a while and settled on commodities, and prices.

"Fine. We have agreed on prices. Now we must discuss quantities."

They argued back and forth, again. Nadine scrunched up her forehead. The quantities that Jake was offering were limited. She knew they had ten or a hundred times that much back in the containers on the freighter, yet he kept the amounts minimal. She wasn't even sure how they could break that small bulk out of the different containers.

LaFerme said the same. "This is not as much as we expected."

"You want to buy more?"

"Yes. We would like to buy four times as much."

"At what price?"

"We expect a discount. We will pay ten percent less, but we will buy four times as much."

"Okay, here's my counterproposal," Jake said. "Per unit, I will sell you ten times as much."

LaFerme smiled. "Now we are trading. At what discount?"

"No discount. I will charge you four times the unit price that we agreed on, but you may buy up to ten times as much."

"Sacré bleu. You are insane. No one charges more when you buy a larger quantity. There's always a discount."

"I guess you're not as smart as I thought you were," Jake said. "That's good to know. But those are my offers. You can have five hundred kilograms of mixed goods, or you can have five thousand kilograms of mixed goods in the proportions set. If you buy the five thousands, you'll be paying four times as much per kilogram as you did before. Any questions?"

The captain's mouth hung open. The others jabbered in Francais, too fast for Nadine to follow.

"Jake," Nadine whispered, "what are you doing? Even I know that's stupid."

"It's not," Jake said.

"You're supposed to give people a discount for larger quantities."

"Yes, you are, aren't you?" Jake said. He waited.

After a minute of back and forth with his colleagues, the captain turned back. "We think you must do a better price."

"You do, do you?" Jake crossed his arms. "But not for you. I know other members of the council…."

The captain said something to his colleagues, then crossed his own arms. He glared at Jake for a long time, then laughed.

"I understand. So I'll pay four times as much for ten times as much."

"Four times as much per unit," Jake said. "For ten times as much. Forty times the money you expected to pay."

"The price per unit goes up the more you buy. Provided I buy five thousand kilograms?"

"Yes, in the proportions we specified. The wool, the linen, and so on."

"What if I bought ten thousand kilograms?"

"If you bought twenty times as much? Rather than charging you four times the unit price, I would charge you eight times the unit price."

"Comprenez." Captain LaFerme rubbed his chin. "And what if I wanted twenty thousand kilograms?"

"I'm not able to deliver that to you at this point," Jake said. He kept his face blank. *I'm telling the truth, technically. It's not an actual lie, not right now.* He made sure not to squirm. He never lied in negotiations, and the feeling was...uncomfortable.

"Understood." LaFerme issued a series of rapid instructions to his colleagues. "They will escort you to the... they will commence assembling the payment. This is a large quantity. We will need to access several containers."

"D'accord."

"We need to have a short discussion amongst ourselves. Perhaps you and your friend will enjoy our hospitality."

"Does your hospitality include booze?" Nadine asked. "And food. But only if its good food. Anything but those stupid trays."

"We do have some beefalo trays," Captain Francais said. "Would you like those?"

"That sounds wonderful while we wait," Jake said. "And Basic, if you have it."

He and Nadine floated in the lounge while LaFerme's crew moved around the ship, continuing to argue.

"Jake, the world has gone crazy," Nadine said. "I know when you buy more of something, you're supposed to get a discount. You told him that you're going to sell him twenty times what you initially offered, but rather than the price going down, the price is going up. In fact, the price is going to be eight times as much."

"Yes," Jake said. "Pretty good trading, huh?"

"How is this working?" Nadine said. "Is he insane? I mean, what, did you drug him?"

"When he asked for twenty thousand kilograms, I said I couldn't deliver. That's the key point. He's not buying products, he's buying exclusivity. He knows we have a lot to trade, but he also knows that he's not the only one we're talking to. He more or less said that he wanted to buy all that we have. That way he can set his own price. When he sets his own price for the first little while," Jake said, "the markup on these is going to be extraordinary. What he wants to avoid at all costs is us flooding the market. So this way, he's going to control the supply." Jake smiled. "Or he thinks he does. He'll make his money, as long as he moves quickly. That's how these things are."

"Jake," Nadine said, "you're the world's best trader. But you're just talking about what was on board *Accounting Error*. You didn't mention the Jump Freighter. We've got tons and tons more there. Plus those other containers."

"We do. But he didn't ask about that. He asked for what we could deliver now."

"You're selling him a fortune worth of goods so he has exclusive control of the market, and then you're going to break his exclusivity with more goods?"

"Yes."

"Won't that ruin him?"

Jake bit his lip. "Yes."

"Jake, that's not like you. You've never taken advantage of people like that before. What would Dashi say."

Jake looked away. "Dashi's dead, Nadine. These people might have helped kill him. I don't owe them anything. I'm not sure Dashi's way is the best way."

Nadine shook her head. "He'll be upset. If it was me, I'd come looking for you with my knives."

Jake grimaced. "I still haven't decoded all the messages I got from Dashi. I can't figure out some of the codes. But the Free Traders had something to do with Dashi dying, and I'm going to make them tell me all about it, or ruin them. And Nadine?"

"What is it, Stewart?"

"I'm counting on them coming back at me, one way or another. You know what happens then?"

"What?"

Jake pointed at Nadine's belt holster. "You're going to show them what happens to somebody who brings a knife to a gunfight."

Chapter 5

"The evidence is inconclusive, Jake," Jose said, over the radio. "I've had an investigator from the militia's regular crimes department, and I had some folks from TGI security check it. They agree that we can't figure out exactly what happened. Dashi was poisoned, but we don't know who did it. The poison's common enough that anybody could have located it and administered it."

"I can't believe he's dead," Jake said, and sat back to await the response. *Accounting Error* cruised the outer system. Jake and Nadine had been quietly setting up trading deals and meeting with some of Jake's old contacts. Jake had changed *Accounting Error*'s orbit to be close enough to get near real-time communication with Jose at TGI Main. But he made sure he moved fast enough that no regular trading ships, or warships, could catch him without being noticed.

Jose's voice came back twenty seconds later. "Yes, it's a problem. I'll send you the whole report. I have queued it up in the data stream if you're ready to receive it. We don't know who did it, but one way or the other, he's gone. The Senate's been elected, and we're debating what to do."

"Who's in charge of the Senate?" Jake made notes while he waited for Jose's answer and sipped his basic. As always they had plenty of basic, and plenty of trays. The only shortage was Nadine's patience. If he didn't get her different food eventually she'd start gnawing on his arm.

"Shutt is the leading Militia voice on the Senate, along with a non-commissioned officer named Chaudhari. There're a couple of Free Traders—Marianne, of course, before she was killed—a couple non-aligned, some other corps, and some other TGI people. We're working together to bring the system together after the current crisis. Jake, I know you've got a lot of resources out there. I'd like to meet with you and discuss how they can be allocated."

Nadine arrived from her room and slid the lights up. "Allocated my fine butt," Nadine said. "He killed the admiral. I know he did."

"Let's see what his report says," Jake said. "And do you need to always play with the lights?"

"Deal with your depression some other way. I don't care what his report says. I'm going to go stick him with a knife. Then we'll see what he reports."

"Nadine, that's not wise."

"Of course it's not wise," Nadine gritted her teeth. "None of this is wise. Going off on a trip to another system isn't wise. Traveling in space isn't wise. If we were trying to be wise, we'd stay home and hide under our bed."

"Nadine, on the balance of probabilities, I don't think Jose killed the admiral. Shutt says she found him dead when she went there for a regular visit."

"And you believe her? The admiral was dead when she got there?"

"I didn't say I believed her. Hang on, got to answer Jose."

Jake turned to the microphones and set up his return communication. He and Jose were far enough apart that they couldn't hold a real conversation. Instead, they asked and answered a number of questions, sent them all in a batch, and then waited.

"Jose, regarding my coming in, That's not possible at this time. Stellar geography is such that—"

Jake carried on blandly with numbers and statistics, discussing his orbit, his fuel requirements, and his unwillingness to tamper with his already programmed course to make a meeting with Jose. He was careful to give Jose believable numbers. Most people wouldn't bother to check them, but he knew Jose would. Jose was smart, hardworking, capable, and intuitive. In other words, a great friend—but a dangerous enemy. And Jake wasn't sure which he was right now.

Could he have killed the admiral? I doubt it, he wasn't there, and I don't think he is that ruthless. At least, he wasn't that ruthless before. People change. But three deaths of prominent people so quickly wasn't a coincidence. And he was there when Dashi died, but so were the others. He's smart enough to have arranged things to work out for him. Jose could be innocent, but he could be my enemy. I have to be careful.

"I suggest an in-person meeting, but it's going to have to be in the Outer Rings. I know you have substantial TGI assets under your control. I'm sure you could arrange to meet me out here. If nothing else, one of the cutters would give you a lift."

Jake stopped the transmission, sent the close command, and then waited.

"I say we go in and kill them all," Nadine seethed beside him.

"We can't kill everyone we don't like," Jake said.

"Sure we can," Nadine said. "It's a public service. If I killed everyone I didn't like, there'd be a lot fewer people in this system right now that I don't like. But in this case, something smells."

"Something does smell."

"Well, when something smells," Nadine said, "you have to do something about it. You clean it out."

"So you're going to go and wash him down with vinegar after you stab him?"

"Yes," Nadine said.

Jake carefully typed another sequence into his board.

"Jake," Nadine said, "what did you type?"

"I'm waiting for Jose's return communication to come in."

"Did you lock the navigation board?"

"I don't want to inadvertently send us on the wrong course."

"You've never inadvertently sent anything anywhere inadvertently in your life. You've always burtently done it."

"'Burtently' isn't a word."

"Shut up. You're worried that I'm going to try to zoom in there and find out what's going on and start breaking heads."

"That was your plan, wasn't it?"

"Well, yeah, but I didn't think I was that obvious about it."

"Nadine. All you want to do is go in there and smash people until you feel better. It's not going to help."

"And all you want to do is sit here and collect data and let people run roughshod over you, That's not going to help either," Nadine said.

"Nadine," Jake said.

"Never mind." Nadine held up a hand. "Jakey, I'm going to go back to my room. You can stay up here. You don't have to worry about me sneaking back and trying to send the ship on some big revenge-seeking, killer, kill-myself type of thing."

"I don't—"

"No," Nadine said. "I've learned. I've learned that revenge is worth it." She stopped as she was climbing out of the control room. "But I've been reading some of those books you gave me. What was it the guy said? Revenge is a dish best served cold."

"That's what he said," Jake said.

"Yeah," Nadine said. "There's a lot of cold in space. I just have to wait until somebody exposes themselves to it. I've got your number, Stewart. Fire and ice." Nadine smiled.

"What's that?" Jake said.

"Fire and ice. I'm the fire, you're the ice, aren't you? I barge in and blow things up or hit people, and you watch and listen and learn, then you edge in and take advantage."

"You were right Nadine." Jake rubbed his head. "We don't know what happened in Delta while we were gone. I'm not sure who to trust now."

"Fire burns quickly, causes destruction, and something new arises out of the ashes," Nadine said.

"And Ice is slow, thoughtful, crunches everything in its path, leaving a whole new environment behind. But it takes time, and people who don't want to be part of the ice can run away."

"Smart, Jake. I always said you were smart. Of course, there's one problem with you being ice and me being fire."

"What's that?" Jake said.

"When you throw the two together in the same spot, it doesn't always work out well, does it?"

Jake spent the next two hours fencing diplomatically with Jose. He almost enjoyed it. Jose was a smart man and a good opponent, and both of them knew that neither trusted the other at this point.

When Dashi ran TGI, Jose had sometimes given Jake direction or controlled the agenda, but Dashi had always had the final say. Now, with Dashi gone, he had to deal with Jose, and he wasn't liking it. And like Nadine, if he wasn't liking something, he didn't do it. He was more subtle, was all.

"Well, I'm sorry, Jose, that won't work for us, but one of your ships will be departing on a regular run soon." Jake rattled off the details. No way was he letting Jose near him with an armed cutter, or two armed cutters. He wasn't willing to chance an ambush. Ambushes were hard to set up if you didn't know where your target was going ahead of time, especially if the other person had sufficient sensors to track the ships that were getting there.

And Jose is interested enough that he would chance coming to see me in person to find out what I suspect.

The freighter that he'd suggested Jose hop a ride on was a long-haul freighter on a steady course to the far rim. Jose could catch a ride with it if he left TGI headquarters right away.

He could also try to divert some other freighters, but Jake had checked. They couldn't make it. The only things that could make it out that far were specific trading ships—or Militia cutters, and they'd have to burn hard. And hard-burning ships were easy to find with sensors. Jake had already identified a half-dozen that could be in the area if they burned in, and had programmed the computer to watch them.

There were eight free-trader ships that could make the rendezvous. Jake was curious to see if Jose called more of them in. They weren't usually armed, but who knew what had happened? *Need to watch out Stewart. You don't know who to trust now.*

Jake closed down the discussion with Jose. They would meet in the Outer Rim where he wanted. He didn't know what had happened while he was gone, and he didn't know what his next move was going to be, but he was patient.

"Which is what Nadine hates about me," Jake said. "Patience. Patience is a virtue."

Chapter 6

"I'm going to shoot him," Nadine said. "I'm going to shoot him in the chest three times. No, he's probably wearing armor. I'm going to shoot him in the head three times. No, that'll be too quick. I'm going to shoot him in the leg. Then I'm going to shoot him in the other leg. I'm going to shoot him in the shoulder. Then I'm going to shoot him in both shoulders, in both legs, both arms. And then I'm going to shoot him in the head. Twice."

She and Jake waited facing *Accounting Error*'s airlock. Jake had insisted that Jose come across to visit them. He said he couldn't leave because his automated systems were down for necessary maintenance and he had to be close by in case of problems.

"That's more bullets than you have in your gun, Nadine." Jake examined the comm pad Nadine was holding in front of her. "You'll have to stop and reload in the middle."

"Don't try to stop me, Jake. I know Jose killed the admiral."

"I'm not trying to stop you at all. I'm only pointing out practical difficulties." Jake unclipped his holster, which Nadine had insisted he wear, and handed it to her. "There. Another gun. You can shoot with either hand. You'll be fine. Blaze away."

Nadine and Jake were facing the airlock of *Accounting Error*. Jake had arranged that the bottom of his orbit would graze the top of Jose's. He'd monitored the approaching traffic closely. No other ships were nearby, and as long as only Jose crossed over Jake felt safe.

"You're fine if I shoot Jose?"

"I'm not fine with it," Jake said. "I'm not going to stop you, though. Good luck. Don't waste too many bullets. Make sure you don't get any ricochets. It's all metal in here. It'll be loud, too. You might want to put on ear protection."

"Jake Stewart, you went to all this trouble to arrange this meeting, and now you're going to let me shoot him?"

Jake shivered and wiped his nose. To back up his maintenance claim, he'd turned off the life support. Water condensed out of the cooling air, collecting on metal surfaces and making them both sneeze. "You're not gonna shoot him. You don't want to."

"I don't want to? What do you mean, don't want to? I want to, absolutely. I wanna shoot him. I wanna shoot him six times. If he's the one who killed Dasih, I want him to suffer. I want whoever killed the admiral to suffer too, and especially whoever killed Dashi to suffer."

"Prove he killed Dashi?"

Nadine grimaced. "He could have. Maybe. Don't tell me he couldn't."

Jake shrugged. "I'm not. I'm still gathering data."

Nadine watched the external monitor and sniffed. "Why did you insist on meeting him in person?"

Jake tapped the environmental controls on the wall and turned the lights down to half power. "Talking to him over comms hasn't worked out. He has too much time to frame a reply, craft his response. I can't get a good read on him." Jake changed the light balance from reds to more of a blue-green. "I've known him a long time. It will be harder for him to lie to my face."

"He's a master manipulator, he knows it's harder to lie in person. Why would he risk visiting you then?"

"Jose, and most other people in this system, think I'm a dumb yokel and they can orbit rings past me. Him less than most, but it's still there. He's coming out from his warm shiny office, sleeping in a soft luxurious cargo berth, wearing a custom skin suit. Then he meets poor Belter Jake, sneezing in the dark, and explains to him what's happening. I'll be impressed by his brilliance and believe him."

"Wow." Nadine looked at Jake. "I forget sometimes how smart you really are."

"Everybody does. It's that famous old saying, never interrupt your enemy when he is making a mistake."

"Now Jose's your enemy?"

"Not sure yet. And, regardless of what those messages from Dashi indicate, I can't go to war with a friend until I look him in the eye. He'll have every chance to tell me the truth."

"What will he say?"

"He's gonna blame the admiral's death on Shutt. Then blame Dashi's death on Shutt. He's gonna say he can't prove either of them, then see if I believe him." Jake held up his revolver. "Still want this?"

"No." Nadine shook her head. "And Marianne was killed in the fighting. Smart, she can't argue."

"Fighting with a Militia-run group commanded by one Sergeant Russell. Very strange coincidence."

"Sergeant Russell," Nadine said. "I know him. He's a Militia guy. Burly guy. Quite attractive."

"I'm sure I don't know," Jake said.

"Big. Handsome. And he's a fighter. Why is it unusual he shot her?"

"There were only a half dozen fatalities on that particular station. One of them being her. She was one of the last people killed in that entire uprising, supposedly by him. Any one of his troops could have killed a bunch of people by accident and I'd believe it. But he didn't strike me as the type of person to lose his cool in the middle of a shooting match. Or at the end after things had settled down."

"If he shot her," Nadine said, "that means he had instructions. It means that Shutt did it. She told him to."

"Certainly does seem that way, doesn't it?" Jake said. "First Shutt arranged to have Dashi assassinated. Then she arranged to have Marianne killed in the fighting. And finally, the admiral succumbed to his wounds from the assassination attempt on Dashi. All blamed on Shutt. But all very convenient for Jose."

"See?" Nadine said. "That's my point. Jose did it. I don't need any evidence. Him and a bunch of others."

"Could have happened," Jake said. Or Jose could have set them up to take the fall. He's smart enough.

The airlock thunked.

"Jose is here. I told him to use a line. I'm not sure how good he is out in the dark."

"Wait," Nadine said. "Jose couldn't have done all this himself. He must have had help."

"I suppose," Jake said.

"And if I kill him, I'll never find out who helped him."

"You certainly won't find out anything after you've shot him," Jake said. "Shooting is kind of final that way."

"Damn it," Nadine said. "That means I can't shoot him."

"You can shoot whoever you want," Jake said. "I'm not stopping you."

"Damn you and your logical manipulation, Jake Stewart."

"I'm not manipulating anybody," Jake said. "You talked yourself into it."

"Yes, but you let me."

"I let you talk yourself into it?"

"Wait," Nadine said. The outer airlock light flashed. "I can torture him. Torture him and get him to tell me who helped him."

"Great idea," Jake said. "How do you torture him?"

"Stab him in the liver."

"At least you know where that is now. What happens when you stab someone in the liver? It hurts a lot, and they die," Jake said, "Die quickly. Jose's smart. Since he already knows he's dying, why is he going to answer any of your questions?"

"I'm going to make it hurt really bad."

"You don't know how to make it hurt really bad. You know how to kill him. Stabbing him is going to kill him."

"Double damn," Nadine said. "I never studied torture."

"Another flaw in your education."

"Shut up, Stewart." Nadine tapped her forehead then pointed at Jake. "You could torture him."

"I could torture him?"

"You must know how to torture people. You must have read a book on it. Torture for beginners, something like that. You've read a book on everything else."

"I'm not going to torture him," Jake said. "I'm not torturing anybody."

"If you don't torture him, I'll do something to you. I'll make you want to torture him."

"So you're going to torture me until I torture someone? Is that it?

"You know, Stewart, every time I talk to you—every time I think about something—it's so simple in my head, and as soon as I start dealing with you, things get turned around backwards and sideways."

"Maybe they were backwards and sideways to start with."

"Fine," Nadine pouted. "No shooting and no torturing. As a favor to you."

"It's not a favor to me," Jake said. "I didn't ask you to do anything."

"I know. You were just so damned reasonable about it."

The inner airlock flipped open and Jose stepped through. His eyes were wide as he tried to unclip his helmet. Jake waited as he struggled with it, until it was stuck, then helped unlatch it.

"Thank you. That's harder than it looks." Jose's hair was frazzled, and grease smeared his custom skinsuit.

"Most things are," Jake said. "Harder than they look, that is."

"Agreed." Jose said. "But, with time and patience and research and effort, you can usually get everything to work."

"That's also true," Jake said. "Welcome to our ship, *Accounting Error.* Thanks for coming so far out of your way."

"Thanks for coming out of your way, Jake." Jose wiped sweat from his eyes. "We've only got so much time before I have to start back. I've read your report about your visit to Magyar. That's fascinating. Destroyed Imperial Station, another abandoned Imperial colony, with no connection with the Empire."

Jake had sent Jose a complete report of their travels throughout the system. Actually, he hadn't sent it to Jose—he'd sent it to Dashi, but on an account he knew Jose had access to. He didn't want Jose to think he was holding back, but he also wanted to be careful what he disclosed. He had left out encountering missile boats, pirates, and the fact that he would soon have a jump freighter arriving.

"Yes," Jake said, leading them into the lounge and pouring some Basic. "It was an invigorating trip."

"Where's the rest of the crew?" Jose asked. "And why is it so dark? And cold?"

"Some of the systems broke when we jumped. I'm patching them. They crew is back at Magyar, doing research and acquiring cargo. We loaded up with everything we could profitably trade and came here. We'll return for the rest."

"If that's what you want," Jose said. "Well, I understand— you understand this is a cooperative venture."

"Of course," Jake said. "Cooperative, but mostly private. My understanding is that TGI, in the shape of Dashi, was entitled to one-fifth of the profits. Rather than doing all the computations, it's simpler to give you one-fifth of the cargo."

"All right. As I said, do I get to pick, or...?" Jose coughed, then sneezed. "Miserable temperature."

"You get used to it. We'll assign it pro rata," Jake said. "You've got the manifest. We've listed everything that's in the ship. I'll give you one-fifth of it as soon as it gets here. We'll have to go back for most of it."

"Of course," Jose said. "There won't be any difficulties with the manifest, will there? Things that are not on it that you might be dealing with?"

"As if you could tell," Nadine interrupted. She'd been quiet until now, seething and toying with her holster.

"Ms. Nadine," Jose said. "I'm so very sorry to hear about the admiral. I knew he was... a figure of great moment to you."

"You knew he was my grandfather."

"That's not widely shared, but yes, I knew that. Again, my condolences."

"Thank you," Nadine said, although it came out more like a growl because her teeth were clenched so hard. Like she might bite through her jaw.

"And I suppose there's no chance of me catching the great Jake Stewart in some sort of cargo scandal. It's well known that's your area of expertise."

Jake shrugged. "I'm sure that's exaggerated."

"Jake, when can we expect you at TGI Main?"

"I'm not sure I'm going to go down to TGI Main," Jake said.

"What? But—I mean—that's the headquarters. The Emperor is dead, the gods save him, he was like a father to me. But work goes on. At the very least, you should report to the new Senate. We could use your input, in an advisory capacity of course. Control rests with the Senate."

Jake nodded and tilted his head like he was thinking hard. *He did it. I think he   killed them all. I don't know how yet, or even why, but he killed them all, or caused them to be killed. Should I let Nadine shoot him right now? No, it's just a feeling, I don't have proof, and that will make more problems than it would fix. What would Dashi have done?* Jake nodded again. "I cared about him, not TGI. And I don't know anything about this Senate. Besides, I'm a Belter boy, born and bred. I never fit in the close orbit stations or on the ground. That's more you surface-born types. I talk funny, I dress funny, and I'm happier out here. I've got a going trading concern now. I'll be able to set up a route between here and Magyar, and who knows? Maybe with the Jump Ship we'll find some other nearby planets to trade with. Do it on my own dime."

"Well, Jake, I'm not sure how we're—"

"This ship is mine. That's understood. You own some of the cargo. That's all. I'll give you your share, the rest is up to me."

Jose stared at Jake, unblinking, then shrugged. "If that's what you want."

"It is. And congratulations on your promotion to chairman of the board of TGI."

"Acting, but thanks."

Jake nodded. "And I understand you are on the Free Trader Council now."

"Yes," Jose said. "They decided it was prudent to have some TGI members in their Captains guild—and on their council—given the current political situation."

"Meaning," Nadine said, "you told them you'd hunt them down—"

"Nadine." Jake's voice was quiet. But he grabbed her forearm with a vice grip. "Jose is our guest."

Nadine took a breath. "With their ships, and TGI behind you, it seems like you're the number one corporate and the number one Free Trader hegemon here."

"I wouldn't use the word hegemon," Jose said. "I'm acting chairman of the TGI board. But TGI still needs an election. And the Free Traders council hasn't elected a leader yet, so that's still unresolved. Which means two elections in my future. There's still so much to do. I'm a senator, but we don't even have a permanent speaker yet."

"Yes," Jake said. "You told me. An interesting list of senators. I double checked the names you gave me. You've got some TGI people, a couple Free Traders. Not many else. No Belters."

"None stood."

"Of course. Shutt's a senator, of course."

"Major Shutt. Senator Shutt."

"And a few others. That guy, Chaudhari, is a senator? I thought he was a corporal."

"He was. Somehow he got himself elected. He's Senator Chaudhari now."

"Well, I'm sure he'll ably represent the Militia on the Senate. What are you going to do for a new emperor?"

"There're lots of discussions about that," Jose said. "Right now we're stalled because nobody has any idea who should be Emperor next."

Jake nodded. *The senate knows you've cowed them into submission, but they're smart enough not to give you full executive control. You've still got a fight on your hands, especially with the Militia.* "Well, I'm sure you'll work something out," He said. "But my plan is to stay out here, handle my trading, and grieve Dashi."

"He was a great man," Jose said. "Jake, there's a place for you at TGI Main. We could use your unique perspective."

"Thanks," Jake said. *Keep your friends close and keep your enemies closer, is that what you want?* "But Nadine and I will be leaving the system shortly, go back to Magyar for more trade goods. We wanted to make a run in to get a feel for the trading situation. We do have some commercial issues to discuss. Would you like another drink?"

Jake and Jose sat in the lounge, drank cups of basic and a glass of wine while they fought—politely—over cargo allocations, shares, percentages, and interpretations of the different documents laid out.

"I'm less concerned with the current situation," Jose said, "than about future opportunities. I was wondering if we could arrange some sort of exclusive arrangement on future goods."

"I won't give you exclusive," Jake said, "but I can give you a much, much higher quantity. I noticed a number of these organizations that had initially been part of this have been folded into TGI. You effectively have a good portion of the Free Traders, so you should have, being a council member, some ability to track with them. But of course, I'll run my own numbers."

"And the Militia?"

"The Militia wasn't part of this expedition," Jake said. "There's no reason why they should be included in future arrangements. Why don't we agree to split the shares that Dashi had allocated between us? Dashi did leave that to our discretion."

"Of course," Jose said. "Dashi would have trusted us to do the right thing."

Jake's expression didn't change. *What Dashi would have trusted us for, is to grind the Militia into dust between the two of us. I'll have all the outer belt and out-system resources when this is done unless you swindle me out of them. You'll have everything on the ground and most of the orbital stuff. And the Militia will be left with a bunch of stations and ships they can barely get fuel or supplies for unless they bow to you. And you're in the process of absorbing the Free Traders, so they'll disappear as a player soon.*

"I'm sure we can work something out, Jake," Jose said. "And again, I'm sorry about Dashi. He was like a father to me. And tell Nadine, again, I'm sorry about her grandfather."

"I will," Jake said. "I will. I'll let her know that you care. She's been broken up by this." *And as soon as she figures out a way to kill you without ruining whatever plan she thinks I've done, she's going to do it.*

But Jake watched Jose's eyes as a shadow passed over them. *That is, if Jose doesn't get to us first, somehow.*

Chapter 7

"It's too sharp." Roi gestured at the wooden frame ahead of him. "Too pointed. Too straight."

Sergeant Russell shaded his eyes and peered into the trees. Work crews from his plant—that's how he thought of it now, his plant—had cut down a section of pine forest near the water. The wood had been cut up and planed down into planks, and the outline of a small sailing ship sat on a cradle. "Good to know, Roi. It should be curved?"

"Yes, sergeant." Roi said. "And it's Colonel Roi." He put his hands on his hips. "I am a Militia colonel. I demand proper respect."

Russell dug in his pocket for a cigarette, and didn't find one. *I hear that Jake Stewart has tobacco. First thing I have to trade with him. After I deal with this idiot who doesn't realize that things have changed.* Russell sniffed the air. Fresh cut pine. *If Kim One were here, she'd say how invigorating it was. Gotta admit, like it better than gun oil. Smells like barracks after the newbies clean them up. Maybe I can get pine flavored cigarettes?* "You're not a Militia Colonel anymore, you're a convicted felon. And you're breaking the terms of your parole by coming here. A word from me, and you're back in jail, rather than on your boat. Or I could shoot you, according to Militia rules."

"If you were following Militia rules, you would not be building sailboats. You'd be trying to fix the monorail. And you wouldn't be hiding your military construction."

"I'm not hiding anything."

Roi pointed at the tree canopy overhead. "You have not cleared out the forest. Some of the remaining trees will do good duty as heavy-lift cranes, if you put block and tackle on them. But the others are there only to hide from orbiting satellites. Otherwise you would have cut them down, rather than stripping the limbs off for half way."

"Ridiculous," Russell said. "I'm not hiding anything. And how could I? There're satellites overhead all the time. Drop ships, freighters, shuttles in orbit everywhere."

"Shuttles don't have infrared scanners," Roi said. "Not working ones. They can check for radio emissions, but there are none here. Visual scans will show trees. But you're careful when you dock your trading ships. That's why you make me come in at night and hide my ship up close to the shore, so nobody will notice what you are doing." He bit his lip and looked at Scott. "And nobody does. I have not heard a word of this. I am somewhat impressed."

"Out in the ocean on your little boat?"

"My little boat has a radio. I send in my updates to Militia HQ regularly. And I can talk to my friends. I still have friends you know. Some very important. Sometimes they smuggle me messages. I have some idea what is going on."

"So what is going on?"

"Things fall apart. The center cannot hold."

"What?"

"Never mind. The last fight was too much for us. The whole system is descending into barbarism. Production is down, we have transportation challenges everywhere. You have more food than you'll need in a hundred years here, and the ability to make more, but you can't get it anywhere. We have more food on the ground on Delta then we'll ever need. But no metals, no ores. That's all in orbit. Our orbital infrastructure is so fragile, one big push and it will shatter into a thousand pieces. Then all the orbital stations will starve, and we will slide into the dark ages without their industrial goods."

"Big talk from a man who tried to kill one of our shuttles. One of our few working shuttles." *Maybe he's smarter than I thought. He might get it.*

Roi shrugged. "I am not the man I was. I ponder now. I have had time on my hands. Things are not going well here. We are this close—" Roi held his fingers an inch apart—"this close to losing everything and becoming barbarians. Do you want to be a barbarian, Mr. Russell?"

"Not sergeant? Weren't you insisting on ranks?"

"This is not a military discussion. This is a commercial discussion," Roi said. "I wanted to know how you view yourself. In the old Militia, a sergeant would never speak as you do to a colonel."

"I'm not only a sergeant anymore."

"Nor am I a colonel. I will call you Mr. Russell if you call me Mr. Roi."

Russell extended his hand. "Call me Scott. Scott Russell."

Roi raised his eyebrows and put his hand behind his back. "I think not. We will be partners, not friends. I will call you Mr. Russell. Mr. Russell, all this is wrong. This is no way to build a ship. Let me explain what you must do."

Roi explained what must be done. Ribs of the ship bent into curved shapes. Round, nearly flat bottoms so they wouldn't tip over when they grounded on mud when the tide ran out. Wooden masts, but with metal fittings. Big hatches, how to rig a ships wheel.

Russell found himself nodding. *He's a pompous twit, but he knows ships. This can work. But I have to keep an eye on him.*

"This can work," Russell repeated. "I can do that. I'll get my people on this right away. You can supervise. What do you want?"

"What every sailor wants, of course."

"You want to be a captain?"

"No, no." Roi smiled. "I want to be an admiral."

Chapter 8

"Jake, you can't go back to trading." Nadine stepped into the computer room and sat next to Jake. *Accounting Error* had been custom-built by the old empire as a Jump Courier and anti-pirate missile boat. Part of the customization was a special central module with access to the jump computer and secured databanks. Jake could control the jumps and do navigation from there, cutting off control room access if necessary. When they weren't in jump, he spent most of his times running simulations.

"Why not?" Jake ran another price-cost analysis on his screen. "I'm good at it. We're making a fortune these days. I don't even have to wait for the *Flandre* to arrive."

"The *Flandre*… it's overdue."

"A little, but things happen in space so I'm not worrying yet. And between what I got from working with Dashi, the money from his inheritance, the other assets he transferred to me, the trading from Magyar, and some of my other endeavors, I'm rich. I could even buy up my old station. I could buy the shares from the station people on the open market."

"Why in the name of a merciful Jove would you buy your old station? I've been there, remember? Nothing but freezing hab units with drab decorations, disgusting food, worthless gravity and poor lighting."

"Poor lighting?"

Nadine tossed her hair. "Doesn't show off my looks."

Jake laughed. "Somebody who hadn't met you before would think you were a vapid airhead."

"You did, when you first met me, and look how that turned out," Nadine said. "Fooled you and all your friends, got the job done, and the admiral took me out for dinner at that restaurant afterwards…"

Nadine sat silently for the next few seconds. Jake glanced sideways. Her mouth compressed and her eyes brimmed with tears. "It's hard Nadine. He was a great man."

"He was a controlling ass who hectored me into doing things I didn't want to. Put me in danger, made me take risks, pushed me to try things that were dangerous. Best thing that could have happened to me." She sniffed.

Jake hugged her, and the tears flowed. She sniffled and whined, and sometimes bawled. Jake held her. *This is the best I can do right now. If I explain any of my plans, she'll want to know when I'm going after Jose and Shutt and all the others with them. I haven't decided yet, and I doubt she'll take that for an answer.* Nadine hugged him back, dried her eyes, and rubbed her arm—the spot where she kept her knives. *And if I don't keep my mouth shut I might say the wrong thing, and she might stab me. She'll be sorry afterwards. I think. But I'll still be stabbed.*

"Nadine, I don't know what to say."

Nadine wiped her face. "Don't say anything. Just figure out some way to get them."

"Get them? What if I can't do that?"

"I know you Jake Stewart. Behind that bland, forgiving exterior is a razor sharp mind. And you've been poring over those communications from Dashi. What did he tell you?

"Not important right now. But there were some surprises. I'm not sure how to best utilize that information yet."

"Whatever Dashi told you doesn't matter. You've already figured out fifty ways to get who ever killed Dashi — everything from them getting arrested for tax fraud to dying in an unexplained reactor core accident. All that's going on is that you're waiting to choose which one to use and when."

"I have no idea what you mean—"

"Jake, I'm direct. I go right at them. I push people into doing what I want, and they don't like it. They're always angry with me, but I don't care. I power through. Your superpower is patience and calculation. You make a spreadsheet of all the options, figure out what will happen, and nudge people into doing what you want, without them even realizing it. I see you do it." Nadine shrugged. "I don't know how to do it, and I don't know how you actually do it, but it happens right in front of me. It's like watching a herd of Beefalo roaming up north, trying to go down those mountains. They're stupid big and clumsy, and the mountains are steep, but leave them alone and they rumble downhill without ever having any problems."

"Beefalo are not people. You can't compare them."

"I spent time on a ranch, remember? And don't change the subject. What *is* your plan? It can't be only trading?"

"What if all I want is to retire to the Rim and run a trading empire? Relax? Retire? Smoke with Skimmer?"

"Skimmer will steal all your cigarettes and there won't be any left for you. But you sound so sincere I almost believe that. Good thing I know you better. But that's a good point. If you're going to keep acting like a trading person, then you must have a reason. Fine. I'll help, just tell me what to do, I need the distraction."

Jake grinned. "Nadine, I can say, without fear of contradiction, that telling you what to do never goes well. You do not like being told what to do."

"Not true." Nadine shook her head. "I've been told what to do my whole life. By subtle experts. The admiral would maneuver me to doing what he wanted. He'd get me angry, point me in the right direction, and let me lose. You do the same thing."

"Nadine, every time I tell you what to do, you do the exact opposite. "

"Exactly." Nadine nodded. "You know that. That's how you get what you want. You set me up, tell me what's best and I should do it, and I immediately don't do that, and I end up doing the opposite, which is what you wanted all along."

"If that's the case, then it won't work anymore, will it?"

"Of course it will. Now that I know that you always tell me the opposite of what you want me to do, I'll do what you tell me, thinking I'm going to make you angry." Nadine held up one finger. "But you know that, and you're always a step ahead, so now you're going first to tell me to do what you want." Nadine held up a second finger. "Then, I'll think you want me to do the opposite, but you're not the boss of me, Jake Stewart, so…" Nadine held up a third finger. "I'm going to do exactly what you say, which is exactly what you want." Nadine shook her head. "It's unfair, even when I know what you're doing, you end up winning. You're always a step ahead." Nadine cocked her head. "That's what we should put on your tombstone, 'Jake Stewart, he was always a step ahead of everybody'."

"If I get a tombstone."

"You'll die in your bed when you're a hundred. You'll outlast everybody."

"Will there be a few pretty girls in bed with me when I die?"

Nadine's arm twitched, and she had a knife in her hand. She held it in front of her face. "There better not be, but even if there is, I'll make sure that all you can do is look."

"Nadine, we're not…"

"I was upset. I'm moody, you know that."

"Fickle."

"I prefer mercurial."

"Volatile."

Nadine shrugged. "Men like that. It's exciting. Know what I am now?"

"No."

"Horny." Nadine grabbed Jake's skin suit and dragged him out of the chair. "Come with me, master trader. We have a few transactions to complete."

A few hours later, Jake wobbled into the galley. Nadine sat and munched on a tray. Or rather, slurped, because there really wasn't anything munch-able on the food trays.

"That was fun Nadine, can we do that again?"

"Long trip to meet up with your smuggling ship, we'll have time. It was fun for me too."

Jake leaned in. "Then why do you look sad?"

"Thinking of the admiral."

"Why do you call him that? Why not grandfather?"

Nadine shook her head. "Family thing."

"Do you want to—"

"No. No I don't. Do you have a plan for getting who killed him?"

Jake tilted his head. "Yes. I've got notes from Dashi. Reports from… employees of his. And as soon as his will is official, I'll have control of some other legal instruments."

"Good." Nadine spooned up green mush. "Go get them, tiger."

"Do you want to know what it is?"

Nadine shook her head. "Before, I would have. But now I know it's going to be too confusing for me to figure out, and I'll only get angry trying to understand. And I'll worry about future problems that you've already built in a solution for. It wastes my time. Just make sure I have a lot of fun things to do."

"Fun things?"

"Shooting things. Stabbing things. Those are fun."

"I'm not sure I'll ever understand you."

"You understand enough, Jake Stewart."

"I do? What do I understand?"

"You never let your friends down. You're always on their side, helping them out. Even if they don't know it. You've got a plan. You'll get them."

"Thanks. I think."

"How much longer until the next course change?" Nadine asked.

"Hours."

"Good." Nadine shoveled the last of the food in her mouth and stood. "You know, you might as well leave that skin suit off. Saves time."

Chapter 9

"I'm disappointed in you Sergeant," Major Shutt said. "I expected better."

"Expected better what?" Sergeant Russell looked at the box of shells in his hand. "Better selection? Quality?" He rattled the box. It was cardboard, previously used for boxed asparagus. "Nicer packaging?"

"You know what I mean."

Russell sighed and put the box of shells back into his pocket. *Gotta keep this box off the shelves here, otherwise I'll be all day answering some stupid questions. Like where did this illegal ammunition come from?*

The Militia armory, inside Militia HQ could easily be confused with a poorly maintained ground-car garage. Grease stained the concrete floor, half opened crates of broken equipment leaned against the back wall, and poor lighting and a burnt fabric smell completed the display. Only the locked racks of shotguns, rifles, and revolvers had been dusted in the last year. And the piled crates of ammunition were barely tall enough to hide behind. Russell had checked out cover and concealment as a matter of course—where would he site a squad weapon, if he had one? Despite now being a factory boss, he still thought of every meeting as a tactical assault problem. "I did the best I could for quality control. They shoot fine when they go off, but I've still got one in ten mis-fire, not sure why. The only test I know of is to fire it, and that's kind of counter-productive, Clarisse."

"That's exactly what I mean, Sergeant. Stop using my first name. Call me Major."

"Why?" Russell raised his eyebrows. "I know your name, you know mine. Makes things easier. And there's nobody else who matters here."

Chaudhari, standing next to Russell, raised his hand. "I'm right here."

"That's exactly what I mean, Chad," Russell said. "Nobody who matters. We're all friends here."

"I remind you, Sergeant," Shutt said, "That I'm a major and a senator, and should be addressed as such."

"Hey. I remind you, Senator," Chaudhari said, "That I'm a senator too. So you should call me Senator as well."

"You're a corporal," Russell said. *What's up with Shutt? Why is she talking to me like this? Does she know that I'm hiding the extra ammo?*

"That's my part-time job now. Scott has me being a Senator for him."

"Oh, *Scott* does, does he?" Shutt scowled. "That's Corporal Chaudhari to you, Sergeant Russell."

"And you want us to call you Major all the time?" Russell grinned. "Use your Militia rank?"

"Yes."

"Even when," Russell waved at the tiny box of ammunition that he'd brought in, "Even when we're discussing the secret ammunition I illegally brought in that you don't want the other groups to hear about, is that what you want." Russell raised his voice. "Is that what you want, Major."

The three people outside of the main armory room twisted to face them. One member of the Free Trader Legion, one Militia trooper, and one member of TGI security. The three factions maintained a twenty-four-hour watch on the weapons dump there, to keep the others honest. They didn't care about hand weapons. The recent 'unpleasantness' as Jose called it had shown there were plenty of actual hand guns available. But they did keep a close count on the amount of ammunition. And the armory had the only on-planet stock of heavier weapons— mortars, rockets, shoulder-fired missiles. Anything that could heavily damage a landing boat or the fusion plant was carefully monitored.

"Everything okay in there," the Free Trader representative asked.

Shutt waved it off. "We're fine. An administrative issue. Not a concern."

"You sure?" the Free Trader frowned. "Should we come in there?"

"Stay out there, on guard."

The three outside muttered between themselves. Ostensibly, Sergeant Russell and Corporal Chaudhari, accompanied by their commanding officer, Major Shutt, were dropping off a newly located crate of ammunition found in the course of their duties.

Russell figured that was the easiest way to show Shutt how good his ammunition shot. They'd dropped the crate inside, loaded up, and then practiced on the adjacent pistol range. Hide things in plain sight. Russell shrugged mentally. *Which is why she's angry at me. She didn't want her new toys to be under joint control of the others. She wanted her own ammunition store back at her office. But it's best for me if I start limiting her options, before she limits mine.*

"Who's going to argue with the Major?" The woman in a worn Militia trooper uniform said.

The TGI security—he had the best uniform, a tailored suit jacket over a skin suit—moved to stand in front of the exit door. "I will, if it comes to that."

The outside door swung open, and Jose stepped inside. "If it comes to what, Nejkin?"

"Sorry Mr. Jose. Sorry sir." The TGI man ducked back into his corner. "We heard noises inside, that's all."

"Noise means spirited debate. I'm in favor of spirited debate." Jose sauntered past the counter and into the armory's main room. "Senator Shutt. Senator Chaudhari. Good to see you, thank you for coming. I'm sure you're wondering why I called you here, and I'd like to take this opportunity—."

Russell folded his arms. "What? He called us here? Clarisse—"

"Senator or Major, Sergeant."

"Excuse me, Major Shutt. Ma'am." Russell stamped to attention and saluted. "Sergeant Russell reporting for duty ma'am. Your orders?"

"Stand by, Sergeant. You were saying, Senator?"

"I wasn't saying anything," Chaudhari said. "I'm confused."

"Senator Jose, not you, Corporal." Shutt shook her head. "What were you saying, Senator Jose?"

Jose's eyes flicked back and forth between Shutt and Chaudhari. "Senators. Sergeant. Corporal. Major. I wanted to discuss some Senate business, so I invited two Senators here, and I wanted Mr. Russell's perspective as the…operator… of a production plant might help out as well. But I appear to have stumbled into some sort of military function. Should I wait outside until you three finish your Militia business? What we're discussing will require your full attention."

"I think we can proceed here." Shutt gestured them back to the rear of the main room, out of earshot of the watching guards.

"Why here? An armory? Why not an office somewhere?" Chaudhari's eyes fluttered around. "We don't even have chairs."

"We have guns though," Russell said. "I like guns. I'd rather get some shooting in than go to a meeting." He laughed. "Much more fun."

Shutt glared. Jose cocked his head and stared at Russell. "You know, Mr. Russell, you always act like a buffoon, but everyone says that you're much, much smarter than you act, did you know that?"

Russell shook his head "Sir." *I don't know about that, but I know that if we meet in a private office somewhere, there might be some gunplay, or some poisoned food, and one or all of us might wind up dead. Shutt is acting squirrelly, and there have been a lot of accidental deaths recently. This armory is the only place in Landing where the Militia, the Free Traders, and the TGI group have a constant presence at, and cameras. You can't have us shot out of hand, not here, Mr. Big Shot-TGI person.* Russell laughed.

"What's so funny Sergeant," Shutt asked.

"Nothing, ma'am."

"Mr. Jose asked you a question."

"Don't remember, ma'am."

"About you being smarter than you look."

Russell shrugged. "Can't be that smart, I'm a sergeant."

Jose smiled. "I hear you're the wealthiest sergeant in Landing right now."

Russell shrugged again. "Don't know. I haven't met all the sergeants in Landing."

"You might soon." Jose lowered his voice. "The Free Trader's council opened their books to me. Things are worse than we feared. With the recent destruction, their supplies are much more limited than they let on. The loss of food production facilities during the recent unpleasantness has affected us worse than we feared. There's going to be another food shortage and famine shortly, if we don't act."

Shutt shook her head. "That's impossible. We've always produced much, much more food than we needed. We have warehouses full of it. That's why we were able to deal with the recent crisis. We had more than enough food, but we lack transport to move it."

"That is all true," Jose agreed. "But the conditions have worsened. It's not critical now, but I'm planning on introducing a resolution into the Senate. We're going to set up a rationing system, assign ration coupons. To make sure everybody gets fed."

"Do we need to do this? It seems… extreme." Chaudhari said.

"We do." Jose extended a comm chip. "The details and numbers are here. You can double check them if you like."

Chaudhari put his hands behind his back. "Numbers, not my thing."

"I'll take it." Russell extended his hand.

Shutt snatched it out of Jose's hands. "Above your pay grade, Sergeant. I'll take care of this."

Jose produced another and slid it into Russell's hand. "Duplicates. Here you go, Mr. Russell."

"Thanks. If I know where the shortages are, I can try to increase production. Once I've got some more things going, I'll let Major Shutt know, and you can buy extra of what you need from the Militia."

"I'll contact you directly, then, shall I, Mr. Russell?"

Russell shook his head. "Nope. I work for Major Shutt, remember."

Shutt nodded. "That you do."

"And I don't even have a real radio that reaches Landing. Something about cells, or local range, or something. All my comm traffic goes through Militia headquarters."

"Does it?" Jose said. "Unfortunate. An extra step always slows things down, but we have to make do with what we have."

"Outstanding," Russell said.

The four of them discussed food, shipping, cargo space, production times, and caloric intake. Jose secured a commitment that they would increase food shipments to Landing, and that the Militia would, along with TGI and the

Free Traders, provide extra guards to help with the food rationing system. Jose thanked them for their time, and left.

Shutt waited until Jose had left and turned on Russell. "You were very quick to agree with Mr. Jose, Sergeant."

"He's a Senator."

"Remember you work for me, Sergeant."

"I do remember Ma'am. I've shot a lot of people for you. Still will, if they have guns. But starving people whose only crime is being in the wrong place? Is that what you want me to do?"

Shutt glared at him. "You don't have to—"

"Is that what you want me to do, Clarisse?" Russell emphasized her name.

Shutt deflated. "Nobody is going to starve. Carry on your duties, Sergeant. Dismissed."

Russell and Chaudhari saluted, she returned the salute and marched out the door. Russell took the revolver he'd been practicing with, checked it was unloaded and opened the cylinder to clean it.

Chaudhari did the same with his. "Was that Major Shutt, or Senator Shutt that was here?"

"Neither. That was some other Shutt. She's scared, that's why she's acting so weird."

"Scared of who?"

"Jose maybe, or Jake Stewart, now that he's back in town."

"I haven't heard that Jake Stewart is a particularly scary guy."

"Me neither. So why is everybody so worried? Jose is scared too. Why did he even set up this meeting? He could have waited, he could have done a whole bunch of things. He should have downplayed the shortages. Last thing we need these days is more drama."

"Maybe he's scared of Jake Stewart too."

"Maybe he is. Feel up to another trip to orbit?"

"What for?"

"Make a new friend. Invite him to visit."

"You know I'm a Senator, right? You can't just order me around."

"And yet, in a day or two you'll be jumping on a shuttle, won't you?"

"Yes." Chaudhari nodded. "I will."

"I'm curious. You are a senator. How come you do what I say?"

Chaudhari flipped the cylinder of his revolver closed. "Whatever happens, you always bring your troops through. If there's any way for it to happen, you make it happen. That's why everybody listens to you. Shutt, I feel like I'm for the high jump when I'm no longer convenient."

"So you understand then?"

"Understand what?"

"We're no longer convenient."

Chapter 10

"Trading is boring," Nadine squirmed back into her chair until she could prop her feet up the console. "How do you stand it?"

"It's not boring," Jake said. "It's fascinating. An endless diversity of products and services in infinite combinations."

He and Nadine had retreated back to the Jump Computer room. Jake sat upright and ran trading simulations using multiple screens. Nadine slouched in her chair, played with fuel consumption profiles, and played the latest music downloaded from the Belt Stations. She stretched her arms and yawned. "Have you been drinking, Stewart? And can I have some?"

Jake shook his head. "This stuff is fascinating." Jake rummaged in a pouch next to him and held up a metal object. "Consider this. What do you see?"

"I see a crazed lunatic with poor social skills boring the crap out of his pilot while taking her on a tortuous path through barely habitable stations at the edge of known space." Nadine snatched the object from him. "Also a screw. A common or garden variety screw.

"It's not only a common type." Jake tapped his console and started a timer. "It's a particular type. It has a certain pitch, a certain length, the distance from one thread is a particular distance. It has dozens of different characteristics that have to be specified if we want things to work out."

"Whoopee, you have a particular type of screw." Nadine rolled her eyes. "Are you going to get rich selling particular types of screws?"

"Yes." Jake nodded. "Richer, that is."

"Richer?" Nadine folded her arms. *What's he up to? I know he's always figuring something out. Dare I ask? It'll be soooo boring but, I've got to figure out how he does it.* "How?"

"I'm developing a database of small metal objects that can be easily machined, are of a standardized size, and in high demand, and assuming that we have a complete set of—"

Jake continued in this line for some time. Helical threads. Gender. Mechanical advantage. Nadine rolled her eyes, sighed, huffed, and finally pinched his mouth shut. "Elastic deformation? Zeus on a plate, Jakey. Can you get any more boring? Stop talking. I don't care. I don't care. And," Nadine threw her arms wide. "I. Don't. Care. Got it?"

"Yes, thanks Nadine." Jake tapped his console and peered at the screen. "Four minutes, thirty-five seconds. Good enough. Double that to be sure, and I'm set. Thank you."

"Set at what?"

"I need to know how long to talk before I get so boring that people give up and will do anything to stop me. I want to be prepared with enough material so that people will stop listening."

"Stewart, you're boring right from the start. Ten seconds ought to do it."

"No, it took you almost five minutes before you cracked. I need twice as long as I talked to you to make sure for others. You're impatient, so you'll be the first to start interrupting my talks and having me switch topics. But after ten minutes everyone will be completely bored."

"I was already completely bored. At ten minutes I'd chew my own arm off to have you stop talking."

"Excellent." Jake typed some more on his console. "That was screws, how much do you know about nuts and bolts? If you can't tell them apart, I can explain the difference."

"Don't make me shoot you Stewart, you know…" Nadine narrowed her eyes. "You know that this sort of thing bores me. You already know that. You knew it before you even started. What are you up to? What are you trying to distract me from?" Nadine shifted tapping through her console screens. "We're still on course, fuel status nominal, all systems online." She turned back to him. "Something is going to bite me, Stewart, what is it?"

"How do you know I'm up to something Nadine?"

"You're always up to something. I know you. It's not a question of are you, it's a question of what. Everything has two and three levels. You're sneaky. Very sneaky. You've got a plan."

"I've got a plan that involves boring everybody talking about metal fasteners and fixtures?" Jake asked.

"Yup." Nadine nodded. "This is some big scam. You're going to use those helical heads to steal a company or destroy a planet."

"It's helical threads."

"Whatever."

"Destroy a planet? With screws?"

"Yup." Nadine pointed her fingers at her eyes. "I'm watching you Stewart."

Watching didn't help. Jake insisted they meander through the outer system. He stopped at the smaller stations, met with the locals, and talked with passing Free Traders. They received plenty of messages. Some from traders, some from Militia ships, and some from unknown addresses on the planet. All were encrypted. Nadine enjoyed the course plotting more than she expected. Jake let her have her head, setting up whatever orbit she wanted.

"I could do it myself of course," Jake said. "But I'm busy working out metal compositions."

"Jakey, you can barely halt a ship with all the docking magnets at full power. And you never met a vector that you didn't think was too fast. I could get out and push faster than you like to maneuver."

"I remind you that I've been doing visual dockings since I was a kid."

"Is that why you dock like a clumsy five-year-old?"

"At least I don't crack the chains when I vector in—"

"Bite me, Stewart." She'd always been a good visual range pilot but the math of the longer trips challenged her. And once he added a fuel budget to their reckoning, it got harder and harder for her to make things work.

"Okay, Mr. spending-fuel-is-like-sucking-blood." Nadine pointed at her final course. Her original, fun course, burned too much fuel. "Hah! See this course? It cuts our fuel consumption by seventy percent! In your face! In your face!"

Jake looked at the displayed course and nodded. "You're right. That's an awesome course. But the direct course takes only six hours, this is six full shifts."

"Yes, but, by waiting the extra two orbits we find that we'll only need a small vector change to come in commo range, and our velocity near them is such that we can hit it in one pass."

"Trading time for fuel, I like it Nadine." Jake grinned. "Exactly what I would have done. Cautious piloting. Efficient piloting. Well done."

Nadine flipped her course back on the screen. "Efficient? Trading time for fuel. I'm not doing that. That's so boring."

"Is it?"

"A hot shot pilot like me doesn't do that."

"Doesn't she? Looks like that's exactly what you're doing. Working within the parameters and restrictions given. Exactly like I would have done. Good for you."

Nadine gulped and gave him a horrified look. *Jove save me. I'm turning into Jake Stewart, thinking like him, piloting like him.* She shuddered. *What if I start dressing like him?* "I can't do it the way I want, because that would use too much fuel…"

"Yes." Jake nodded. "It would."

"Well, that's no fun, it would…" Nadine flipped back to her original layout, then flipped back to her new one. Then back again. *It's true. I've become Jake Stewart. Saving fuel. Taking the cautious way. He tricked me. Next thing you know I'll be measuring boxes to fit them into containers…*

Nadine checked her board, then methodically re-calculated all of her vectors. First she calculated the direct routes, the fast burns, the full G force with a mid-course flip then a full retro burn. Those came naturally to her, often times she had a good estimate of course and distance before the computer even suggested a vector.

But the minimum fuel courses were harder to calculate. She'd guess, but all of her guesses were wrong, sometimes spectacularly so. "Stewart!"

Jake looked up from his screen. "What is it Nadine?" He was researching size and pricing of different shaped eyeglass frames.

"How come I can almost beat the computer with the fastest courses? I figure them out right away, and I just need the computer to refine the details. But the slower fuel courses… they're weird."

"Delta is small. The stations are in similar orbits, and you're always chasing them. Slow down or speed up to match orbits, that's all you need to do. Almost every course you calculate you blast full to speed up and drop lower, pass your target, then retro blast to climb and slow down to meet it. You can almost do it by eye, you're that good."

Nadine beamed. "I'm amazing, aren't I. That's what I do. But why do I do it this way?"

"You think I know?"

"Spill it Stewart. Why do I do this?"

Jake started a price simulation program running on the main computer, leaned back and folded his hands. "That's the way you learned, it works, and it's easy to explain. And you've been practicing it for years. But you only had to get a solution, you've always been on Militia ships, or special corporate couriers—fuel was no problem. Cost was no problem."

Nadine nodded. *That makes sense. I do what I was taught, and my only limit was time. I spent fuel to save time. Because I thought fuel was free. It's all a question of perspective.* She bit her lip. *But I can learn. Show me your evil ways, Stewart.*

Their last adventure, at the planet Magyar, she'd had to manage a revolutionary group and keep them from making stupid mistakes because of poor logistics. She'd been frustrated until she adopted a new mantra. WWJD? What would Jake do? After that, things got easier.

She looked at Jake. "Everything costs something, doesn't it? Fuel. Money. Food."

"Right." Jake nodded. "We have to keep things balanced. If we don't, we'll run out of something important. Air. Water. Food. Fuel. Run out of too much too often, and we're in big trouble. Not only our ship. Everywhere really."

Aha. That's why he's doing it. Nadine grimaced. "Jake, all this fighting. Delta's running out of things, isn't it?"

"Yep. After the abandonment, we were lucky. We had surpluses of everything for passing ships in our warehouses, and we could produce limited replacements. But that's only because the people who founded Delta were smart and built things up, and left things here. We've been working with our capital, not our income. And we're running out of capital. Dashi knew this, that's why he did what he did. He wanted us to reach equilibrium. More resources, more efficient use of our existing resources, or fewer people."

"Fewer people how?"

Jake shrugged. "War. Famine. Plague. That's the traditional way."

"He was trying to stop that." Nadine rubbed her forehead. "You're trying to stop it. You're continuing his work."

"Yes." Jake's program beeped, and he brought up his screen to check the results. "That's why all this trading. We've got a trading ship and access to external resources. If we bring in the right tools, the right inputs, we can stop the decline, and maybe reverse it. We have to get the numbers right, and everyone to work together."

"And you're the best man to do it?"

"I'm the best man to do the strategy. I'm the one who sees this the best. Somebody else needs to be in charge of the working together, the tactics, the day-to-day things. The Senate seems like a good idea."

"And you think you can solve this by trading?"

"Helps everybody." Jake said. "And I get rich. Doing well by doing good, as they say."

Nadine blanked her board, leaned back and put her hands behind her head, then put her feet up and stared into space.

Jake waited in silence for a minute. "Nadine, are you okay?"

"Don't bug me Stewart. I'm thinking."

"Is that what that grinding noise means? And that's why steam is coming out of your ears?"

Nadine scowled at him.

"Sorry."

"Don't be." Nadine nodded. "It's funny because it's true. I'm not what you would call a deep thinker. I get bored too easily."

"Okay...and what now?"

Nadine swung her legs off the console. "Jake, you're wrong."

"Wrong? About what?"

"Nearly everything."

"Could you be more specific?"

"Why was Dashi killed?"

"We don't know who did the actual—"

Nadine shook her head. "Not how. Why. Somebody needed to kill him. Never mind who. Why did they need to do it?"

"Well, because, because.."

"You said yourself that Dashi was working for the best of Delta, and everybody knows that. I knew it and I'm some dumb pilot who thinks bolts grow on space trees."

"I never said you—"

"Shut up Stewart. I know exactly how dumb I am. Anybody who spends time with you gets an immediate education in what a smart person sounds like when they talk. I know I don't sound that way. Not how. Why. Why was Dashi killed?"

Jake blinked once. Then again. "Resource constraints are affecting the political structures. With a surplus of resources, everybody gets along. But as soon as there is any sort of shortage, different groups fight for what they need. The shortages have been temporary, and unequally balanced, so only limited fighting is required to reach a new equilibrium."

"But fighting is inefficient, isn't it? It destroys resources that could otherwise be pooled together for mutual benefit. Rather than being shared to maximize utility, it's removed from the resource pool damaging everybody."

"Yes, that's true—Wait." Jake glared at her. "Where did you learn that?"

"That book you made me read—Capital in the twenty-first century? The old empire one. It talked like that. That phrasing stuck in my head."

"Long phrasing."

Nadine tapped her finger. "Point one. Somebody removed Dashi to protect themselves, their position in the power structure. And the same with the admiral. And Marianne."

"We don't know for sure who killed Dashi," Jake objected. "And the admiral could have been an accident. And Sergeant Russell shot that trader woman in the middle of a confusing battle."

Nadine tapped her second finger. "Point two. The Free Traders were decapitated, their leadership is scared now."

"He said it was an accident—"

"Might have been for him. Not for somebody else."

"Nadine, we can't prove anything—"

Nadine tapped her third finger. "Point three. Grandfather had a saying. Once is coincidence. Twice is enemy action. Three times is a war."

"You have no proof."

"Don't need any. I've got all the validation right here." Nadine pointed at Jake. "I've got the smartest trader jump-ship guy right here, and he says things are going to Hades in a basket, and that all the different groups will tear each other apart and then fight each other for the bloody carcass. Isn't that right?"

"Well, I wouldn't be that poetic…"

"Cause you haven't got my skills." Nadine nodded. "Right, I know what we need to do."

"You do."

"Yes, well what you need to do." *Better make it explicit. He's clueless sometimes.*

Jake sighed. "I know you're going to tell me whether I want to know or not. Fine. What should I do."

"Kill them all," Nadine said. "Jose. Shutt. Russell. The Free Traders council. The Senate. All of them. Kill them all, let Jove sort them out, and you become the new emperor."

"Nadine!" Jake's eyes widened. "I can't do that."

"I know, I know." She grinned at him and patted his cheek. "Not by yourself. Don't worry, I'll help you." She grinned again. "It'll be fun!"

Chapter 11

"Jake, your friends are here!" Nadine yelled from the control room. "Check out their ship. Why can't we have a ship that nice?"

"They're not my friends Nadine, they're business associates. A Belter trade Captain and his cargo master. They come well recommended, but I've never met them before."

"Belters like you? Can we shoot them then?"

Jake tied down the last of the selection of woven fabric samples he'd collected from the Magyar traders onto the galley table. This potential customer had called two shifts ago, asking for tree-silk in quantity. He'd festooned the galley with samples while Nadine had maneuvered hard to meet with them. It made him a tad uneasy—he was now displaying, purely as a demonstration, more wealth in clothing than his entire family had owned when he was younger.

"Nadine, you can't kill everyone we meet." Jake made sure his samples case was mag locked to the wall. With her new fuel consciousness, Nadine now drifted whenever possible. *Feels like I'm at home with Skimmer, floating for ten hours to save a cup of fuel. I do miss her crazy flying. Don't miss his smoking though.*

Nadine ducked under the overhead water pipes as she floated into the galley. "I said shoot them. Not the same thing. Have you decided on my proposal? Kill everyone and let Jove sort them out."

"We are not going to do that."

"We don't have to. I can. But I'll need your support. You know I'm right."

"I know no such thing."

"You've been attacked. You need to defend yourself."

"Nadine I...we can't..."

Nadine grinned. "You'll come around Jake, you always do. Once you've figured out a sufficiently complicated way to defend yourself that nobody expects. I can wait." Her grin widened. "But while I'm waiting, as practice, can I—"

"No shooting, but keep a close watch on them."

"Normally you're super careful with these meetings. Only trusted people."

"I checked them out with a contact, and they said they were legit. They're from a shady merchant family. He said they were unfriendly to strangers, but they knew how to do business."

"Sufficiently shady for us then," Nadine said.

"Shady is as shady does. They were in a hurry to meet with us, which is unusual. And my contact didn't recognize their names, but he did vouch for the codes they used."

"So I've still got a chance to shoot them?"

Jake ignored her. "At least they're on time."

"Right on time. Look at that snazzy ship they have." Nadine pointed at galley display.

"Snazzy?" Jake shook his head. "What do you mean, snazzy?"

"Ships all clean outside. Shiny. Just been painted or patched with new metal or something."

"It's a tug. Tugs should be all beat up."

"Modified tug, like you said. It matched that picture you sent me. And the lights they showed matched."

"Show me," Jake said, stepping over the transverse support beam to get a better view. The display hung from the overhead, across the middle of the galley. Nadine obligingly put a picture on the screen and then split it with an exterior camera shot. As a veteran of dozens of secret meetings during her earlier career for the admiral, she was even more particular than Jake on identifying strangers before meeting them.

"Front catcher cage, control cabin with a door but no airlock, lockers and bins open to space, then all the drive parts external. Standard tug." She flipped back and forth comparing the two pictures. "Only difference from the picture is the coloring. They must have painted the catch cage. Bright silver isn't a great idea, I would have darkened that. And the locker doors have been painted or sandblasted or something. Maybe they clean them?"

Jake flipped the pictures back and forth. *You can't clean things in space. And who would bother?* "Do the lights match?"

"Suck it Stewart," Nadine said. "I was checking lights at meetings before you, well before you…whatever. The pattern matches what you told me to expect."

"Double G's?"

"What?"

"Long-long-short. Long-long-short. GG. Matches what was supposed to be there."

"What do you mean, double G?"

"Morse code. Long-long-short is a G. It's a code. The flashes mean numbers."

"Morse code? Flashes mean numbers? Stewart, I've told you to stop making things up."

"I don't—Never mind."

Nadine pointed at the front of the tug. "The crash cage looks brand new."

Jake nodded. "It does, doesn't it?" The door of the tug swung open and a white gas vented—internal humidity rich air cooling so rapidly that the water froze out. A suited figure rolled out of the hatch behind it, then another. The two of them pushed off from the tug toward *Accounting Error*.

"Looks like your cousins, Stewart. Or some such. That's one of those heavy suits you Belters wear. A Hard suit."

"Hard suit," Jake agreed. His eyes never left the screen. The two figures floated across the void. "Harder to work in than a skin suit but worth it in case of damage."

"You've gone all soft now, Stewart. You barely ever wear that hard suit thing. Mostly you wear that custom skin suit. Quite the dandy you are now." Nadine ran her hand down Jake's covered back. He'd stopped wearing his hard suit after Nadine complained about the smell. He didn't like the lack of pockets for his tools, but Nadine said it made his muscles stand out.

"Dandy, yes." Jake kept staring at the screen. "Not the greatest piloting though. Zero-zero rendezvous, but they're too far away. Most Belter captains would have brought their ship in closer."

"Maybe they're not good at Navigation."

"This isn't Navigation, it's piloting. Close in piloting. That's all we do in the belt." Jake bit his lip and watched the screen.

Nadine waved her hand in front of his face. "Jakey…"

Jake blinked. "Huh? What?"

"How did they clean that catcher so well? It's not like they can wash it. Did they paint it silver?"

"Paint flakes off right away, you have to keep renewing it if you want it to be seen. Micro strikes, radiation, that sort of thing. That's a new catcher grid. And new locker covers."

"Well, they match the pictures we got."

"And the light code is correct. Even if they flash it all the time…"

"Other than that, their tradecraft is stellar," Nadine said. "The admiral would have been proud. A good clandestine setup."

Jake turned to Nadine. "How so?"

"No markings. They must have filed them off, or whatever. Maybe that's why they put on the new locker covers, to hide the numbers. With so many tugs in this system, it would be hard to identify a particular one without Id numbers."

"True."

"And even if they are identified, they could drop that catcher grid, remove it and you'd never find this tug again."

"True—" THUMP "Emperor's scrotum."

"What was that?"

Jake flipped through the screens. "They're on the hull. That's fast. They must have jumped off right away, not waited for a travel line or a tether."

Nadine looked at the darkened picture. "Why is he on one foot?"

"Bad landing," Jake said. "Only one of them locked on, and only with one foot. He caught the second one. Sloppy. With no tether he could float away."

"Who cares?" Nadine said. "You hardly ever use a tether."

"I've been doing this since I was a baby."

"Shouldn't they?"

Jake nodded. "It's odd—"

CLANK CLANK CLANK.

"Weird," Jake said. "They're cranking the outer airlock open."

"Why didn't they wait for us to open up. They're expected."

"Don't know. Let's go meet our guests." Jake bit his lip. "Have you got your knives?"

Nadine flipped one out of her sleeves. "Do I ever not have my knives?" She smiled. "And as far as guns go, as long as I have my boots, you know I always have my backup—"

Jake shook his head. "No shooting on the ship. You'll blow a hole in the hull, or blast some irreparable part, like the jump computer."

Nadine pouted, but nodded.

Jake led the way down the central corridor, bypassing the inset ladder. After the lounge deck came a habitation deck with staterooms, then a storage hold stuffed full of trade goods. Farther aft was the oversized airlock and adjacent ships locker. Fuel storage, engineering, and the engine truss continued aft.

Nadine twitched the camera display next to the airlock door. "Nobody left in the tug, only the two chowderheads out there. They left the door hanging open."

"Sloppy." Jake pointed at the airlock lights. "Green means go, let's air up and let our guests inside." He punched the fill button and waited for the pressure light to turn green. He swung the airlock door open, stepping back as he latched it against the bulkhead.

Two men emerged. Both were shorter than Jake, bulky in their hard suits, with a selection of shiny tools on their belt. The first stepped through and stared. "This is a nice ship," he said, through his external speaker. He didn't remove his helmet.

"Thanks." Jake pointed at the helmet. "You going to take that off?"

"Not until I know it's safe." The helmet swiveled. "This is a very, very nice ship."

"Safe?" Jake looked around. "I'm breathing here, you worried about the smell?"

"You core types don't understand. These hard suits can't be pulled on and pulled off, easier to leave it on."

"Is that so?" *No, it's not so. I've got a bad feeling about this.* Jake had worn hard suits his whole life — there were a whole number of dangerous situations where you had to get a helmet off in a hurry. Every Belter kid knew how to do an emergency release by age three. "Didn't know that. Well, come on up to the galley then, we'll show you the goods, and you can have a glass of basic, or would you rather orange juice?"

"Orange juice?" The helmet nodded. "You have orange juice? I love orange juice. Lead on."

Jake turned to Nadine. *I let them onboard without checking. This is bad. Very bad.* "You heard the man. Let's go to the galley. More room for you. You can show him your tool kit as well."

"Jake," Nadine propelled herself backwards. "These better be good customers. We don't want to waste any orange juice on just anybody."

"You know how we Belter Boys love our orange juice. Brings me back to when I was a kid, end of week dinner. Especially the lime juice, that's the best. I love the taste, same as you." *Remember Nadine, please remember.*

Nadine's head swiveled so she could look over her shoulder. Jake had told her that he never saw orange juice out on the Rim, he was too poor. And she'd described how she'd gagged on lime juice-she'd ordered it because it was the most expensive item on the menu, and hated the taste.

Only real Belters wore hard suits. And real Belters never tasted either juice. *This was a problem. These men weren't Belters…*

"Of course, Jakey. Let's get to the Galley, I'll show these two everything." She pulled herself up to the galley area.

Jake followed at a sedate pace. *I need to give her time to get anchored.* The man behind him bumped into Jake's feet.

"Hey!"

"Sorry," Jake said. "I'm out of practice." Nadine cleared the door ahead of him, then rolled forward and twisted mid air, landing feet-first, upside down on the bow water pipe. Jake followed her into the galley, grabbed the overhead electric line and pivoted left to the basic tap. "Let me get you your orange juice." He grabbed a metal cup and filled it with pale yellow basic from the sip spout, then extended it to the man. "Here you go. I think I'll get one for myself. You'll need to take your helmet off if you want some."

Seeing the juice cup floating in front of him, the first man reached up and undid his helmet spring, and tried to twist it off. The helmet rotated counter clockwise and came loose. At the same time, his body counter rotated, he'd forgotten to lock his feet. He grabbed the helmet in one hand, which made the rotation worse.

Jake ignored the spinning, cursing figure. He balanced with one hand on the counter, the other held another metal cup of basic. "Does your friend want a cup too? And do you two have names?"

The second suited-figure had cleared the hatch. He stuck both hands out to stop from crashing into the galley table and ended up pivoting feet first to the ceiling.

Jake assessed the situation. *Idiot number one is floating, no threat. Nadine's anchored. With his helmet off, she can hit him any time. Idiot number two has a hand on the table, so he can maneuver, but he's in an awkward spot. We have time, and I need information.* "Do you two have names?"

Idiot number one—the floater—continued spinning, his arm's flailing. "A little help here."

Jake twisted and extended his foot, stopping the other man's spin. "Having a few problems with your new suit?"

"These are harder than they look," the man said, sweat beading his face. "You're Jake Stewart?"

"Nope." Jake shook his head. "I'm Norman. That's Jacky," he pointed at Nadine, "over there. Some people call her Jake, isn't that right Stewart?"

"Absolutely true." Nadine continued to hang upside down at the front of the compartment, her arms loose. "Jacky Stewart. What do I call you two? Spin and Roll?"

"I thought Jake Stewart was a guy?" Spin, the free floating one asked. His companion, Roll, struggled behind him to drag his boots to the galley table hook-rail.

"Who told you that?" Jake asked.

"That Militia guy…" Spin tried to get a view of his companion over his shoulder, and succeeded only in starting a slow roll. "Crap."

"The Militia sent you?" Jake asked. "The Militia? They want to do a little clandestine trading."

"Jove's knees," Spin dropped his helmet and scrabbled at his tool belt. "I'm going to get sick if this keeps up."

"You've never been in space before, have you?"

"Not like this." He snapped open a tool pouch and produced a revolver. "Doesn't matter though. Look, could you stand still while I do this? Otherwise the blood gets everywhere. Nothing personal, but this ship is so much nicer than ours, it'd be a shame to mess it up."

"You're not the people that Bobby-one-thruster mentioned are you?"

"Don't know a Bobby one-thruster," the man said. "All I know was I'm supposed to get in this tug, come out here and take care of business." He pointed the revolver at Jake. "And you're the business. I don't know who's who, but I can take care of both of you easy."

Jake stared at the barrel. *He's not aligned on me yet. And the trigger pull will pivot him up. He'll miss, I can duck under it. There's nothing important behind me, only the basic dispenser. I can risk talking more.* "Who sent you?"

"Thousand credits sent me, that's who. Friend of a friend of a friend, get in this tug thing, come out here, shoot everyone in the ship. Nothing personal, just business. Look, why don't you step back, make this easier? I promise that I'll make you go easy if you do. No mess, no fuss, last thing you want is problems. I hit you in the stomach with this, takes you a long time to die." He looked beyond Jake to Nadine. "And can she stop being upside down? I'll make her go easy too."

"Of course. Nadine?" He glanced at her. She nodded. The man's eyes followed.

Jake hooked his feet under the galley rail, and squatted. Squatted, not ducked. The squat dipped him down without unbalancing him. He checked his motion and threw his cup of basic as hard as he could. It flew past Spin's shoulder and smacked into his companion. Without seeing where it hit, he launched out. Spin waved his arm, the gun tracking. Jake slammed into it, got both hands around Spin's wrist and twisted. Spin yelled, and rolled into Jake, then screamed. Warm liquid splashed Jake's head. Jake twisted again and the revolver dropped loose.

"Jules," Spin yelled. "Get them Jules."

Jake pushed off the galley table and dove to the deck, hitting, rolling and bouncing up across the table.

"Shoot Jules, Shoot them—GURRG."

Jake snatched a two meter wide swatch of dark blue tree silk and shoved off again. He bumped off Spin. Jake noted one of Nadine's throwing knifes in Spin's throat, and what looked like an ear floating next to him in a cloud of blood globules.

Why'd she cut off his ear? The blood will get everywhere.

Jules raised his revolver, but Jake carried past the windmilling arm, and smacked into the man's chest. He grunted as Jake hit him, but the armor absorbed the hit. Jake pushed the helmet's quick release catch, and the spring half lifted it off his head. Jules cursed as it banged on an overhead pipe and stuck, his helmet half off. Jake stuffed the swath of tree-silk over his head, blinding him.

BOOM. Jake's body shook from the gunshot next to his ear. His hearing blanked.

Jake couldn't hear the next two shots, but saw flashes and felt the recoil, pushing them to the stern of the ship. *Keep shooting, keep shooting. Aft is where I want to be.*

The revolver fired again and again, bouncing them from side to side and backwards down the central tunnel. From long experience, Jake reacted to each shot, continually driving them sternwards, and squirming under Jule's grasp. *If he thinks, he'd try to shoot himself in the chest. The chest piece would stop his shot, especially if it went through me first.*

Red and green lights burned ahead, Jake threw out an arm to adjust his spin, then shoved off the wall with one foot. Jules slammed back-first into the open airlock hatch. Jake stomped the ground, kicked a magboot on, and rolled the cursing Jules into the open air lock. Then he grabbed the airlock door and slammed it shut.

Nadine appeared beside him. Her hair was covered in blood. "Nadine, are you hurt?"

Nadine shook her head and spoke. Jake didn't understand, his hearing was still gone. Nadine's lips moved again. Jake shook his head. Nadine screamed at him. "Not mine. Ears bleed a lot. Thanks for ruining my aim."

"Sorry," Jake mouthed. Nadine ducked back. Jake realized that he'd shouted, and her hearing was in better shape than his.

"Who sent them?" Nadine yelled.

"Militia, I think." Jake said.

"Outstanding." Nadine smiled. "Now we have a target. We'll execute your daring plan." She shrugged. "Whatever it is. Don't need him anymore." She looked at the airlock, then slapped the external vent button.

"Nadine." Jake was back to screaming. "His helmet isn't latched. And I don't think he knows how to fix it."

Nadine smiled and leaned closer and yelled so Jake could understand. "Well, he has the rest of his life to fix it."

She slapped the control. The airlock lights all flashed red, and the outer hatch vented.

Chapter 12

"But they said the Militia sent them." Nadine thrust out an arm to adjust her spin and tapped feet-first onto the defeated killer's tug. "That's what he said…"

Jake dropped in beside her. The tug's cab was wide enough for both of them to lock on. "Before you killed him. Yes, that's what he intimated, yes."

"It's not my fault that he's dead, Stewart. They came to kill us, and I reacted to it. There's no difference between stabbing them with a knife, or pushing them out an airlock. They brought it on themselves, stop blaming me." Nadine twitched her belt. *He does have a point. I can be quick on the draw, sometimes. But those guys were scary, and they killed grandfather.* Nadine's eyes teared for a moment, then her spirit hardened. *I'm tired of people trying to kill us. I need to convince Jake to do something about that, soon.*

"I'm not blaming you." Jake detached the far side of his tether—they'd stayed attached to *Accounting Error* when they jumped—and reeled it in. Then he stepped sideways and grasped the frame of the open cabin door and swung in.

"Yes you are. You're using weird words again, Stewart." Nadine reeled her own tether in. "You only do that when you're angry with me. That's what he 'intimated'?" She tapped his suit. "When you're using words like that it means you're angry. Shove over and let me in."

Jake slid to the left-hand seat and brought up the tug's computer. He put the fuel and maintenance log up on the screen. Nadine slammed the door before activating her screen. She started the re-airing sequence and brought up a course plot while she waited. "Slowest air system I've ever seen. Going to take ten minutes to fully air up in here."

"There was no need to kill him." Jake flipped through screens, stopping at the fuel log. "They got fuel at Transit-17. The receipt said it was paid by a corporate account."

"Which corporation?"

"Numbered company. Never heard of them. I can look them up back on *Accounting Error*, but I'll bet it's some shell company."

"Whatever that means," Nadine said, checking her plot. "They took a standard course to here from Transit-17. Same course I would have mapped when life was cheap, fun and I didn't have to account for every liter of fuel to an anal-retentive trading fanatic, if that matters. And you're welcome."

"Welcome for what?"

"Saving your butt from those killers."

"Nadine, you can't—"

"Yes, Yes I can Jake." Nadine spun her helmeted head to face Jake. "I'm not out there killing everybody I see, no matter what you 'intimate'. These people snuck on board, lied to us, pulled a weapon, threatened to kill us, and then shot at us. They're part of the group that killed granddad. They deserved to die." *And I panicked, just a little. But I'm never going to admit to that.*

"Thrown out an airlock?"

Nadine lifted her hands to her shoulders, a suited person's hand signal for a shrug. "That was a bonus, I'll admit."

Jake regarded her. "Thanks. Thanks for looking out for me. I should have been more careful. You saved us. I'm glad that you killed them. It was us or them."

"Told you so Stewart, told you so." She leaned in and touched her helmet to his, so she could look him in the eye. "Glad you recognize how awesome I am. And since you've admitted that, I will say I do kinda sorta wish I hadn't spaced him right away. It would have been nice to have a few more questions answered. Earless certainly didn't help."

Before coming to the tug, Jake and Nadine had searched the other body on board, finding only some money and a cheap generic comm unit. Jake had shoved him into the black. He'd kept the ear.

"He didn't have anything personal on him at all," Jake said. "No ID, no custom tools, no personal comm unit, not even a favorite snack in his pouch. Who travels like that?"

"Professionals, that's who. Professionals who are trained to not leave a trace behind."

"Like Militia people," Jake said.

"They did say they were from the Militia." Nadine flipped through the course settings. "Or intimated it, as you would say. Jake, these course settings were loaded from an external source, like a course chip."

"How can you tell?"

"The way the waypoints were entered. If you're doing manual course setting, you put in the first waypoint, then calculate the vector changes and enter them, then the second waypoint. The creation times are different. These creation times are all the same, down to the millisecond. They were given this course on a chip."

"Anything special with the course?"

"It started at Transit-17, it's the same course I would have calculated if you told me where to go."

"You told me that before, and I'm not sure—oh. In other words, not a course put in by a Belter," Jake said.

"Or Free Traders," Nadine said. "If what you say is true. This was done by somebody with my training, Militia or a big corporation, not you fuel-obsessed belt people."

"Fuel-obsessed Belt People, thanks Nadine. And speaking of fuel…" Jake tapped through screens. "This tug is almost empty. They would have run out of fuel if they hadn't found us."

Nadine brought the screen up herself. "Well, they did find us, but they're still nearly out of fuel."

"Who sets up a course into the black without enough fuel to come back?" Jake asked.

Nadine twisted her shoulders side-to-side. "People who don't care if they come back or not."

Jake and Nadine sat silently while they digested this.

"People," Jake said, frowning, "Who don't care if they come back or not. But those bruisers didn't seem like the suicidal type to me."

"Nor to me. Not enough imagination," Nadine said. "Especially since they didn't create their own course…"

"They would have checked it," Jake said. "Double checked it to make sure that they weren't going to get in trouble."

"That's Jake Stewart the paranoid Belter talking." Nadine gestured at the board. "Until you forced me into indentured fuel servitude, I would have assumed we had enough fuel to get me there and back, especially if I was given a course." *One more thing to worry about now whenever I fly. Thanks for increasing my paranoia, Stewart. Then again, paranoid people live longer.* She had a mental vision of a long ago fight. She'd known that woman wasn't harmless, but decided to give her the benefit of the doubt. She still had the burn scar from the hidden laser. And Wayne hadn't made it out at all. *Better to be judged by twelve than carried by six.*

"And you said they were trained like you," Jake said. "So they—probably—wouldn't have checked the fuel either."

"But why give them a course and not enough fuel? It's not like they can't get on the radio and call somebody? We're in the outer system, but we can record a message and send it inward. Somebody will hear it in time to come get us."

Jake tapped through the screens. "Radio screen says not installed."

"No radio?" Nadine asked. "Even I would have noticed that when I did pre-flight."

"Maybe they were told not to." Jake reached underneath the control board and fiddled with the latch. "Nadine, did you bring any tools?"

"When do I ever bring tools Jakey?" Nadine gestured at her form fitting skin suit. "There's nowhere to put them that doesn't mess up my look. Besides, you always have tools."

"Not when I don't have my hard suit on, I don't," Jake said.

"That's stupid, not wearing your hard suit."

"Didn't you say that the smell was—"

"Shut up Stewart. I can't be responsible for all the things that you think you heard me say."

Jake bent down and fumbled with his mag boots, then pulled out a multi-tool from a concealed slot. He selected a screw setting, then unfastened a panel on the board. "Give me a hand, try to pry this off as I loosen it. I want a better look at the radio components."

"You said you didn't bring any tools?"

"This is my emergency backup tool. I keep it in my boot."

"Meaning you have tools."

"Hardly any. Wait one." Jake braced his feet so he wouldn't spin and twisted the screws free. He collected each screw as it came loose and handed them to Nadine. "Put these somewhere you can find them again."

Nadine grumbled, but set them to one side in a line. "Look at me, organizing screws by size. I've become Jake Stewart. Next thing you know I'll have a spare screwdriver strapped to my wrist."

"We can only hope." Jake jammed his multi-tool under the edge of the panel. "It's stuck. Get your fingers under here and pull."

"I'm in a suit, Stewart. Not simple. Not easy." Nadine jammed her fingers next to his, and together they levered the panel up until it popped loose in a shower of white flakes.

"Glued in," Jake said. "Weird."

Nadine looked inside. "What's a radio look like?"

Jake tapped his temple to turn on his suit floodlight, then leaned over, but was blocked by Nadine. "I can't see. Is there a metal box about six inches long with a blue-red-blue stripe on the top, plugged into the expansion bus."

"No metal box, no." Nadine tilted her helmet forward. "There is three—no four—brown cylinders with red ends, with wires stuck in them leading to a circuit board. The circuit board has a countdown display on it."

"Not a radio then?"

"Nope." Nadine shook her helmet. "It's a bomb. And we've got one minute left."

Chapter 13

The countdown clock reflected red Nadine's visor. "Bomb. I hate bombs. Time to go, Stewart." Nadine fumbled for the door handle on her side. "They're going to blow the ship."

Jake grabbed his door handle. "My door's stuck."

Nadine yanked on hers. "Mine as well." She pulled again, and the handle snapped loose. "Some assembly required, handle not included. Jakey, get your magic tool out over there and unlock the door."

"It's a screw driver and pliers, not a magic wand." Jake pulled out the biggest screwdriver, stretched over her waist and tried to fit it to the door lock. "And it's too small for these bolts."

Nadine rolled sideways and lay her head on Jakes lap. "Grab my shoulders."

"Nadine, now is not the time—"

"I'm not horny, you imbecile. Brace me so I can kick my door open."

Jake wedged himself into his seat and braced his feet, the hooked his arms behind Nadine's shoulders. "Go."

Nadine kicked hard. And again. Again. The door didn't budge. *This isn't working. I'm not kicking hard enough. All those exercise classes are going to waste, we're going to die here. Harder. Kick harder.*

"Kick the lock, Nadine. Not the door."

"And kiss my hairy—" Nadine gave him instructions on where to kiss. She didn't stop kicking. "Emperor's hairy armpits. Who builds these things this strong? How long have we got?"

Jake peered into the open panel. "Twenty-two seconds. I don't suppose you have any of my tools hidden in your boots?"

"Your tools in my boots?" Nadine looked up. "I don't carry your tools." *I never carry his tools, but I do carry mine.* She squirmed up, pulled her legs back, reached down, and fumbled at her boots.

"Nadine much as I enjoy this, I don't think we have time. Oh!"

Nadine popped her left heel off. Inside was a coil with a mini-power pack—half of her backup gauss pistol. "Other side."

Jake rolled her onto her right side. She grabbed her other heel and pulled the magazine of nickel-tungsten needles out and slammed it into the coil.

Nadine extended her hand and fired a burst at the door. The accelerated needles chewed up the door latch, but the door didn't move.

"Ten seconds, Nadine," Jake said. His voice was level but his faceplate clouded with condensed breath.

Nadine kicked out, hard. *How do you know when it's time to panic? When something in space makes Jake Stewart breathe fast.* "Still stuck."

"Blow out the window."

"We won't fit."

"Do it. Trust me. Do it."

Nadine raised her aim and fired in a circle, shattering the window. Shards blew outwards. The air foamed into cloud as the pressure dropped, then became deathly clear as the air evacuated.

Jake grabbed Nadine's shoulder and shoved her to the roof of the cab. She flailed her arms trying to get a purchase.

"What the hell? Stewart?"

Jake swept his hand under her, grabbed the loose radio panel, and punched it into the window, smashing the remaining glass out. The panel continued out in the void. Jake ducked under Nadine and stuck his hand outside the door. He groped outside for the emergency hinge lever. He found it and pushed down, lifting the hinge pins out of their sockets.

"Kick!"

Nadine kicked out. One foot hit the top of the door and wrenched it loose. The other slammed into Jake's shoulders and pushed his shoulder into the door. The door exploded outwards. Jake's inertia making him follow, but he grabbed Nadine's foot and pulled her along with him. They blasted out into the void, spinning and pinwheeling through space, toward *Accounting Error.*

"Hang on," Jake said. "We've only got seconds."

"We're too close."

Jake grabbed the spinning door, rolled it to face the ship, kicked out a foot to balance and dragged Nadine behind him, all in one motion. He'd almost got her behind him when the ship exploded.

Chapter 14

"More basic?" Jake reached for Nadine's glass. "You'll be dehydrated."

"Not dehydrated enough to drink more of that." Nadine picked at her food tray. "It makes even this mush taste good. Red-Red-White? Apples, and.. What?"

"Apples, beets, and that's porridge. Made with rye." Jake slurped up a spoonful. "Try it with some soy sauce. Unless you're saving all our soy sauce for recreational purposes."

"That's me. Nadine, recreation consultant." Nadine lifted her arm, then clenched her teeth as the pain hit. Explosive debris hadn't penetrated their suits, thank the Emperor. But it had smacked them around and disoriented them. Both had slammed sideways into *Accounting Error* in the confusion. After climbing out of the airlock, they'd headed for the med pod. Jake had a sprained ankle. Nadine's shoulders were bruised, and the med computer said multiple pulled muscles in her arms. The pain drugs made them both sleepy and hungry.

Nadine took a bite of beet mulch and gagged. "Jake, why would the Militia blow up that ship?"

"We're not sure it was the Militia."

"Jake." Nadine waved her fork at him. "Dashi's dead, that Militia woman was the last person who was with him. The admiral's dead, that Militia woman was the last person to see him. Marianne, that offspring of a diseased beefalo was shot by the Militia. The Militia has launched two different coups in the last while. They're trying to take over the system."

"Your grandfather wasn't trying to take over the system, he wanted the status quo back. Have you looked at the make-up of Dashi's new Senate? It's split between the Big Corps, some unaligned ones, Free Traders, and only a few Militia people. If the Militia was going to take over the system, they would have done it before the election. That's hard to square with somebody who wants to take things over." Jake grimaced. "Even if one of the Militia Senators is a corporal."

"That Chaudhari guy. I met him," Nadine said. "He isn't that bright. He worked for that Sergeant, Russell. We need to watch him."

"I know why you watch him, but why do I need to?" Jake grinned.

Nadine stuck her tongue out at him. It was no secret that she had a major level crush on the Sergeant. "Because he's up to something. Plotting."

"My information is that he's out in the boondocks somewhere getting some damaged factories up and running."

"Big job for a simple sergeant. But he's smarter than he looks." Nadine set her spoon down. *I find the smart ones attractive now. Oh no. Am I... maturing?*

"He'd almost have to be," Jake said.

Nadine stuck her tongue out at him again. "Back to the ship. Fine, I'll play. The Militia didn't blow up that ship. Who did?"

"Somebody who didn't want the Militia to be blamed for killing us. They sent out those thugs, and they were supposed to kill us and then vanish."

"Why didn't they kill us and vanish then? As long as they don't tell anybody, who would know?"

"Save money by not paying the killers?"

"Jake." Nadine waved her fork again. "Even I know that a tug is worth a lot more than a thousand credits. That's what they said they would get paid. Dump them in an alley somewhere, sure. But blow up an entire tug?"

Jake nodded. "You're right. Somebody wanted them to disappear."

"After they killed us."

Jake pointed at the tray in front of Nadine. "You going to eat that?"

Nadine shoved the tray across to him. "Be my guest. But why would the Militia do that? Kill us and then pretend they didn't?"

"Could have been the Free Traders."

Nadine flipped one of her knives out of her wrist sheath and spun it. "Could have been the ghost of dead emperors manifesting in space and overloading the fusion drive. But the same question, why the double-blind?"

Jake put a mouthful of red mush in his mouth, chewed, and swallowed.

Nadine watched him chew. "You don't have to chew it. It's mush, just swallow it."

"You do if you buy cheap trays, the end runs, sometimes they have chunks of stuff in them, you choke on it."

"These trays come from our supplies before we left Delta. Finest money can buy."

"Habit, I guess." Jake stared off into space. "I'm not sure what's going on. I'm not sure who is after us, or why. I'm not sure what can happen." He nodded again. "That will be our strategy."

"Confusion is our strategy?" Nadine spun her knife again. "Cause if it is, it's working great on me right now, I'm completely confused."

"We don't know who sent those guys to kill us?"

"Nope."

"We don't know who sent the bomb to blow them up."

"Nope."

"And even though we have suspicions about who, we don't have any idea why Dashi, the admiral, and Marianne were killed."

"Right."

Jake scraped up the last of the mush on his tray. "Good, well you know what to do."

Nadine raised an eyebrow. "I do?"

"Sure you do."

"Why don't you remind me then," Nadine said. "I mean, I remember, but just in case you don't why don't you tell me…"

"Paranoia. Assume everyone is our enemy. Assume they're all out to get us. Take the battle to them, every one of them."

"A big fight! I like it." Nadine thumped the table with the hilt of her knife. "In fact, I love it. When do we start?"

"Right now," Jake said. "We're going to take the battle to them."

"Wonderful." Nadine thought for a moment. "Jake?"

"Yes?"

"Who are the 'them' that we're taking the battle to?"

"All of them. The Militia. The Free Traders. TGI. The unaligned corps. The Militia. Sergeant Russell. Even that corporal guy."

"Um…" Nadine bit her lip. "That's a lot of enemies to take on at once."

"Not up for it Nadine? You were the one saying to kill them all earlier."

"Well…" Nadine squirmed. "That would be nice, a great idea, of course it is because it's my idea. But that's a lot of people to take on at once."

"Don't think you can do it? You said you could."

"Jake." Nadine frowned. "I say a lot of things. Nowadays, I sort of count on you to rein in my more… ambitious ideas."

"Don't worry about ambitious," Jake said. "I'm going to be more ambitious than you even suspected. We're going to war." Jake drank his basic off in one. "War. But war Jake Stewart style."

Chapter 15

"Jake, I thought we were going to war?" Nadine punched the code into the docking truss airlock on Transit-33. The light stayed red.

"We are. You got that entry code wrong. Add two threes at the end. That's the station number, they always add that here."

Nadine laboriously re-typed the code, adding the extra threes, then watched the lights flash green. It took both of them to shove the door open before they could step into the airlock. Pushing it shut was no easier. The fans whirred as the air system attempted to drop the pressure down to one third of the stations regular pressure. By the look of the indicator lights, this would take a long time.

"No, I mean people are trying to kill us. And you're not even armed."

Jake pointed at the harness over Nadine's custom skin suit. "You've got enough weapons for both of us. Three revolvers?" Nadine had two thigh holsters, and another one visible behind her right hip. "You've only got two hands. And two knife sheaths? Why bother?"

"Because, Jakey, the next time somebody sneaks up on us and captures us, I'll be able to keep shooting longer without reloading. There's a shortage of ammo in this system, not weapons, remember."

"If somebody sneaks up on us, by definition, you won't see them coming, so they'll hit you on the head and knock you out."

"And if that happens, then when they search me they'll take the three visible guns off me, and those crappy knives in the sheath. They won't bother to search farther. I've got my gauss pistol in my boot heels, a knife hidden in each forearm, one down my back, and two others hidden as well."

"You've got six knives? Even for you that's paranoid."

"Somebody needs to be." Nadine surprised herself with a stifled sob. *If he'd been more paranoid, maybe grandfather would have survived. Well, nobody will get the better of us after this. I'll kill them first.* "Why don't you take at least one revolver?"

"Nadine, you've seen me shooting. I'm more likely to shoot my own foot, twice, than to shoot anybody else."

"Not everybody knows that." *Well, except for everybody who has met you. I can keep an eye out for physical trouble, but it would be nice if he could at least distract them.*

"Everybody I'm going to talk to will. Besides, I have my tool kits."

"You don't look even vaguely threatening."

"That's the point, isn't it?" Jake typed the code into the far door in the airlock and waited until the lights flashed green before hauling it in. "Nobody suspects me. I'm free to do what needs to be done. And I've got the tools for it."

He passed through the airlock hatch, climbing up a step to enter the docking truss. After their explosion incident he'd switched back to his battered hard suit. Nadine surveyed his new look. *He's got two different electronic repair kits on his belt, and at least three wrenches. He spent two hours on trading plans before we got here. And he can kill more people with those than I can with all my ammunition.* Nadine's stomach clenched as she followed him. *I'm okay with fighting things I can see. This war from the shadows isn't something I'm good at. Half the time I don't know what I should do with these people—shoot them or give them a cup of basic.* Nadine grimaced. *Give them a cup of basic? Wonderful, I'm half Belter now.*

The noise increased tenfold as they climbed up to the docking truss. This was the shared truss, not the main ring section, and it teemed with crew, merchants, passengers and thieves.

Militia ships, Corp ships, Passenger drop ships, even big Free Traders with money docked at proper airlocks on the Stations outer rings. Each got a dedicated airlock, and the bigger ships could get two - a large cargo airlock and a smaller passenger one.

But this was not the regular cargo concourse. This was the discount docking truss. One airlock for three dozen hatches. Cheap construction and limited safety interlocks—but within the budget of the smallest Free Traders,

"This place is a zoo." Nadine covered her nose. "A smelly zoo."

"I like it." Jake smiled as they walked down the central corridor. "Reminds me of home."

Nadine stepped past a stack of crates piled in front of a hatch. An open crate displayed a complete set of galley dishes in steel—plates, cups, knifes, forks, all laid out for inspection. At the next dock a dark-haired woman knitted on a chair. A locked glass case at her feet displayed mittens and socks. The man holding a shotgun next to her looked enough alike that he had to be her brother.

Jake stopped and exchanged pleasantries with the woman, and admired her work. Nadine scanned the crowd. The crowd scanned her right back. Most people wore hard suits like Jake. The regular skin suits that she saw were badly fitted collections of random pieces thrown together. Her custom outfit stood out. Many of the lock denizens pointed her out to their friends. Their expressions were not welcoming.

"I stand out here," Nadine said.

"Yes Nadine, yes. You're beautiful, I get it, and you look so much better than these other women, you have better fashion sense—"

"Bite me Stewart. I stand out as different. Not good looking, but rich. Somebody to rob. Not somebody to trust." She unconsciously reached for her revolvers. "Everybody's looking at me."

"You're with me," Jake said. "They recognize my type, if not me personally. We'll be fine. Don't shoot anyone. At least not without asking first."

"I promise I'll ask first." Nadine stepped past different sizes of pipes laid out on the deck. "But I'll ignore your answer. Anybody could steal these pipes. Steal the steel! Hah! Don't they need a guard?"

Jake shrugged. "Where are they going to take them? Back to their ship? Everybody will see them do it. Besides, pipes aren't worth stealing."

"What about that guy with the shotgun guarding those dinner sets?"

Jake laughed. "He wasn't guarding the dinner sets. He was guarding the mittens."

"The mittens?"

"The dinner sets are steel. We've got so much steel in orbit we can almost give it away. One of the orbital factories has a press that churns those plates by the thousands. But mittens."

Jake shook his head. "That needs wool. It has to be lifted from dirtside. That costs money. And then to size it specially for somebody costs even more. It's a luxury item. Most Belters and a lot of Free Traders inherit their clothes. Skin suits last forever, so do most station items. In fact—" Jake stopped to look at a set of pumps.

Nadine watched. Water, fuel, or air, she couldn't tell which.

He exchanged greetings with the vendor and moved on. "In fact, I'll bet those mittens are the most expensive items here. Maybe the seals for the pumps there. Notice the owner has the pumps laid out all over the table, but the plastic washers are right in front of him where he can keep his eyes on them."

Nadine's eyes followed Jake's gesture. Now that she knew what to look for, it was obvious. Metal and ceramic items were thrown out with abandon, barely noticed. But small pockets of electronics, wooden or fabric items were closely guarded. "You continue to amaze me Stewart." They passed a table of carved wooden chopsticks. "Why, I think that—oh." She grabbed Jake's arm. "That's why you brought back all that fabric and silk and stuff."

"Yes."

"And coal." Nadine hadn't been able to figure out why Jake brought so much of the dirty rock back. She'd been making jokes about coal-burning spaceships for weeks. "I get it now. You can make plastic from coal. But is it worth it to lug all that coal back here?"

"Check the prices of the washers for those pumps and tell me what you think." Jake stopped at a closed hatch and checked the number. "The *Kaskaskia*. This is who we need to talk to." He punched a call code into the ship comm.

"Yes?" A female voice said.

"I need to talk to the captain."

"Are you here to buy fuel?"

"I'm here to buy something." Jake introduced himself and Nadine, and asked to speak to the captain on a 'confidential matter.'

"Wait." The intercom clicked off.

Nadine waited with Jake. Jake crossed his arms and surveyed the crowd. His eyes lingered on different groups of spacers wandering around. "Lots of business being conducted here. All sorts of groups operating."

"How can you tell?"

"Nothing special," Jake said. "I just know it. I'll have to handle things a bit differently this time."

The airlock door swung open behind them. Like all ship airlocks it opened in. The interior lights were off, or dimmed. Nadine squinted and peered inside. "There's nobody there."

"I'm right here," a voice said.

Nadine looked down. A freckle-faced young woman in a patched skin suit stared back at her. Her name tape said E Lopez.

Nadine bent down. "Kid, we need to talk to your parents."

"Do you want to buy fuel?"

"No, I don't want to buy fuel."

"Then we don't have any business, do we?"

"What?" Nadine glared at her. "Listen, kiddo. I want to talk to your father. Or your mother. Some adult."

The young woman glared at her, then crossed her arms. "They won't give you a better price. I know all the prices for our fuel. If you don't want to buy any, then go away."

"Listen, you little twit, we need—"

Jake tapped Nadine's shoulder.

"What?"

Jake eased her aside. "Thanks Nadine, I've got this for now. Thank you." He stepped in front of Nadine and nodded at the young woman . "Free Trades—" he checked her name tape—" crewman Lopez."

The young woman narrowed her eyes. "Free Trades."

"Are you a watch officer?"

Lopez nodded.

"And do you have the watch?"

Lopez nodded again.

"Good. Then you can act as your ships commercial representative. I'm in the market for a specific atmosphere mix. I need ten thousand cubic meters of standard nitrogen-oxygen mix, but with all the argon frozen out. Can you give me a price?"

The young woman 's eyes were still narrowed. "That's custom mix. We don't have it in stock."

"This is the *Kaskaskia*? you're a tanker?"

She nodded.

"Then if you don't have it in stock, you can mix it up with your fuel processing plant."

"We'd have to dump the argon," Lopez said. "Not worth storing, cause not much of a market for it. Unless you'll take it. Do you have dual hose connections on your ship?"

"Nope," Jake said. "Single hose, single mix. You have to get rid of the argon yourself."

"We're processing right now," Lopez said. "You'll have to wait until we finish the main tank."

"I'm in a hurry," Jake said. "I need it soon. Very soon. You can abort your primary processing run."

Lopez shook her head. "Main tank processes first. We've got contracts here for water and oxygen, other ships to fill."

Jake shrugged. "Well, if you can't do it, I'm sure the *Salamonie* can. I'll go and talk to her captain. I'll bet he'll give me a better deal, and faster too."

"Nope." Lopez grinned. It made her freckles stand out. "Sal's too busy. She has even more of a backlog than we do."

"And you know that because…." Jake tilted his head.

"He's my uncle." Her grin widened. "He an my dad, they work together on contracts. Won't get him to dump regular station contracts for some dirt sider."

"Do I look like a dirt sider?" Jake tapped the chest plate of his hard suit. "And did I mention I want this delivered to a Belt station?"

"That's gonna cost a lot," Lopez said. "A big lot."

"Give me a price. I'll put down a deposit to cover the processing, and the delivery."

"What type of deposit?"

"Copper." Jake said. "Or fabric, if that's what you need."

"Fabric?" Lopez smiled. "Fabric, and we can talk. Dad's across the station helping fit hoses. He won't be back for a shift, but we can get the particulars laid out now. How do you want it done? Wet lease or dry lease?"

Nadine lost interest in the discussion as Jake and the young woman talked about things like 'deposits in escrow' and 'allowances for reasonable wear and tear'. *Why is he negotiating with this child? Shouldn't he be talking to her parents? There's got to be a reason. Every stupid, time-consuming, infuriating, unimportant detail that he obsesses over ends up being something that he makes bank on. I have to be patient.*

She stood side on to them to keep an eye on the crowd behind them on the truss. Three younger spacers had walked down from a bulk freighter two locks up. They sauntered along, pretending to shop, but neither of them examined any items on display. Two wore tool belts, one carried a backpack in his hand. They drifted among the tables, coming steadily closer, eyeing Jake and Nadine. As Nadine watched, one picked up a candy from a table down the row and popped it in his mouth. The table clerk glared at him. No money changed hands.

"Jake," Nadine said. "We may have a situation here. The natives are getting restless."

Jake ignored her. "Deal with it Nadine. We're conducting a complex commercial negotiation here, now isn't a good time to interrupt."

"Not a good time?" Nadine glared. "Jake, we might be in a fight in a moment. Not a good time? This is not a good time to be trying to conduct a 'complex commercial negotiation' with a nine-year-old, that's what's not a good time. Let's wait for her parents to come back."

"I'm fifteen." Lopez put her hands on her hips. "Not nine. And Dad left me in charge, so if you don't want to talk to me you can shoot all your talk out your thrusters and back into your intakes, as far as I'm concerned."

"Missy," Nadine turned to the young woman. "We're not looking for trouble, but we need to move things along."

"You're not the boss of me." The woman stepped forward and into Nadine's space. "You don't tell me what to do."

"I'll tell you what to do if I have to," Nadine said. Lopez shrunk back. "And I say speed it up. Stewart, are we done here yet?"

"We're at a delicate point in our negotiations," Jake said. "Ms. Lopez and myself need to agree on the delivery parameters."

"Bite your delivery parameters," Nadine said. "This kid needs to speed things up or get her parents out here."

"This is a family ship, and I'm part of the family—"

"Everything okay here, Elly?" The spacer boys had slouched up to the airlock entry. "Need a hand? We can help you out."

"I'm fine." Lopez snarled. "Go away Jimmy."

"Maybe you need a hand with your negotiations here." Jimmy smiled. "Hi dirtsiders. I'm Jimmy. We help with the cargo negotiations on this truss."

"Is that so?" Jake blinked. "I thought this was a family ship."

"It is, it is." Jimmy grinned. "Pretty girls in this family."

Lopez blushed, but didn't say anything.

"Well, I'm talking to a member of the ship family," Jake said. "Which means that we won't need your assistance."

"Oh you will need our assistance." Jimmy's grin widened. "One way or another. See, old man Lopez isn't here, so Elly here will need us to help interpret things."

"She hasn't had any problems interpreting things so far," Jake said.

"She will."

"Go away Jimmy," Lopez said.

Nadine turned to face the three young men. "Yeah, go away Jimmy. We're doing business here."

Jimmy turned to Nadine. "Nobody asked you." He stepped forward and bumped her. "Move along and you won't get hurt."

Thank you, Jove. This is exactly what I need. "I asked me," Nadine said. She shifted her stance to face her opponents. Jimmy scowled in the front, two others lagging behind on either side. Jimmy was her height, and beefy. The others were plain fat. All three wore mean scowls. Jimmy crowded her while the others made fists and cracked knuckles.

No firearms, no visible knives. Nadine focused on their tool belts. Wrenches festooned Jimmy's belt. His partners carried a similar, but smaller selection. *He'll threaten me with the wrench first.* She looked farther down. They wore station slippers. Jake had insisted she wear her mag boots, even walking in the station. *Low gravity, and they're not balanced properly. A shove will send them flying.*

Nadine shifted her feet again and stepped back a pace. Jimmy's sneer widened. *He wants to scare me. He doesn't know I can use the space.*

The concourse was a long thin rectangle, with single hatches for each docked ship. Faded red and blue lines painted on the floor demarcated a central walkway and pads to drop cargo deliveries. A pallet loaded head high with rusted cylindrical hydrogen tanks flanked her on the right, and a dozen stacked six-foot lengths of steel water pipe came up to knee level on her left. *Not enough room for them to flank me, only enough for one to come at me at a time. Perfect. I'm going to enjoy this.*

"My friend here is conducting some business with Ms. Lopez. He doesn't want to be interrupted, neither does she. Go away, this is our business, not yours."

Jimmy's snatched the wrench from his belt and held it up in front of Nadine's face. He did a fancy finger twist that spun the wrench. "We're making it our business, understand?"

Nadine waited. *He's going to do that again, to prove how tough he is.*

As expected, Jimmy spun the wrench in his fingers a second time. Nadine's right hand shot out and snagged the wrench. Her left grabbed his now-empty hand and held it tight. "Understand this, dirt bag." She rammed the wrench into his gut, pulling the thrust at the last second. *Disable him, don't kill him. Not that I care, but Jake would be upset.*

Jimmy doubled over, grabbed his stomach, then toppled over and was noisily sick. His two friends stood there, eyes wide.

"Catch." Nadine lobbed the wrench at the third kid, the farthest back, a gentle underhand throw. He got both hands up and caught it, but it threw him off balance. He stumbled backwards, tripping over the water pipes and smacking his head. The other's eyes followed the toss, his mouth gaping.

Hands free now, Nadine whacked her palms on the second kid's ears, hard. He screamed and dropped his backpack, grabbing his ears.

Nadine got an arm on his belt and another on his shoulder and rammed him headfirst into a tank labeled 'Compressed Hydrogen. Explosive. Fragile. Handle gently.' The tank gonged, and the boy flopped bonelessly in her hands.

"Behind you, Nadine," Jake yelled.

Nadine spun. Jimmy was up, bent at the waist, and with murder in his eye. He fumbled for another wrench. "Dirtsider scum. I'm gonna smash you." He swung the wrench. Nadine hopped back. The wind of the passing wrench dusted her face. *Almost got my nose. He's faster than he looks.* She stepped inside his extended arm and stomped down on his foot. He screamed, and she grabbed his wrist and broke it with a quick snap. He screamed again as she propelled him into the third kid.

The third kid was bleeding from the scalp and had climbed upright. Jimmy smacked into him, knocking him back into the pile of pipes. This time he stayed down.

Jimmy bounced off the pipes and hit the ground with a yelp, and crawled away. *Wrist won't support him for long, he'll have to use his elbows. Bet his foot hurts too.* Nadine followed behind, kicking him until he was crawling at walking speed.

"You won't need this." Nadine rolled him over, produced a knife, and reached for his crotch.

Jimmy's face turned white. "No, no—" He tried to squirm away. Nadine grabbed his belt and cut it free with a quick slash. "Have to find some new weapons." She held up his tool belt. "These are mine now." She marched back to the lock, grabbed the dazed kid in the pile of pipes and hauled him upright. She used her knife to slash his belt, and the tools dropped. She held the knife up in front of his face. "Take your friend on the ground and get off this truss. If I see you here sixty seconds from now, I'm going to finish what I started. Understand?"

The boy nodded and staggered way, grabbing his groaning friend before stumbling down the walkway.

Nadine crossed her arms and turned to Jake. "Stewart, can we please move along? I'm getting bored."

The crowd clapped and cheered. None moved to help the incapacitated boys. One woman from the crowd sneaked close and kicked them in the butt as they passed.

Lopez covered her mouth with both hands. "That was awesome. So awesome." She looked at Nadine. "Will you show me how to do that?"

Nadine nodded. "If you want. Provided you process some argon in a forward-cost averaged transaction, or whatever Jakey here wants you to do. Can you do that?"

"Sure!" Lopez nodded repeatedly. "Wow. That was great. Sure. As much fuel as you want. Ten percent off. I'll even take care of the argon disposal if you show me how to do that."

Then she frowned and turned to Jake. "But no discount on the delivery. You have to pay full for that!

Chapter 16

"Stewart, you set me up," Nadine said, sitting at the jump computer console next to Jake. He had four display screens up, showing vectors to the nearest stations, a list of commodities, and a real time news feed.

"Argon." Jake made an entry on his trading list. "With all this new supply of argon, the price is going to dive. I'll sell cheap futures to some corps, they'll stock up before they realize it's not a deal." He saved the list. "And set you up for what? I have no idea what you're talking about."

"That whole fight at the freighter." Nadine took a deep breath. *I shouldn't hit him. I'm a grown woman, in control of my actions. I shouldn't smack him, just because he's being a manipulative ass.*

"Tanker. *Kaskaskia* is a tanker."

"Tanker. With Elly."

"You mean crewman Lopez?" Jake shrugged. "She didn't like you very much. Not at the start."

"Because of how I was dressed."

"Well, you didn't fit in there."

"And why didn't you tell me that ahead of time? Tell me to dress differently, and tell me to not come on so strong."

"Nadine, I'd never tell you what to do. I trust your reactions."

"You trust my…." *Maybe a little smacking is necessary.* Nadine reached over and snagged his ear between her fingers, and twisted.

"Ow! That hurts."

"It's supposed to." Nadine twisted his head until he faced her. "That fight was fake."

"Not from where I sat. You for real knocked two of them out, and could have burst an eardrum on the other guy who attacked you."

"I mean that fight didn't have to happen. You could have bought them off. You pay bribes all the time. Why didn't you pay them to stay away? You have plenty of money."

"It wasn't in the budget."

"Your budget includes whole freighters, and starships, and crews and jump ships. You have more money than…" Nadine tilted her head. "Jake, are you the richest person in the system?"

"Not at all, not at all." Jake said. "There are several family trusts that have much more money than me. Well, some with more. A few. Not many. Well, maybe one. But not much more. But their holdings aren't as liquid, and a lot of it is in corporate shares that are entailed, so in my ability to—OWWW."

Nadine had twisted his ear again. "Why did you set up that fight?"

"Let go of my ear."

"Not till you explain."

Jake twisted, and Nadine tightened her grip. "OWW."

"Spill it."

"Fine. Let go."

Nadine released his ear and raised her eyebrows.

Jake rubbed his ear. "I need to corner the market on starship fuel, only for a little while. That family, the Lopez, they and their clan are big in that market. I wanted them to be grateful to us. You impressed Elly. Those thugs won't push her around next time without a lot of trouble. They're traditional Belters, extended family corporation. Look out for each other. Her mom died years ago, so her dad raised her. She's a great crewman, and her dad's been teaching her to run the ship—she'll inherit after all. But he's worried that she isn't as tough as she could be. At least that's what Skimmer told me. He dated her second cousin for a while when they did a belt sweep, a few years back."

"You started a fight where I nearly killed three random traders because you wanted somebody to like you?"

"To like you, not me. And technically, you started it." Jake rubbed his ear, then looked at his hand. "Am I bleeding?"

"It's only a scratch. Jake, I nearly killed those three."

"Nearly doesn't count. Besides, you said you'd ask permission before you shot them, so I figured I could head things off if they got too dangerous."

Nadine closed her eyes. *Count to ten. One, two, three..* At twenty she opened them again. "Stewart, next time you want somebody roughed up, tell me why ahead of time."

"It's not about the roughing up, it's about how Ensign Lopez would respond to you, and you to her. And it worked out beautifully. We're in with the family. They've sold us a cargo of fuel, and they're off to deliver it. And she very much appreciated your training."

After seeing off the thugs, Nadine had stayed while Jake and Elly finalized their order. Elly had agreed to transfer some of the station's order to fill Jake's, and arranged a delivery schedule. In return he'd paid a hefty deposit, and convinced Nadine to show Elly some self defense moves. Nadine had taught her a couple of stances, and set her up with a training program for fitness and building up the right muscles. She'd also shown her some basic drills, and agreed to coach her virtually. And bought her a new outfit and introduced her to a station hairdresser. In return for that, Elly had steamrolled her father and uncle into assigning extra processing time to Jake's order and arranged an immediate departure from the station for both ships to make their belt delivery as soon as possible.

She hadn't budged on the transport and shipping fees, though. Jake had to pay full fare on those.

"Stewart, you've told me over and over again that fuel is cheap. And it's everywhere in this system. Melt some water and you've got fuel. How can buying a single cargo of fuel make you… what are we doing, anyway?"

"Going to war," Jake said. "That was stage one. A station brawl."

"Great." Nadine shook her head. "What's stage two?"

Jake didn't answer, but instead highlighted a station on his screen. "Can you get us here before end of second shift tomorrow?"

Nadine leaned over. Transit-9. A hub for the drop ships. "Sure, but not on your fuel saving suck every last gallon out of the tanks course."

"Direct course is fine. But we have to be in the bar next to lock one-five-five drinking at the start of second shift. No later.

"I can do that," Nadine nodded. "But you never answered. What's stage two in your system war?"

"A traffic accident," Jake said. "I need a small thruster-buster."

Nadine was true to her word. Second shift, they sat in a greasy spacer bar on the outer wheel of Transit-9. Jake had ordered a belter beer for her, because she hated the taste and not drinking it would keep her sober until they met his contact. She'd retaliated by ordering him an expensive mixture of pure-alcohol cut with fake lime juice. Unfortunately, he liked it.

"It makes my mouth feel fresh," Jake said. "Who would have thought that I'd like a lime flavored drink?"

"Not me," Nadine said. "And definitely not at this price. I expected to get ripped off, but not this badly. Nor this quickly."

Jake signaled the bartender. "Another." He pointed to her. "The lady is paying."

"Jake, you're like a zillionaire, and those are expensive, you should be paying."

"We need the verisimilitude. I need you looking like money, so you have to buy expensive drinks. And that's why you're dressed the way you are." Jake had insisted she wear one of her best outfits, complete with wrist and neck ruffs, an embroidered over-vest, and a giant opal ring on one hand.

"I looked up what verisimilitude means," Nadine said. "It means the appearance of being true or real."

"Yes. So?"

"Means like make something appear true when it really isn't."

"It means making something appear true, but it doesn't mean that it isn't true. It just means that it doesn't appear to be untrue. It could still be true."

"I'm dressed like a rich girl so that we appear to be rich?"

"Nope. We're already rich."

"But we have to look rich?"

"I don't care what we are. I care what we look like. This way we appear to be somebody who is rich, without actually giving information that we are rich, which means that we're probably not rich, otherwise we wouldn't have to appear so. If I came here by myself, our contact would assume that I was actually rich, because I don't appear to be. But because I appear to be, he'll assume that I'm not, because you're here, pretending to be rich."

"So I'm, that means that I'm…" Nadine shook her head, then took a slug of Belter beer. "You're confusing me, Stewart."

"That's the point. When people are confused, they react on instinct. I'm counting on people reacting to you a certain way."

"What should I do."

"Follow your instincts."

"My instincts say drink a lot, start a fight, then puke on your shoes."

"Yes, I wore old shoes because of that. Here's our friend." A fat crewman in a Militia undress uniform had stopped at the door. He scanned the crowd, until his eyes lit on Jake, then he waddled over.

"That's the fattest Militia trooper I've ever seen," Nadine said. "How does he fit into the control seat?"

"He barely does," Jake said. "Doesn't meet service weight requirements at all."

"How does he get away with it?"

"He bribes people," Jake said. "And he needs money for bribes, which is why we're talking to him."

The man arrived at the table, breathing heavily. "You're Stewart?"

"Call me Jake." Jake stood. "You're lieutenant Dee?"

"Yes." The lieutenant looked over at Nadine. "Who's she? You said come alone, no witnesses."

"She's my employer," Jake said. "She's hired me to do a job, and she's here to make sure that it's done right."

Dee gave Nadine a once over. "She looks fake. That skinsuit can't be real. Not a real custom job. Custom jobs are smoother. That's a knock off."

Nadine bristled. "What do you know about good clothes, dirt bag? The closest you ever came to high fashion is when your laundry got mis-delivered." She tracked him up and down. "Nice outfit. Does it come in men's sizes? Or only beefalo sizes?"

The lieutenant reddened. "Look lady, this is a real militia coverall. It's not supposed to be nice, it's supposed to be functional. Not like the trash you're wearing. Nobody will believe you're a corporate executive. I mean, look at that ring. That's gotta be fake."

"This?" Nadine held up the opal ring she was wearing. She'd collected a few dozen on her and Jake's last adventure, and he'd counseled her to keep them hidden until the market climbed. But he'd made her wear one with her outfit. "This is real. It's worth a fortune."

"What is that supposed to be, an Opal?" The lieutenant bent his chin to examine it, then shook his head. "There's no way a stone that big is real, it's got to be fake."

"Fake? Listen you little space bug, I'll—"

Jake grabbed her arm. "You can have that instead of the thousand credits we offered."

"You can't fool me," Dee said. "I studied gemology. That's not real. No way. I want real cash."

"If you insist." Jake slid a credit chip across the table. Jake and Nadine sat with their backs to the bar wall, Dee across from them. He reached for the chip, then twisted to see if any of the bar patrols were watching. His arm knocked a chair over and it clattered on the ground. All eyes in the bar swung to them.

Nadine rolled her eyes and looked at Jake. "Stewart? Can I—"

"No." Jake shook his head. "Not yet. Well Dee?"

"I need to check it."

"It's all there."

Dee put the chip in his pocket. "Thousand credits?"

"Half now, half when it's done. Remember, no big accident, just a small tap. I only want your departure delayed for a few hours while you check the pipes for cracks."

"You said all in advance."

"The boss here—" Jake indicated Nadine—"Changed her mind. She wants it done before end of shift. Come back here and we'll pay the rest."

"No way. I want all the money in advance!" Dee turned to Nadine. "You're trying to trick me."

Nadine laughed. "You'll get your money. I don't care about you one way or another. But if my friend here says he'll pay you, he'll pay you."

Dee called Nadine a not nice name. Nadine stood, hands on her holstered revolver. "I don't care what you call me, but you better do as my friend says."

"Or you'll shoot me?"

"Why not? I haven't shot anybody in hours. And you're hard to miss."

"If you shoot me, who'll set up your little accident? Can't shoot me."

Nadine narrowed her eyes. "You just told me that you're not going to do anything. If I let you leave, nothing happens. If I shoot you, nothing happens. Kind of the same, except one would be more fun for me."

"No deal," Lieutenant Dee said. "You promised a thousand, I want a thousand. No deal." He held up the credit chip. "And I'm keeping this for my time." He got up and stalked off. Nadine made to follow—Jake's arm held her back. "Not now Nadine. Sit and wait."

"Jake, he's getting away with five hundred credits of our money."

"No he's not."

"He's not? Oh." Nadine sat. "You gimmick'd the credit chip?"

"Kind of." Jake sat back and surveyed the bar.

"He doesn't have five hundred credits.

"Nope."

"Good."

"He has a thousand. I put a thousand on that chip."

Nadine turned to Jake. "If I run, I can still catch him. He won't get far the way he waddles. A good beating and he'll give up the chip."

"I don't need the chip back. And if you beat him up, everybody will know you did it, and the Militia will put you in jail."

"How will they know?"

"You had a loud argument with him in public, you're standing up, armed, and at least twenty people here are watching you."

Nadine thumped into her seat, glared at Jake, then glared at anybody who stared at her across the bar. "Jake, why in Jove's name did you have this meeting here."

"So everybody will see what happened and blame Lieutenant Dee for what happens next."

"What happens next? He spends all our money on bowls of beefalo stew and a lifetime supply of antiperspirant." A group of three women across the bar were looking at her. She gave them a fiery glance until they looked away. "What does happen next?"

"The other pilot—here she comes."

A blank faced woman in a worn but starched and clean coveralls slid into the chair across from Jake. "You're Stewart?"

"I am." Jake pulled another credit chip from his pocket and slid it over. "Here you go. Two thousand credits. All in advance."

The woman pocketed the chip without checking. "What was that last thing all about?"

"Your lead pilot is a moron," Jake said.

"Tell me about it." She shrugged. "We drop at start of next shift. That soon enough?"

Jake nodded. "Don't blow up the station, but I want the whole fueling dock out of commission. For two weeks, at least."

The woman nodded. "He always gives the wrong commands, anyway. A retro fire at the wrong time and we'll scrape the whole fueling valve set off the truss. The station crew is careful. They'll have it shut off at the feeder before they let us decouple. No chance of an explosion, but we'll knock valves and pipes everywhere."

"Outstanding."

She stood. "Pleasure doing business with you."

"If you ever need more money," Jake said. "I have more work like this from time to time. Let your friends know and word gets back to me."

The woman laughed. "It's not about the money. That one thinks because his grandad was a colonel he's hot stuff. He isn't, barely got out of pilot's course. I'm always fixing his problems. They'll can him for sure after this."

"You might mention," Jake said, "To somebody after this accident, to check his credit chips and see where they came from. His chip is coded differently from yours. He might be in more trouble about the chip than about the accident."

The woman gave Jake a wicked grin. "Your friends said you were smart. Smart and generous." She got up to leave. "Outstanding. He's for the trash heap for sure."

Nadine watched the woman stride off, whistling. "Jake, did you pay two different people to crash the same ship?"

"One to crash a ship, one to get caught. Two different jobs. Of course, the one who's going to get caught doesn't exactly know that is what will happen to him."

"Care to explain?"

"I need a big crash, mess up the fueling system here. This is a central hub for Militia ships on patrol. Fuel issues here will cascade. Any accident that I arranged here will get close scrutiny. That Lieutenant Dee was never going to bump the station. He'd know that he'd get hung for it. He had no intention of doing anything except taking my money and laughing at me. The second woman wouldn't have done it, except now she knows that she won't get blamed. The whole bar saw an argument between the lead pilot and some mysterious lady. She'll do the job, he'll get the blame—if nothing else a search of his room will reveal untraceable cash."

"Isn't her cash untraceable too?"

"Nope. Gambling payments."

"She gambles?"

"She does now." Jake smiled. "I have a friend at the casino. He took some money from me, linked the deposit to her account, and a payout as well. That's where the chip came from—the casino."

"Will this station run out of fuel then?"

"Militia will have to bring it in on tankers for a while. Of course, a lot of the tanker capacity in-system has either been reserved or is on a long trip to the outer belt. And the militia has limited fuel processing capability."

"But there must be a lot of fuel in storage, all over the system.

"There is." Jake nodded. "All over the system. But somebody has been buying it up for the last while, and he doesn't like the Militia."

"Anybody I know?" Nadine asked. "Is it you?"

"Jake Stewart enterprises, heating and fueling supplies and service. Repairs guaranteed." He smiled a grim smile. "Revenge included, free of charge."

Chapter 17

The wave washed over the bow and crashed onto the wooden deck, soaking the cargo. Pine trees and metal beams don't suffer from being immersed in water, nor by waves crashing on them. But people, Sergeant Russell reflected, were neither waterproof nor crush proof. He leaned close to Roi, holding the wheel next to him. "Are we going to sink?"

"Sink?" Roi hauled the wheel left one spoke. "Why would we sink?"

Russell gestured at the ocean. Sharp sided waves ran down on them from the western horizon, pitching the bow up, then slamming it down. The next wave came right behind it, and the bow couldn't rise fast enough, so the wave crashed onboard and flew along their length, soaking everything on the lower level and draining through gaps in the deck beams. "I'm not much of a sailboat person, but shouldn't the water be outside the boat and not inside?"

"This abomination is not a sailboat." Roi glared at Russell. "Never, never, ever, ever, call it a sailboat."

Russell pointed up at the gray fabric flapping overhead. "Got a sail."

"It is not a sail boat. A sailboat is a thing of beauty, a balance of nature's forces that sends us into a delicate ballet between wind and water. This is a barge. A flat, slab sided cargo carrier, useful for nothing other than moving freight." Roi looked right, at the brown water draining between the sand flats to the north then sniffed. "Smell that?"

Russell took a deep breath. "I smell rotting plant. Smells like every Militia transport cutter I've ever been on."

"That's the mud flats. The tide is ready to turn, and we have not traveled nearly as far west as I wished. We will have to continue under engine for some time." Roi pulled a lever on the control pedestal, and the engine note deepened as the motor revved up.

"Whatever you say, Admiral," Russell said, saluting with the arm not holding the rail.

Roi frowned, he knew he was being mocked. "Captain will do for now."

"As you say, Captain." Russell looked ahead at the dark, turbulent sea. *I'm getting so soaked. It's like splashing across a muddy training field in the rain, but we're not sinking. Gotta hand it to the pompous freak, he knows boats, and this was an outstanding idea.* Russell had started building a fleet of sailboats to carry produce and trays from his factory—he thought of it as his even though the corp had never sold it—to Landing. But sailboats required skilled labor, specialized parts, and lots of time on the building stocks. Roi had put a stop to that and shifted to a different project--barges.

Roi designed them with side walls to keep out the water—he called them bulkheads, and a raised tower to keep the crew dry, or at least drier. Then he added a covered housing for an engine, and a stub mast to hoist a simple sail. The whole thing could be knocked together in a few days. Especially if you had electric power to run saws, metal printers to make nails and reinforcing brackets, and technicians who understood motors to mount them.

And a team of cosmically connected mules to drag lumber from the forest. Kim One got up and walked into the forest every day with timber cutting crews, and now all the mules followed her like she was some sort of mule messiah. It was eerie to watch.

Roi was yelling at the crew. The deckhands splashed across the bow, and the dirty gray sail dropped. Russell waited until they finished tying it down. "Don't we need that up to move us along?"

Roi shook his head and pointed at a headland visible in the distance. "Watch that."

Russell stared at it. Nothing changed. He counted to sixty to be sure. "A point of land with rocks and trees. I don't get it."

"Use this. Take a bearing like I showed you." Roi handed him a compass.

Russell pointed the sighting line at a prominent tree on the headland. He waited longer than a minute this time until he was sure. "Bearings changing. We're going to pass it."

"Yes." Roi adjusted the wheel slightly. "Ebb tide is still running. The current is pushing us west."

Russell pointed at the waves, breaking on the bow. "Waves are coming from the west, won't they push us back?"

"Wind makes the waves. Tide makes the current. They're fighting each other right now, but current beats wind."

"Always?"

"Usually. Big winds can beat a smaller current."

"If we're being pushed by the current, why the sail, why the engine?"

"Current isn't everywhere. It's stronger in some places, weaker in others. And we need to steer. The current will take us generally west, for now. The ebb current at least. The sail lets us move side to side within the current, control where we end up."

"That makes sense, now." And it did. Earlier Roi had tried to explain, and Russell hadn't got it until he was out on the water. "Tide goes out, takes us out of the river into the ocean, and generally west. Tide goes in, takes us into the rivers, generally east."

"In these waters. It's different elsewhere. But it will work here, to and from Landing. We can't pick when we sail, but we can pick where we drift if we're careful."

Russell grabbed for the rail as a double sized wave rocked the boat. Behind him, Chaudhari leaned over the rail and retched onto the deck. Five seconds later a flood of water washed the vomit away.

"Chad, ready to do your thing?"

"This is worse than the shuttles when they land," Chaudhari said. "I told you that I wasn't going out in bad weather anymore."

Roi chimed in. "This isn't bad weather. Just regular chop."

"See?" Russell grinned. "It's just regular chop. And also, I don't care what you say."

"I'm a Senator."

"Which is why you're the one going to see that Jake Stewart guy, and why you're going to find out what he wants, and work out some sort of arrangement."

"I'm not a diplomat."

"How difficult is it going to be to agree to stay out of each other's way? I sell him food, he sells me metal, and as long as that continues none of my Militia people go off planet. So simple, even you can explain it."

"I can…" Chaudhari gulped, swallowed, then ran to the rail again. After he'd dry heaved, he came back wiping his mouth. "I'm not sure that I can convince him. I'm not good at negotiations."

"Yeah, but I hear he is. Master negotiator and all that. He'll tell you what he wants. Don't agree to anything, just say you'll bring it back to me."

"What if he asks me about Militia business?"

"Tell him you're a corporal and for him to talk to the Major."

"You should go, not me."

"Too busy. I've got a plant to run." *And Landing is too dangerous for me right now. The last few radio calls from the Major have been difficult. She's already asking for more ammunition and resources I don't have, and my excuses are wearing thin. If I went to town, I'd have to bring a squad for protection, and I'm not ready to break openly with her. I need Chad to run interference. Besides, I like being out in the woods.* Russell liked running a factory. It was like running a squad or a platoon. Set the mission objectives, make sure the specialists got what they needed, and stand back and let them do the work. And savagely beat any non-performers. He liked that part the best.

"You should radio him."

"Radio can be intercepted. And I don't have one that will reach that far." That sort of higher-tech equipment was still in the Militia HQ's hands. Or the big corps. "If he wants to talk to me, he can give you a radio."

"What if he asks about… that other thing."

"What other thing?"

"You know, that thing." Chaudhari looked to Roi. "That thing we don't talk about."

Russell grabbed Chaudhari and dragged him back out of earshot of Roi. "Listen up. You don't go spilling the beans on anything unless you're asked. But if you are asked tell the truth. The rumor is this Jake Stewart guy is always straight with you if you are with him."

"I need it spelled out, Scott."

"Fine." Russell stared him in the face. It was widely known that Russell had personally shot and killed the former head of the Free Traders guild, Marianne, while retaking a station she had seized. What wasn't widely known was that it was a mistake, the result of mislabeled ammunition. Russell had thought he was firing frangible ammunition, which hurt like blazes, but didn't kill. He'd fired thinking he was knocking her down and putting the wind out of her. Instead he'd put two solid slugs through her chest.

Jose had given him the doctored ammunition, and been standing next to him when he did it. Afterwards, somebody had leaked to the Free Traders exactly who killed their leader. Russell suspected Jose behind that.

"If he knows enough to ask, you tell him everything I told you. What the ammo was, where it came from. Who was there? And the second thing?"

"Yes?"

"Everybody believes that she strangled her boss. She probably did. But she wasn't the only one who could have poisoned him to start with. She was in the room when he was poisoned, true. But so was Jose."

"You think Jose poisoned them and blamed it on her?"

"He could have. Or she could have. It's confusing. But let that Stewart guy know what's what."

"Why? Why are you doing this?"

"So that he knows who to trust."

"And who's that?"

"Nobody." Russell looked at the headland on the horizon. "Trust nobody."

Chapter 18

"I'm sorry Lieutenant that's all I can spare right now in the way of fuel. You can have all I have warehoused there at the current market price, but I have commitments elsewhere for the rest. I won't be shipping more in." Jake leaned back from his board and waited for a response. After a crazed buying spree where he'd bought more fuel than was actually available in the inner system, he and Nadine had taken *Accounting Error* into a farther orbit. He'd leased or hired two dozen ships and sent them on futile delivery runs. System fuel production wasn't so much depleted as over committed. Some Free Trader and corporate stations and ships could still process fuel, and reserves remained intact. But the bulk of the systems capability belonged to Jake, at least temporarily.

The Militia Lieutenant responded with a higher offer. Jake waited long enough to make him sweat and then turned it down. The conversation continued on, with the far-away lieutenant offering higher and higher prices, and Jake continually demurring.

Nadine wandered back from the bridge. "Want some Basic?"

"Sure." Jake took the glass from her and took a big gulp. "Wow, that's, what is that? It's flavored like that drink you got me back at the station."

"I was able to get some lime-flavored basic powder before we left. Got a deal, not a popular product apparently."

"Is it safe to drink on duty?"

"No alcohol in yours."

"Good." Jake took a big slurp. "I do love that taste." He looked at her glass. "What are you drinking?"

"Same." She took a dainty sip.

"But you hate lime."

"Well, I need something to relax me."

"Relax you how?" Jake looked down. "There's no alcohol in it, you said."

"None in yours. We need you to stay sharp with all those numbers to deal with." She took another sip. "But mine, that's another matter. This is the only taste strong enough to mask that engine room alcohol your friend makes. How goes the taking control of the orbital economy?"

Jake explained his success with cornering the fuel production market, his win on selling overpriced argon to some of the corps, and the sky-high prices his recent trading goods from Magyar were bringing. "The Free Traders perked the market up and attracted interest. Now everybody wants more fabric. And I've got a buyer for the coal. Things are looking up."

"Are we rich?"

"Richer," Jake said. "I bought a couple of ships, and a station."

"You bought a station, good for you." Nadine stared at him. "How's this fitting into revenge for Dashi's murder?"

"The Militia are taking it up the shorts," Jake said. "Their ships need pre-processed fuel, and they don't have enough refining capacity. By my calculations, they'll have to idle thirty-four percent of their ships. That will lead to disillusionment in their crews, and they'll lose those to the corps or the Free Traders, and that will cut further into operations."

"Can't they stockpile fuel for the future and re-activate their ships?"

"Not at these prices. And these prices will continue for a while. I've made enough from the sale of the luxury goods that I can permanently idle a big chunk of refining capacity. With the new, higher price of fuel, and the fact that they will have to compete with the corps and Free Traders for it, they'll lose staff and clout."

"They'll get smaller? That's not much of a punishment."

"As they get smaller, they lose prestige. Lots of Militia people worship prestige. They didn't join for the money. As people respect them less, the rank and file will hate the leaders who put them there even more."

Nadine laughed. "Classic Jake Stewart. Put them in a position where their own people will take care of their leaders for you. You won't have to do a thing, but they'll end up shooting their boss because they're angry. Who will do it first, do you guess?"

"That's not what I meant to happen—"

"Jake." Nadine interrupted. "That is exactly what you meant, you just don't want to admit it. You're not trading to make money, you're trading to put people in a position where they'll do bad things that will benefit you. You're ruthless enough to do it, but too embarrassed to admit that you're doing it. And enjoying it."

"Nadine, I am not enjoying it."

"Then why are you so angry at me? You're nearly shouting." Nadine nodded. "Face it Jake, you're manipulating these people, and you're enjoying it."

"I…" Jake closed his mouth. *I am manipulating these people. I'm not making fair trades, I'm making trades to force them to do something.* Jake bit his lip. *Am I a bad person?*

"It has to be done, Jake. Don't beat yourself up."

Jake took a deep breath. "To answer your question, a number of people will be angry," Jake said. "I can't guarantee any sort of violent reaction, of course. But past patterns allow me to extrapolate."

"I'll bet you've got the shooters, and the replacements picked out already," Nadine said. "You think this is enough, enough for Dashi?"

"Anybody who harmed Dashi will suffer," Jake said. "Don't worry I'm still on target for that." *I'm not morally ambiguous about those people suffering, at least.*

"You think it was Shutt?"

"That's what Jose thinks. I've read some of his internal files. He thinks she did it, and he has evidence."

"Uh huh." Nadine nodded. "Does he know that you can read those files?"

"In theory, no. In practice, he could have set them out as a honey trap."

"A what?"

Jake explained about honey traps. Data that was sufficiently interesting that it attracted hackers who tried to break in and steal it. Exposing fake but realistic data was a traditional way of finding out who was trying to get it, and by making it harder to get, planting fake information with the thieves.

"Jose is smart enough to be able to do that," Jake said. "I'll need collaboration. But I'm working on that."

"You think Jose is smart enough to dangle lies in front of you so you'll think they're truth?"

"Precisely," Jake said.

"Think that Sergeant Russell is smart enough to do that?"

"He could." Jake drained his glass. "Why do you ask that?"

"Got a message from a friend of a friend. Guy wants to talk to you. Friend of Russell."

"Does he have a name?"

"Chaudhari. And get this, he's a Senator." Nadine grinned. "Senator Chaudhari wants to talk to you. Says he wants to discuss 'arrangements'"

Chapter 19

"It's a totally different motion," Chaudhari said. "Space doesn't make me sick. Even sustained zero-G. But on that raft, I puked my guts up. And I didn't feel like eating for two days after. You understand what I mean." He'd been explaining his recent sea voyage, and why he seemed to have lost weight.

Nadine nodded, wiping sweat off her face. She'd met Chaudhari at *Accounting Error's* airlock. Jake had arranged to meet up with his rented tanker, *Kaskaskia*, in a high orbit. *Or maybe it was leased. Or chartered. I don't understand the difference. Whichever one makes him the most money, that's what it was.* Either way, the crew family was glad to see their trading benefactor Jake Stewart, and crewman E. Lopez was happy to see her. Nadine had spent the last hour knocking the youngster across the compartment in fighting drills. The young lady would have plenty of bruises, but she'd got some surprising shots in.

"Good try." Nadine had told Lopez before leaving. "If I wasn't expecting it, it would have worked. Keep working on it." *That young woman will be causing people lots of problems. Which makes me weirdly pleased for some odd reason, kind of makes me proud. Am I getting maternal? Yuck, I hope not. That's not a skill that runs in the family.*

"Yes. I was sick as a dog too, on Roi's stupid ship." Nadine had also spent time throwing up on a sailboat crewed by Roi. "You're right about the motion. I never get sick, but that time. Sheesh." She pulled herself up the ladder. "Jake's in the lounge. Have you two met?"

"In passing, back when Dashi was in charge. And Scott, I mean Sergeant Russell respects him a lot."

"He does, does he?"

"He talks about him all the time. His trading, that type of thing."

Nadine paused on the ladder. "Talks about Jake all the time, does he? Does he ever talk about me?"

"Sure. He respects you too," Chaudhari said. "But in a different way."

Nadine glared at Chaudhari. "You're lying."

"He does. You can ask him."

"I'm asking you." Nadine continued to glare.

"Nadine?" Jakes voice came from above. "Is our guest here yet?"

"Right behind me," Nadine yelled. "Showing me some respect, and staring at my ass."

"Everybody stares at your ass Nadine. The respect thing is new, though."

"Bite me." Nadine climbed up the rest of the ladder then stepped aside. "Jake Stewart, Chaudhari. Chaudhari, Jake Stewart."

Jake stood from behind the lounge table and shook hands. "I know you, we've met before." The two exchanged pleasantries. Jake offered some Basic. "All we have on the ship, it's all I drink when I'm trading."

"No thanks. The traders who ran me out to the tanker fed me."

"Well then," Jake said. "To business."

Chaudhari nodded. "You're probably wondering why I'm here."

Jake shook his head. "Nope."

"Sergeant Russell said—wait, what?"

"Not wondering at all. Not wondering. Not interested. Don't care." Jake picked up a soft paper bag on the counter and extended. "But glad you came out all this way. We have something for you."

"You have something for me?" Chaudhari took the bag, opened it, and peeked inside. "Crap, this is a—" He froze. Nadine had slid behind him, and he heard the click of a revolver being cocked. "No need for that. This was supposed to be a friendly meeting. Talk things over."

"It is." Jake stepped back, out of grabbing range. "Except I'm doing the talking. That sound you heard. You know what that is?"

"Nadine is behind me with two revolvers, cocked." Chaudhari didn't move, didn't reach into the bag, didn't take his eyes off Jake. "By the sound, close enough to guarantee a hit, but far enough away I can't grab the guns if I spin and reach. Maybe two meters, she'll be back by the hatch. I can't stop her before she gets a shot out. If I wanted to take you out, I might make it across that table and grab you, might not. But if I try, she'll shoot me in the back."

"Excellent tactical understanding." Jake said. "Is that why Russell keeps you around?"

"That and the senator thing." Now Chaudhari looked into the bag. "Why are you holding me at gunpoint and giving me a severed ear?"

Nadine was impressed. *He didn't panic and try anything stupid. He knew the sound of a gun cocking, and he recognizes a freeze-dried severed ear when he sees it. Better than I did.* When Jake showed it to her, she'd thought it was some sort of special dried leather thing he'd imported. *I'm not tracking as well as I used to. I miss grandfather. They're still talking. Focus, Nadine. Focus.*

"That's all your assassins left behind when they tried to kill us, a while back."

"I don't understand."

Jake explained about the recent failed trading mission, the boarding, the fight, cutting off the ear, and pushing the other man out the airlock. Chaudhari listened attentively, and didn't make the slightest move. Nadine was disappointed. *Can't he sway or stretch or something so I can yell at him? Must not be his first time held hostage at gunpoint. He knows how to stand still and take it. I wonder if he could teach future boyfriends how to do that…if I have future boyfriends.*

At the end Chaudhari shook his head. "I don't know any assassins."

Jake raised an eyebrow. "Given your past history, That's demonstrably not true."

"Okay." Chaudhari shrugged. "I know lots of assassins. I'm kind of one myself. But I don't think the Militia sent any assassins after you. I certainly didn't."

"What about your boss?"

"Scott? I mean Sergeant Russell. He wouldn't do that."

"I meant Major Shutt, acting head of the Militia. Isn't she your boss?"

"Right. Right. Her. Yeah, sorry, I talk to Sergeant Russell a lot these days. He's like, my tactical boss. But Shutt, I don't think she would do that. And certainly not Russell."

"I'm curious why you think Russell wouldn't have me killed."

"Well, I mean, yeah. He'd have you killed if necessary. But he'd do it himself. And he certainly wouldn't do it and then send me out here."

Nadine spoke. "Why not send you out here to be killed? Does he love you that much?"

"He'd do it himself, not farm it out. Besides, he paid me the money he owed me before I lifted. He paid it early. He'd never have done that if he was going to get me killed."

"Maybe he was being subtle," Jake said.

Chaudhari chuckled. "Yeah, right. That's what everybody says who met Russell. That Russell guy, he's super subtle. It's like his middle name. You know what he called his pet mule?"

"What?"

"SPD. Slow, painful death. He says it cheers him up every time he says that. You think that's a guy who has deep schemes? Nope." Chaudhari shook his head. "Don't care what this ear guy said. Militia didn't send them."

"Interesting." Jake drummed his fingers. "On another topic. Word is that your boss, your real boss, Shutt, killed the admiral personally."

"I heard that too. I don't lose much sleep over what happens to the high muckety-mucks. Maybe he deserved it."

Jake stiffened. His eyes flickered back and forth between Chaudhari and Nadine. "I haven't heard that."

"I've heard that." Chaudhari nodded. "Could be true. Could have been her. Up close, personal, watch the light go out of his eyes, she could do that—"

Jake shoved Chaudhari backwards and yelled. "NO NO NO"

BOOM. Nadine didn't realize she'd pulled the trigger until the shot blasted onto the far wall and smoke filled the room.

Chaudhari rolled over and got one arm onto a chair, but froze as Nadine touched his head with a revolver. "Move and I'll blow you out the thrusters." She was yelling now.

"Nadine, don't shoot him." Jake coughed and waved the dust away. He was yelling too.

"Why not?"

"We've had to clean this room up already once. Remember how long the blood took to get out of the lounge chairs? Besides."

"Besides what?"

"He's going to tell the truth now. If he doesn't, you can shoot him." Jake turned to Chaudhari. "Isn't that so, Mr. Chaudhari?"

Chaudhari took a deep breath. "Why are you so concerned about the admiral? I didn't do it."

"The admiral," Jake said, "Was Nadine's grandfather and only living relative. Mind what you say."

"Didn't know that. I say I didn't kill him," Chaudhari's stared Nadine in the eye. "I say I wasn't there. I couldn't have. It was her—Shutt—or nobody. And I certainly didn't tell her to do it, and she wouldn't have listened to me if I had. And why would I do that? I barely knew the guy. And I must be the most incompetent political guy ever. If I killed an admiral for personal gain, why am I still a corporal?"

Nadine kept the revolvers pressed to his head, then stepped back and pointed them at the ceiling. "Good point. You're still a corporal. You're a sucky politician. How did you become a senator?"

Chaudhari waited until she had stepped back. "I liked the cheerleaders. I talked to them. Mr. Pletcher helped me out. He spent some money on me. I'm only interested in the Senate as far as it affects the Militia. Everything else, I'll listen to him. Corporal Senator, that's me." He turned his head to Jake. "Thanks for the shove. Can I get up?"

Jake looked at Nadine's poker face, then nodded. "Yes."

Chaudhari climbed up, adjusted his clothes, and coughed. "Too much smoke. That's substandard ammo. Sergeant Russell can get you better."

"The admiral?" Jake asked. "You were saying?"

"We don't do subtle. We're the Militia. We're not going to sneak somebody up into your ship and try to shoot you, or hire some weird Free Trader dudes. We'd send two squads with mortars or rifles, or a half dozen ships and chase you across the system until we could blow you up with lasers. We're so subtle last time we started a rebellion we burned down half of Landing and almost starved everybody on Delta. No way we snuck two guys up here and tried to do things secretly. That's not us."

Jake looked at Nadine, then back to Chaudhari. "That makes sense. It's not your style. Fine. Anything else to say?"

Chaudhari dropped into a chair without asking and wiped the sweat off his brow. "I'm telling Scott I want a raise. Being a senator is way more dangerous than I thought."

Two hours later, Jake sent Chaudhari back to the Free Trader sent to retrieve him. He then sat for an hour with the crew of the *Kaskaskia* settling some minor trade issues, while Nadine showed Elly how to break someone's finger.

"Try it out on your brother's pinky finger," Nadine said. "Pinkies aren't all that necessary unless they play musical instruments or are doctors. What does he do?"

"Moves cargo and teases me about my hair," Elly said.

"Break both of them, then." Nadine tossed her own hair. "Serves him right."

"Nadine." Jake returned, stowing a portable projector in a vacuum safe bag. "Back to our ship for now."

"You brought your own projector? Why not use their screens?"

"Too small," Jake said. "We've got some elaborate delivery schedules planned, I needed the extra visual real-estate for an optimized display of pricing parameters."

Nadine sealed her helmet. *That's not a sentence I ever thought I'd hear. 'Optimized display of pricing parameters'.* She eyeballed the jump and made a lazy leap back to *Accounting Error,* keying their private suit-radio channel on the way. "Jake?" *Best get this over with while I don't have to look at him face to face.*

"Yes?" Jake rolled dead-slow end over end. It looked random, but Nadine knew he'd touch down softly feet first at the far end. His spatial senses were second-to-none.

Nadine's face burned red. "I'm sorry I shot Chaudhari. I was upset."

"You didn't shoot him."

"I tried, and I only missed because of you. I'm embarrassed."

"That you tried, or that you missed?"

"Stop making fun of me." Nadine rolled by him and kicked his arm. "I nearly killed him. I shouldn't have done it."

Jake drifted to one side. "You did promise to ask before you shot anybody. Is that rule still in effect?"

"I will. I won't get as angry next time. I'm still upset about the admiral."

"You mean your grandfather?"

"The admiral."

Nadine's kick had added a roll to Jake's spin. He stuck an arm out, gradually extending it until the roll slowed. "Why won't you call him grandfather?"

"None of your business. Let's talk about those shootings."

"You'll talk about shootings but not about names."

"Nope. Do you think what Chaudhari said is true? That the Militia isn't behind killing Dashi? Or the others?—Crap!" Nadine hadn't been paying attention and suddenly the ship was there. She slammed into *Accounting Error's* hull shoulder first. Not hard enough to break anything, but she still bounced off. Only a sudden back twist brought her magnetized boots into contact with the hull. "Stupid ship."

Jake extended both arms, and floated down, tagging with both feet on the first try. "You overextended your legs on the roll over."

"Bite me Stewart. What about the shootings? Did the Militia kill the admiral and the others?"

"I'm sure that Russell shot Marianne." Jake stared out at the Dragon, visible in the distance. "I've always known that. I have independent confirmation from somebody else who was there. But there are also questions about his ammunition. It could have been switched, he could have just wanted to incapacitate her. He was firing frangibles for that whole melee. Almost all their ammunition was frangible. But he had a selection of slugs onboard his ship he could have loaded earlier if he wanted. He didn't. So why change at the end? It's not like he's shy about shooting people, so I tend to believe the story that Jose switched the ammo on him."

"Why would Jose do that? Why not arrange to have her shot during the fighting."

"I'm considering that. Something to do with the Militia being blamed."

"And my grandfather?" Nadine tilted her head. "Shutt killed him."

"Almost certain," Jake said. "And almost certainly not planned. She left him alone in headquarters for weeks without visiting when he wasn't expected to recover. Then when he seemed to be stabilizing, she concocted a reason to visit. And then only after she'd solidified her control of the Militia and had people taking her orders. She took advantage of an opportunity more than tried to create one."

Nadine nodded, then realized Jake wasn't looking at her. "What do you mean by 'not planned'?"

"If she'd planned to kill him, she could have done it the night Dashi died. There was enough confusion and time there that she could have fed him more poison or dropped him down the stairs in the rush or put a pillow on his face. She didn't, and according to my sources she was as surprised as anybody when it happened."

"What sources are those? Do you have somebody in the Militia?"

"I have somebody everywhere, Nadine. Every organization. And anywhere I don't, Dashi did. I have access to some of his people now."

"Who?"

"People who want things to go smoothly. People who don't like revolutions, coups, revolts, fights, mutinies or insurgencies."

"But they appear to love thesauruses," Nadine muttered

"What?"

"Never mind. Jose arranged all this? The shootings? The coup? The two men sent to kill us? Not the Militia?"

"Could be," Jake said. "Could be. I'm considering it."

"What happens now?"

"We set a trap," Jake said. "We arrange things to see who takes advantage of us."

"Nobody takes advantage of Jake Stewart, everybody knows that."

"Not with trading or pricing or anything like that," Jake said. "I'll have to try another way."

"What's your other way?"

"I'll have to arrange for somebody to get hurt," Jake said. He twisted on the hull so he faced her. "And you'll have to help do it."

Chapter 20

Jose leaned over and looked down at the shooting range from the upper gallery. His guard, Nejkin, adjusted his earplugs, stepped up to the line, and aimed at the far target. Jose frowned. "Was this really necessary?"

"Fifty credits says he misses the target at least once." Shutt crossed her arms. "You corporate people can't shoot." Shutt's crews had built the second story of the armory as a viewing area for the shooting gallery. It was next to the armory itself, but not in the secure area where the heavier weapons were stored. That allowed a group to arrive at the armory, and be issued hand weapons and ammunition to train, while their bosses watched the results from above.

"Come on. Two to one my guys beat yours." Shutt pointed out the window at the shooting range.

The groups continued firing below. The room was supposed to be soundproof but faint bangs echoed through the glass. *Her troops are much better with small arms than mine are. She knew that ahead of time, and she's sending a message to me. But the betting thing is new...* "I don't bet on training exercises."

The gun below banged. A single hole appeared on the outer ring of the target. Nejkin squared himself to the target, then fired twice more, quickly. Two holes appeared on the target, near but not in the inner ring. The hammer dropped again, but this time the gun didn't fire. Nejkin checked the revolver and mouthed a silent curse. After fiddling with it, he gave up and left the shooting gallery. Jose frowned. He'd fired only five shots.

"You could be up fifty credits by now."

"Why did he only shoot five? Those were six shot revolvers."

"They are." Shutt bit her lip. "Ammunition isn't as reliable as it could be. Sergeant Russell is working on it. I told him he better get it fixed soon."

Jose saw two other misfires while he watched. "Better get it fixed soon? Or what?"

"Or he won't like it. I have ways of dealing with subordinates who don't follow orders."

Jose nodded and smiled. *Idiot. Don't bother technical people while they're doing their jobs. If it can be done, they'll get it done. You might know how to run a militia, but not how to run a trading concern. Or a factory. Yelling at them won't make things go faster. And building a VIP viewing area to criticize them from will make it go slower.* "Of course. Of course. I wouldn't want to be Sergeant Russell right now." He smiled wider. "I'm sure he'll come up with something."

Shutt's eyebrows lowered, then she turned to the bar at the end of the room. "Drink? We have some decent wine."

"No thank you. I'm trying to cut down."

"You spend a lot of time in space. Want some Basic?"

"Never got the taste for it."

"Water?"

Jose shook his head. "Not thirsty."

Shutt's eyebrow's narrowed further. "Don't trust me? Afraid I'll poison you?"

Jose smiled. After Dashi was poisoned, none of the senior people on Delta, Traders, Corporate execs, or Militia people, would drink or eat anything they hadn't brought themselves. It made corporate meetings long and dusty. "You asked me to come here, what did you want to talk about?"

"Jake Stewart and his trading empire."

"It's hardly an empire," Jose demurred. "Just a few ships and some contracts. He has the Jump Ship, *Accounting Error*, of course, and interesting imports, but only that. Not enough to disrupt any sort of trading flows here."

"He's disrupted mine," Shutt said. "I've had to idle some of my ships to deal with the price of fuel. And there're all sorts of problems with commodity prices. My quartermaster people are idiots, but they're right, prices are crazy. Some have gone through the roof, others have dropped to nothing."

"I'm sorry to hear that."

"Any advice?"

"Maybe find a better quartermaster."

"Already done that," Shutt said. "The last one won't be making stupid purchases anymore. He's on an extended asteroid inspection tour. We took a bath on all sorts of things. How about you? Is Jake Stewart stealing your shorts?"

"We have a sophisticated mercantile department at TGI." Jose said. "Very experienced in market fluctuations. They're used to changing prices, and plan accordingly." *Which makes me all the angrier that I've got tanks and tanks of near-worthless argon. How did Jake convince everybody that argon was going to go up in price? Is it because he always talks like he's too stupid to be a smart trader? He's one of the richest men in the system, if not the richest, but he always dresses like a homeless station hick. Every report has him wearing that stupid hard suit and carrying a wrench.* Jose shot his cuffs and felt the fabric of the custom fitted jacket he wore. It was gray and black, and his favorite, and silky to the touch. *Jake doesn't ever wear anything this nice. Could that be why? More data points needed.*

"We having fuel shortages," Shutt said. "And parts problems, curtailing our operations. I assume you'll make that good."

"Me? Make it good? How so?"

"Give us what we need," Shutt said. She looked him in the eye. "As we discussed, a while back. When we dealt with the Free Traders."

After Dashi's death, Jose had combined with Shutt and the Militia to crush the power of the Free Traders. Giving Marianne free rein had allowed Jose to pinpoint the troublemakers. Most of those that joined her little rebellion were dead now. The other leadership was either dead or cowed, and they'd reverted to being single ships or small family groups scraping out a living from the crumbs that the larger corps left.

"I promised you some logistical and political support, yes," Jose said. "And we've delivered on that. The Free Traders have to side with us in the Senate now. We can smoothly go about setting up the Empire that Dashi dreamed of."

"I don't give a crap about Dashi's dreams. I need more fuel and supplies. And if you don't get it to me, I'll send in my boys to take it. I've got friends all over. Some that you'd be surprised with. I know where you keep your supplies."

"We've agreed, at least here on the surface, to co-operate." Jose pointed down below. "Three different armed groups keeping the peace in Landing. The corps are producing the products we need, you supply system security and keep piracy, and the Free Traders under control. We march forward to prosperity. Everybody wins."

"We don't have enough fuel, but we do have weapons." Shutt said. "My people need support."

"We have weapons too," Jose said. "We will defend ourselves."

"Not enough," Shutt said. "You got a lot from the Free Traders, but not enough to make a difference."

"You sure of that?"

"Like I said," Shutt smiled. "I have spies. Some in places you wouldn't expect. They tell me what you have. Not enough."

"Enough to make a problem for you. That's all we need. A draw is as good as a win for now. Besides." Jose smiled. "There's no reason to take us on directly. This situation won't last forever. Jake Stewart can't keep his fuel trading going indefinitely."

Shutt stared at him in silence. Jose let it stretch. Finally Shutt nodded. "No he can't. But while he does this market manipulation thing, we take it in the guts."

"We're suffering as well."

"Not as much as we are."

Jose shrugged. "You could always retaliate against him."

"What do you mean?"

"No Jake Stewart, no problem."

Shutt shook her head. "Oh no, we're not doing that again. You're not talking me into fixing your problems. I'm tired of being manipulated by you."

"What do you mean?"

"I see your game. Want to fight the other corps? Have the Militia revolt and burn down half of Landing. Want to fight the Free Traders? Let them revolt and then send the Militia after them. It's always someone else doing the dirty work, and Jose never gets the blame."

"I have no idea what you're talking about." *Dammit. She's smarter than she looks, or I've been too obvious. Need to find another Militia person to take charge. Chaudhari? No he's too dumb. Somebody else. Russell? He's too straightforward. Have to think on this. Who out there has it in for Stewart?*

"No idea, huh? Well idea this, Mr. Custom skinsuit. We're not doing your dirty work on Stewart. He's taken us on economically, and it's hurting. But he can't beat us with weapons. Long term that's what counts. I'm already making my own plans to deal with him. And his friends. He'll soon be under control. But in the meantime you need to support us with supplies."

"If I support you economically, you need to support me politically," Jose said.

"What do you want now, Jose? Another vote? Or more shooting?"

"No more shooting." Jose shook his head. "Things are precarious as it is. No, I've got an economic proposal for you. Let me explain."

Jose brought up a document on his screen and showed what he wanted—export controls from the surface to orbit. The main shuttle port in Landing lifted ninety percent of their exports. It was controlled by a consortium: the corps, the Militia, Free Trader families, a union, the tiny university staff, and the ground-car mechanic's union, all had a piece of it. It effectively lifted what people were willing to pay for, regardless of content. Jose proposed to keep the charges the same but issue 'export permits'

"Just to make sure we lift the right mix of goods," Jose said.

Shutt shrugged. "I thought the freight rates took care of that."

"With the current shortages, we'd like to more efficiently utilize the space by issuing export controls."

"You want to control what's being lifted in the shuttle?"

"Not me." Jose shook his head. "A commission. TGI will appoint one commissioner, you'll appoint one, the Free Traders, the unaligned corps, and say... the university. Each would get a few permits they could issue themselves, but the bulk would require a vote." Jose smiled. "Of course, this could morph into a larger corporate entity. A mega-corp to handle all trading from the ground to the surface." *With me in charge of the new mega-corp of course.*

Jose saw Shutt furrowed her brow while she did the math. She and Jose plus a token Free Trader would form a majority. Let the other members use their personal permits for their groups, or trade them to the triad for special treatment.

"That could work," Shutt said.

"You said this problem with Jake Stewart was economic, not military," Jose said. "More control of exports will give you an economic lever to use. Without using any of your precious resources." *And since the Free Traders listen to me, I only need to bribe the university people or threaten the other corps to cripple you when it suits me. One final thing. She's rank happy, so…*

"What do you think?" Jose smiled at Shutt. "Grand High Commissioner?"

Chapter 21

"When do I get to shoot somebody?" Nadine asked. "Is it today?"

"Later," Jake said. "I'm saving that for an important meeting."

"Next shift?" Nadine rummaged through the cupboard in the lounge, looking for something to eat. *Shipboard food is boring. I miss all those meals on Magyar, and the planets, even here. Space isn't as much fun as it used to be. And I always looked forward to that welcome home dinner with grandfather...don't think of that.*

"Later than that."

"Two days?"

"No."

"Next week?" Nadine took her holstered revolver out and spun it in a circle and then dropped it back into her holster. "Come on Jake, give me a clue."

"I shouldn't have told you that. I'm working a complex plan here. I need time."

"Fine. Fine." Nadine reached for her revolver again, but stopped and closed her fist. "The anticipation is killing me."

"Maybe see a doctor about that." Jake checked his screen. "Price of food is up. Trays and portables. We're going to have to switch to basic for a while."

"Which I hate. Why?"

"Jose's started his counter offensive. He's raising the price of everything."

"I thought there were contracts..."

"He's being clever. Rather than raising prices or trying to break contracts, he's restricting the supply. Cutting back on what's being lifted on the Shuttles. Smart move by him. He controls eighty percent of the orbital lift capacity now, and the remaining twenty is afraid of him."

"He's going to starve us out? Didn't he try that before..."

"And it didn't work before. It won't work this time, only make some things pricier. Well, truthfully, it will make everything pricier. Everyone has to eat. And with me jacking up the price of fuel, it's going to get very, very expensive to eat and breathe in this system. Anyway, it's not about that. He's announced a council to run things. Complex setup. A balanced committee, members from all the factions. But we'll have to respond."

"Who's we? There's only the two of us, and we don't have much cargo."

"It's not how much you have, it's how much you control. And I have lots of things under my control."

Jake brought up more of his spreadsheets. True to form, he hadn't bought much in the way of actual goods. What he'd traded for was shipping space. And he'd traded a lot. "And remember, there're people behind him who expect to be paid. If he's not allowing them to make money one way, they'll have to make it another. Time to make some calls. You ready for some piloting?"

"Regular piloting or your fuel-saving crawling piloting?"

"Fuel optimized travel."

"Miserable crawling. Fine." Nadine strapped herself in. "What are we going to do?"

"Take advantage of other people's misery and stupidity," Jake said. "By scaring the crap out of them."

The next two days were long. Jake had Nadine flying a twisty outer belt course, dashing within range of a dozen stations, and five times as many ships. Most of them Nadine had never visited, or even heard of. Many of them had never heard of Jake either.

"Who are you again?" The Free Trader Captain, Spranger, asked, as Nadine closed with the orbiting station he was docked at. "Stewart. I've heard of you. TGI's golden boy. Own that big trading concern. A Jump Ship too."

"That's me," Jake agreed. "So you know I like to do business."

"What type?"

"Captain Spranger, I understand that you have a contract to provide fuel to Rim-87? In quantity?"

"We might." Spranger shrugged. "But that would be confidential if we did, and I'm not likely to break a non-disclosure clause because you ask. You might have been something to Dashi, but you're vapor out the nozzles to me."

"Of course." Jake nodded at the comm display. "And I'm not asking that. But I notice that the cost of fuel has been skyrocketing recently. That will be an expensive contract to fulfill."

"Only if you haven't secured a supply of fuel for this, theoretical contract, which, theoretically, I have."

"You reacted before the current price change?"

"I don't follow the prices," Spranger said. "Because I always offset a sale with a purchase, and take my cut in the middle. Which everybody does on any contract, so I'm not telling you anything you don't know.

"Of course. Of course. Can your supplier still deliver?"

"That's none of your business, Mr. Stewart."

"Indeed it isn't." Jake nodded. "But for the record, if they don't supply to you, I'm willing to step in, and take over the supply contract from you."

"No good if they can't supply," Spranger said. "If they can't supply me, then you're back in the same spot I am."

"That would be my issue." Jake smiled. "Assuming there *is* a shortage. I won't take it over for free, of course," Jake said.

"I don't need your help."

"You could always enter the spot market and buy what you need to fulfill that contract." Jake watched Spranger's face. He didn't look happy. *Guess he does know the price of fuel right now after all. I almost feel sorry for him.*

"If I ever find myself in that position. I'll let you know."

"Thank you for your time, Captain."

"Free Trades, Mr. Stewart."

"Jake," Nadine said. Jake took four similar calls in a row. "What are you doing?"

"Buying fuel."

"But I thought you were selling fuel. That's why we met up with all those tankers."

"Processing ships, and yes. But I've contracted them to sell me fuel. I'm contracting with these people to buy fuel from them."

"But you can't sell and buy the same thing."

"Sure I can." Jake grinned. "That's what I've been doing all day. Buying fuel. Selling it."

"Nope." Nadine shook her head. "If you have a cup of basic, you can't sell it, and then buy it back. Not and make money."

"Yes I can. I sell the cup to you for two credits. Then later, I buy it back for three credits. That way I make one credit profit."

"You mean you buy it back.. What? That makes no sense." Nadine shook her head. "You mean you lost a credit. You sold it for two and bought it for three. You lost a credit."

"Not the way I do it. I make money at every step."

Nadine shook her head. "Even the great Jake Stewart can't do that."

"I can. Watch me."

"Jake, are we going to be poor, will we have to sell the ship?"

"No. We're going to be rich. Well, richer. And we'll have more ships."

Nadine had no idea what the heck Jake was doing. He'd call people and buy and sell some sort of commodity from them. Or sell it. One call he'd be buying bulk titanium. Next call he'd sell it. Sometimes at a loss.

"Jake, did you make money on that last contract? I heard the prices…"

"Lost my shirt." Jake grinned. "Well, lost some on that transaction. There will be others."

In the middle of all this trading, Jake would offer to buy fuel contracts from them. Or sell them fuel. Or both. Nadine meandered the ship across the system, bringing them into comm distance of different stations. Transmit delay wasn't much in such a small system, but even five or ten second one-way delays messed up discussions. But traders lined up to speak to him, some of them even went so far as to contact Nadine directly and ask for a personal call with Jake. She fended them all off, until a voice from the past called up.

"Miss Nadine. It's always a pleasure to speak to such a pretty lady." The figure on the screen smiled at her. It was her old pal Vince Pletcher, the trader who had previously helped her deal with Roi. He was still a militia officer then, and was trying to shoot down shuttles.

"Vinnie! How are you doing?" Nadine grinned at him. "Got any more of that wine?" He'd shared a memorable bottle of old earth wine with her some time ago. The taste had been strange, but she liked it. It was also the most expensive drink she'd ever had.

"Alas. Not of that exact vintage, no." Pletcher smiled at her. "But I have some that I think tastes as good, and I'd be happy to share them with you over dinner. Amazing wine for an amazing woman. Will you be dirtside anytime soon?"

"Don't think so Vinnie." Nadine grinned back. The dinner had been fabulous. And Pletcher knew how to treat a lady. "We're busy trading things right now. Jake is doing some sort of evil plan that involves buying things."

"And selling things." Vince nodded. "The selling things is very important to his plan."

"He has a plan?" Nadine asked.

"An astute plan." Vince grinned. "I wish I'd thought of it, but I don't have the background for something this elaborate."

"If you understand his plan, can't you take advantage of it?"

"I've already taken as much advantage of it as I can," Vince said. "Any more operations and I'll leave myself open to too much downside exposure. That won't be a problem for Mr. Stewart, but it will be for me, because I'm late to the party. But well done on his part. Would it be possible to speak to him?"

Nadine shook her head. "He's got a message queue a mile long. And getting longer."

"I could arrange a… private contribution to the Nadine's personal recreation fund for distressed children? As a purely charitable endeavor. We all love your work with the children."

Nadine blinked. *What was he…oh. A bribe.* "How much of a donation are we talking here?"

Vince named a sum. Substantial, but not life changing. Nadine sighed and shook her head. "I'd love to take it, but I wouldn't be able to deliver. Whatever his nefarious plan is, it seems to be working. Jake's message queue is longer than high elliptic transfer, and getting longer. I wouldn't be able to get him to speak with you until he's done."

"Well, keep me in mind if he gets some free time. And remind him that I have what he really wants out of this."

"What he really wants? He wants to make money."

"Oh no." Vince shook his head. "This isn't about money at all. He has plenty of that. This is about influence, and power, and control." Vince smile widened. "Please remind him I have some of that, if he needs it."

Chapter 22

"But why is it lifting nearly empty?" Chaudhari watched the single container of food get shoved into the mass driver. "I hear the price of trays is way up in orbit, why isn't there more going up there?"

Vince Pletcher clapped him on the shoulder. "Shortage of shipping space."

"But the train's empty." Chaudhari pointed at the line of cargo containers waiting for their spot on the mass driver. Usually an orbital insertion was at least ten, sometimes twenty containers. He'd seen forty during the old days. This train was four.

"Lifting space is completely spoken for." Pletcher smiled. "The permit holders have booked 110% of the lifting capacity for the next month. It's oversubscribed. I was lucky to get my two containers on this launch."

The last container slid onto the flatcar with a thump, and the locking arms engaged and the nosecone slid into place. They'd hold it down until it reached the launch point seven kilometers away. Once the maglev got going fast enough, the loaded containers reached orbital velocity. Releasing the levers and giving them an upward toss, they'd head out into orbit to be picked up by the orbiting tugs.

Chaudhari shaded his eyes as the maglev speed off into the distance. Everyone said the magnets didn't affect people, but the hairs on his arms always fluffed out when a train passed. "You're lifting half of the food the orbitals need?"

"Half today." Vince smiled again. "I have another shipment tomorrow. Or, at least you do."

"What?"

"You and Scott. You're both in the Militia, and you're a senator. You're entitled to a permit under the new system. I applied for one for you. You're welcome."

"What new system?"

"Do you pay any attention to the debates in the Senate at all? Have you been following the allocation crisis?"

"The allocation crisis? What's that?"

Vince opened his mouth, then closed it. "How did you ever become a Senator?"

Chaudhari shrugged. "Your money. And a lot of Militia people wanted more representation in the Senate, but they didn't trust Shutt's people, and they were kind of tired of the admiral. They figured I'd be a good rep for the common folks."

"They believed that?"

"Scott helped. Everybody knew I was his corporal, and that he trusted me. And that he'd stand up to Shutt."

"They figure they elected Russell, not you."

"They kind of did, Militia wise." Lights flashed in the distance and Chaudhari squinted at the glare. The train reached the lift point, and the catapulted containers burned lines of fire into the sky. *I wonder how many trips they can make before the heat breaks them up. And how much metal do they use? Scott would know, he's more a trader and less a Militia guy these days. He runs that factory like a big squad. It works. For now.* "I mean, I mostly do what he says."

"Why not do more of what you want and less of what he wants?"

"Because he scares me. If I don't follow orders he'll shoot me."

"Aren't you scared of Shutt?"

"Shutt's too important to notice the likes of me, even if I am a Senator."

"And Russell pays attention to you?"

"Russell cares. Shutt doesn't." The blinding containers passed over the horizon, and Chaudhari reopened his eyes. "And Russell takes responsibility for cleaning up his own messes. What do you need for your food lift tomorrow?"

"Food. Have you got any?"

"More than you need. My barge will be at your dock tonight, after it gets dark." One of the faster schooners had met the barge and rushed Chaudhari ahead to meet up with Jake in orbit.

"How much is a barge load?" There was some confusion while they talked back and forth, mass versus volume versus shipping size versus calories, but eventually they settled on 'lots' and 'two containers a day for a long time'

"I can feed twenty-thousand people a day at that rate," Pletcher said. "With my cargo space alone. If we get it up there."

"Jake Stewart has some shipping capacity that we can use, according to a message he sent me. He'll take that same volume every day if you want. And as long as the mass driver keeps firing, we'll be fine.

"We'll be more than fine." Pletcher nodded. "Prices keep going up. Jose is restricting other shipments with his permit system, the only people lifting food right now in bulk will be me and him. Everyone else is going to be shut down for the next month."

"How come you know who will be shut down?"

"How come you know that Jake Stewart has shipping space?"

Chaudhari shrugged. "I talked to him, a while back, on Scott's behalf."

"About trading?"

"It was a… security issue that had to be addressed. He and Russell are co-operating on some things now."

"Like Russell and I are co-operating?"

"Something like that. By the way, how much are you paying me for this food?"

"What price do you suggest?" Vince gave his widest smile.

"Whatever, just make it fair."

Vince laughed. "That's it? Whatever?"

"Yup. That's what Russell told me. Don't waste time arguing. Tell Pletcher to give us a fair price and take it. Just tell him to make it good, or else?"

"Or else what?"

"Or else Scott will come into town and clean up his messes. Like he always does."

"Should I be scared?"

"If you want." Chaudhari shrugged. "I would be."

Jose reviewed the prices on his office screen. Everything was up. His permitting system was having the desired effect. He wasn't restricting the food shipments—starving people get desperate, and if they thought it was his fault, they'd revolt. And his own people wouldn't put up with him killing their own relatives.

"I have to be aggressive, not stupid." Jose spoke aloud. He'd started talking to himself recently. Now that he was in charge of planning everything for TGI and many of the other corps, he understood why Dashi used to have him in to discuss matters. Saying things out loud to another person helped solidify your thinking.

His message light blinked. The private line. "Jose here."

"Senator Jose. How lucky I am to have you lower yourself to speak with me."

"Major Shutt." Jose rolled his eyes. Thank the gods this was audio only. "How can I help you?"

"Deliver that fuel you promised."

"It's already been delivered. In fact, your people accepted the last shipment… more than five hours ago. And started distributing it to your ships, at least according to my agent's reports."

The channel was quiet. Jose counted silently in his head. He got to thirteen.

"You're right. The fuel got here."

"That's what I said."

"We've already given it to the ships."

"As I mentioned." Jose rolled his eyes. "Was there anything else?"

"This meets our immediate needs. How come the price isn't going down? We're not buying any more fuel."

"You're not the only organization that needs fuel." *Does this idiot not know how a market works?*

"Well, the price should go down."

"Blame Jake Stewart."

"I will. Little—" she used an uncomplimentary word. "I'll bet he's responsible for the rise in food prices as well."

"Things are unstable right now," Jose said. "We can expect fluctuations."

"I'm going to tell all those Free Traders and the other Corporate people this is all his fault."

"You do that." *Do that and they'll laugh in your face. They all know how a market works, and they know what the permitting system is doing to supplies. Is this woman that dense? How did I ever end up in partnership with her?*

Shutt read his mind, or rather his tone. "Jose, you think that you're Mr. Smart Guy manipulating things from his office, but remember, you need me more than I need you. We've got the ships and guns, and you have hardly any. Keep this up and our relationship might have to change."

"We have some profitable dealings here. No need for things to change." *Yet.*

"Just remember that. We're in business together. We both win or we both lose."

"I feel the same way. It's better for both of us to act in concert." *Until it isn't. Which will be soon.* "I'll send you more fuel as discussed. But in the meantime, anything you can do to discredit Jake Stewart will be welcome."

"Discredit? Oh, I'll discredit him all right," Shutt said. "He'll be so discredited that it will be like he wasn't here at all. Him and all his friends. Including Sergeant Russell. I want a long, private talk with that man."

"Don't do anything rash, Major Shutt. Senator Shutt. Remember, you're a Senator as well. Senators don't take precipitate action."

"Don't you worry your pretty little head, Jose boy." Shutt's smile was in her voice. "Senator Shutt is relaxed and waiting for the Senate to re-open so that we can debate important matters."

"I'm glad to hear it." Jose said.

"Me too." This time Shutt laughed. "But Major Shutt, acting commander of the Delta Militia, she has other plans."

Chapter 23

"Prices are up all over," Captain Spranger said over the channel from his ship.

"Indeed." Jake nodded at the pickup. *Accounting Error* was close enough to Spranger's ship that a real-time video call was possible. If Nadine cooperated and didn't do any crazy piloting. "Increases in commerce are good things for the system. We all benefit in an expanding economic environment."

Nadine, out of sight of the video pickup stuck a finger in her mouth and fake vomited.

"Sure kid, sure." Spranger tilted his head. "We all love an expanding economic environment. Why, a day doesn't go by when I don't hope for more economic enhancements to the current trading system."

Jake grinned. "You too? Wowser. I thought I was the only one."

"Yes, nothing like a good…trade expansion to get me excited."

"I agree, I agree." Jake's grin widened. "Thanks. That made my day. Always happy to hear economic opportunities increasing."

Nadine, watching, didn't make another fake vomit motion. She was too worried she might do a real one. *How stupid does this guy think Jake is?*

"As you say. Listen, kid, I find that I've got too many opportunities on hand right now, so I have to shed some of my deals, my arrangements. You understand, these are still money makers, but with all the changes happening, I felt it was proper to associate myself with some of the more lucrative opportunities. But I was going to have a problem meeting all my requirements, then I remembered, that smart young man I spoke to, Mr. Jake Stewart, why, I'll bet he'd jump at an opportunity to make a little extra profit. I've been doing this for a while, and I'm sure that I could show him a few things. He could learn a lot from me."

"Thank you so much for considering me." Jake nodded at the screen. "I'm always happy to learn from more experienced members of the merchant community."

"For a suitable fee, of course." Spranger tilted his head.

"Of course, Captain Spranger. A suitable fee could be arranged. What exactly did you have in mind?"

"Well, we discussed fuel last time. I have an arrangement..." Captain Spranger explained the details. If he delivered fifty tons of fuel to a contracted station, they would pay him one hundred credits a ton. Or, if he couldn't deliver, he could get out of the contract by paying a cancellation fee of the same amount.

"I'm trying to take advantage of some emerging opportunities in the third-company debt market, so my capital is stretched right now. Would you be willing to take over the delivery contract?"

"Of course," Jake said. "I'd be happy to."

Captain Spranger looked relived. "Good, good, I can send you the paperwork, and put you in contact with the client."

"I won't be doing the delivery myself of course," Jake said. "I'm not a tanker. I'll have my agent do it."

"The client won't care, as long as they get their fuel."

"And what do I get?" Jake asked.

"Well, I figured I could put a few things in your way, opportunities."

"You could, could you?" Jake smiled at Spranger again. "I have a few suggestions."

Nadine had been watching closely. Jake's grin, sometimes goofy, had suddenly turned...different. *He looks like those happy little beefalo cubs do, when they're hanging out in the pasture playing with each other, right before they get together with their friends and trample you into paste.*

"My first suggestion," Jake said, "Is that you pay me the full five thousand credits of cancellation fee, and I arrange to deliver the fuel to your customer. Current market rate is a smidgen under two-hundred credits a ton, not one hundred, so fifty tons would be ten thousand credits. I get five thousand from your customer, I get five thousand from you. I lose money because I have to pay for shipping, loading, storage, that sort of thing. Not as much as you do, not the whole cancellation fee. But at least your reputation with your customer is intact, they don't have to know you took a bath. They'll think you're a good guy. And you'll only be out five thousand. What do you say?"

Spranger's face sagged. "Listen kid…"

"Call me kid again," Jake grinned, "And I'll cut the call and you can explain to your customer why they aren't getting either the fuel, or a cancellation fee, because you don't have the money to cancel, do you?"

Spranger's face paled. "Listen ki—Mr. Stewart. Mr. Stewart. Can you supply me fuel?"

"As much as you want." Jake glanced at his screen. "I've got thousands of tons, all across the system. Say where and when, and I'll get it there."

"I can't pay two hundred credits a ton."

"That's okay." Jake nodded. Spranger's face opened for a moment. "That's okay because the price is rising. It's up to two-oh-six now. You'll have to pay more."

Spranger's face sagged again. "I don't…"

"Here's the deal." Jake put a display up on the screen. "I take over the delivery. I deal with your customer directly. You pay a thousand credit cancellation fee, to me, and I'll make sure your customer is taken care of. And a couple other things."

"Yes?" Spranger said.

"There are some Free Trader council meetings coming up. I'll need your voting proxies, and your extended families voting proxies assigned to me. I have some other minor carriage contracts I want you to sign. Minor things, delivery and transport, of passengers and cargo."

"Only transport? Not fixed price delivery?"

"Transport only." Jake made a motion to the screen. "The details are in the packet I'm sending you."

"I'll need to review them," Spranger said. "That will take some time."

"Of course." A red light flashed on Jake's screen. "Our orbits are diverging, and there will be some stations masking our comms shortly. We'll lose real-time video in ninety seconds." Jake smiled at the screen. "The offer stands until then. Wait longer, and you'll be liable for the full five-thousand credit cancellation fee."

Nadine waited until after Jake had dealt with that contract, and given her a new course to follow. Now she was heading for a new group of stations, prominent in his message queue.

"Jakey?"

"Hmmmm?" Jake had another set of prices on his screen.

"How are you going to get the fuel for that station? We're not a tanker."

"I'll buy it," Jake said.

"But I thought the prices were out of whack?"

"Well, it's straightforward. I buy fuel at a price of..." Jake checked his screen "Two hundred and seventeen credits a ton. Then I sell it at one hundred credits a ton. That way I make a profit of one hundred seventeen credits."

"Jake." Nadine punched up the acceleration profile on her screen. "That's not how it works. You're paying more than you're selling it for."

"Yes. Buying at two hundred, selling at one hundred. I make a hundred profit."

"Jake, you're supposed to buy low and sell high, not buy high and sell low."

"That's how it works now." Jake looked at his screen. "Food prices are up too. Have to move some of that."

"But, but, but..." Nadine locked her board. *Is he drunk? He could be, but he couldn't be drunk all day long, he's too much of a lightweight. And he keeps doing this. It's not a onetime thing. Can he stay drunk all day?* Nadine shook her head. *Maybe he is drunk.* When she got drunk, she started fights in bars. Maybe when Jake was drunk, he did obscure stock-market manipulations.

"Jake are you sure you know what you're doing?"

"Oh, I know what I'm doing." Jake grinned. "It's everybody else that is confused."

Chapter 24

"Thank you for your business, Cargo Masters. Free Trades." Jake cut the connection and made a note. "Nadine, are we on target for our next meeting?"

"Nope." Nadine sat at the other console in the control room. "Not going."

"Great, I want to...wait. What?"

"We're not moving?"

"Why not?"

"Because." Nadine pointed at the screen. "You've gone insane and I need to do something about it."

Jake looked at his screen, frowned, then back at Nadine. "What do you mean?"

"I listened in on your negotiation."

"Nothing in here is private to you Nadine, listen to what you want."

"Those Cargo Masters had a contract to sell fuel at two hundred fifty credits a ton."

"Yes, and?"

"The price of fuel is now..." Nadine craned her neck to look over Jake's shoulder. "Three hundred fifty-seven credits a ton."

"Correct."

"You just assumed that contract from them."

"I got their cancellation fee, and their proxies, and a promise to deliver—"

"JAKE," Nadine yelled. "You'll have to buy fuel at three-hundred and fifty credits and then sell it at two hundred fifty credits. You'll lose a hundred credits for every ton you deliver. We're going to go broke. Not only are we going to go broke, we'll go broke quickly."

"I get it," Jake said. "You don't understand the transaction. See, we buy a three-fifty, then we sell at two-fifty, and we make a profit of a hundred credits."

"Jake." Nadine closed her eyes and took a deep breath. "Can you do that math again? Exactly."

"Sure." Jake typed some figures. "Let's see, buy the fuel from them at three fifty, sell at two fifty, plus the cancellation fee. Hah! I see the problem."

"You do?"

"Yes." Jake nodded. "We don't make a hundred credit a ton."

"Thank Jove." Nadine closed her eyes and took a deep breath. "You're finally getting it."

"Right." Jake checked his result. "It's not a hundred credit a ton profit."

"Good."

"It's even better." Jake's grinned widened. "With all the costs, expenses and other charges factored in, it's a hundred and eighty-seven credits. Almost double."

Nadine and Jake had been arguing for an hour. Nadine had shut down the board and refused to enter helm controls. Jake used his override code to re-activate it. Nadine cleared the planned courses from memory. Jake recovered them and used a special fuel saving program to improve on them. Nadine screamed abuse at him. Jake ignored it.

Nadine finally got angry. "Jake, I didn't want to do this." She unzipped her skin suit, down to chest level, then grabbed his hand. She squirmed a bit so that her suit started dropping.

"Nadine," Jake said, "I'm flattered, but I don't think—Yaaagh."

Nadine had a spare set of knives strapped to her back inside her suit. She'd had to unzip to get at them. Now one of them was jabbed into the table, between Jakes fingers. The other was in her hand, inches over his arm, which she had locked onto the table. "Explain. And go slow, I'll jab you if you go too fast."

Jake nearly lost his mind in the next half hour. He'd explained, he thought, what a 'short squeeze' was, using appropriate technical terms. But Nadine kept looking confused and threatening to knife him. She was going to run out of patience soon, and he was going to run out of blood shortly thereafter.

"I'll make it as simple as I can," Jake said. "Assume you are a trader. You don't have any fuel."

"Got it." Nadine nodded. The knife hovered over his arm. "No fuel."

"I approach you. I ask to buy fuel. The market price is 100 credits. Got it?"

"Yes."

"Will you put the knife down?"

"No. Keep talking."

"Fine. You don't have any fuel. The market price is one hundred credits for a ton of fuel. I approach you, and offer to pay two hundred credits. What do you think?"

"You're a moron. You could buy it for a hundred."

"I'm not, but never mind. I'm not buying it for a hundred right now. You and I set up a contract, you agree to sell me fuel in two days time, at two hundred credits a ton. What would you do?"

"Show up in two days, buy fuel for a hundred credits a ton, sell it to you for two hundred. Pocket the difference."

"You got it. Good. What if the price of fuel has risen?"

"Well…"

"What if it's now two hundred credits a ton? What happens then?"

"Well." Nadine nodded. "I buy it for two hundred on the market, and I sell it for two hundred, so it's kind of a wash for me. You're out of luck though, you could have bought it for a hundred."

"Well, I didn't. Could you at least move the knife to the left, if you sneeze you'll hurt me."

"Sissy." Nadine moved the knife a quarter inch. "That's far enough. Keep talking."

"What if the price is three hundred?"

"Then I'd lose a hundred. Not worth doing the deal."

"But you have to, because we have a contract."

"So I lose a hundred, you lose two hundred because you could have bought it for a hundred."

"Not exactly, but close enough." Jake nodded. "Nadine, that's three hundred credits in losses. Which means somebody made some money. Where does that three hundred credits go?"

"Who ever owns the fuel, I guess." Nadine said. "They sell it for three hundred…" She stopped. "Jake."

"Yes?"

"How much fuel do you own? Right now?"

Jake grinned. "Now you get it. All of it."

"All of what?"

"I own all of it. All the trade-able fuel in the system belongs to me."

Chapter 25

"That's it, that's the last of it." Chaudhari watched the new crane lift the last pallet of food off the barge. "It belongs to you now."

"Owl Trading is pleased, and proud, to do business with you. We look forward to assisting you in your future endeavors. Meaning, we'll take as much food as you can ship for the next two months. Or to be precise, the next fifty-seven days. But nothing for two weeks after that."

The pallet slammed down, and the pier creaked and swayed underfoot. "Jove." Chaudhari cursed and stumbled to one side. *Why can't he build a decent pier? We're going to be coming back here again. If I tried to march a squad on this, it'll shake apart. And we'll end up in the mud below.*

"Nothing for two weeks? Is it because of the smell?" They were downriver from Landing. Sailing ships and loading crews dumped trash overboard, and high tides meant it had plenty of days to bake in the sun. The smell was…pungent.

"Nothing I can do about the smell." Pletcher watched the unloading. The wind shifted, and the barge banged into the dock, which swayed enough that Chaudhari held his arms wide for balance. One of the waiting loaders fell to their knees. Pletcher waited until the swaying stopped, then motioned his crew to pull the boxes of food trays off the pallet and load them into his truck.

"Why the two-week delay?"

Vince stamped his foot on the wooden beams. "High water. Spring tides start in fifty-seven days. They'll wash all this away."

"Should have built them better," Chaudhari said. Rather than modifying the existing stone quay, Vince and his company had built a smaller, custom designed pier for the barge shipments. The old concrete quay was built into the riverbank, creating a lengthy docking area that ships tied up to and rose and fell with the tides. They were designed for even the highest tides. Vince's pier was wooden piles slammed into the water, with a rickety ramp leading down to floating docks.

"Why?" Vince said. "We did all this in two days, cheap. It won't last long, but it doesn't have to. We can build it again."

"Wood's expensive."

"Not any more." Vince shook his head. "Jose and company have embargoed the lifting of wood to orbit. No off planet market now, so the producers are scrambling, they have to sell to somebody. Plus a lot of the riverside factories have forests they don't need. They'll cut me as much wood as I want, cheap. And float it down here. Two days after the tide washes this away we'll be back in business."

"You'll have to build this every three months, forever. Building another concrete quay and you'll only have to do it once."

"Which needs concrete, concrete mixers, special binding agents, iron rebar reinforcements, and a dredged waterfront." Vince ticked each item off on his fingers. "All of which are pre-abandonment technologies, which are going away. With wooden beams, hammers, and a lot of nails, I can keep this up forever."

"You think all the pre-abandonment tech will go away?"

"Don't you?"

Chaudhari had a mental visual of the last factory shutting down, leaving him and his crew to forage for food. "What? We'll all end up chasing animals and killing them with sharpened sticks?"

"Some people will. Not me."

"We've got guns."

"For as long as those last. And guns need ammunition. Trees replace themselves. And our buddy Scott can supply me nails forever, provided I get him iron ore. Which I have a source for in orbit." Vince sized up the barge. "How much can you carry? By weight?"

"Displacement or mass for orbital lift? And what about volume?" Vince and Chaudhari talked size, and weight until they settled on an amount.

Vince agreed to splash a container of ore on the mudflats near the factory next neap tide, and have Chaudhari and a barge crew pick it up. "Just be nearby with a crane. They'll be in pre-formed ingots- whatever size you want. Hundred, two hundred pounds. I get them made in orbit, drop them down to you."

"You have a foundry in orbit?"

"I own most of two big ships and part of a station now. And I'm a shareholder on a belt station, they have a foundry."

"How did you manage that?"

Pletcher shrugged. "Traded them some fuel. They resold it and made a fortune. They got a pile of credits, I got equity."

"I hear fuel prices have gone insane."

"It's our friend Jake Stewart playing games. Smart guy. I've met him before, but he and I need to have a serious talk." Vince looked over at Chaudhari. "You and Russell should come along."

Chaudhari perked up. "Stewart is coming down to Landing? Scott could come here and meet him."

"I don't think that's healthy, Stewart coming to Landing. Might be best if the meeting was somewhere else, not here. And I hear Shutt wants to have a talk with Russell in person."

"Does she?" Chaudhari had heard that too. "What type of talk?"

"Not a fun talk either. A special type of talk." Vince grimaced. "One he might not survive."

Chapter 26

Nadine spun the knife in her hand. "But who is buying the fuel?" They were sitting at the lounge table of *Accounting Error*. Nadine had canceled her threats and cleaned up the remains of her tray, but she hadn't put her knife away.

"Ultimately, it's me." Jake leaned back. "I'm the last, or the top customer, the one at the end of the chain. Could you put that knife away?"

Nadine's brow clouded, and she blinked, then raised her hand. "This knife?"

"Yes. You promised that you wouldn't stab me if I explained."

"Jake." Nadine sighed. "This is confusing. Having something to fiddle with helps me think."

"It doesn't help me think. It kind of slows my thinking, in fact. Makes it hard to concentrate."

"Fine." Nadine twisted sideways and slid the knife back into her lower back sheath. She'd unzipped her skin suit to reach it, and Jake's eyes tracked the movement.

Nadine leaned forward. *Can't get him one way, get him the other.* She stretched over the lounge table for his tray and made sure that he got a longer glimpse. Then she bent to slip it onto the metal recycle pile, picking the lowest locker on the wall. *The more distracted he is, the more he'll let slip.* "You're the ultimate buyer of all this fuel?"

"Yes. I buy from somebody, then I sell to somebody else, then I buy it back from them. I do that a couple of times. Since I'm the last person in the chain, I pay the most."

"But you said you're selling it as well."

"Fuel is a consumable. It's manufactured, then people use it, then people manufacture more. I have a monopoly on eighty percent of the fuel production in the system, but only for the next few weeks. I didn't buy the production equipment, just all the output. I've arranged to restrict the supply, so everybody on the chain has to pay a higher price to get the fuel they need to sell to the next person up the chain."

"But the next person is you. Ohhhhh." Nadine nodded, then zipped up her skin suit. "Since you owned the fuel to start with, the price doesn't matter to you, because you had it to start with. The price has gone so high, for anybody to sell to you, they have to buy from you. You've manipulated the buying price so high that you're making money from back when you bought it."

"That's more or less the way it goes. Most of the time I don't want the fuel itself, I'll take the cancellation fee and their voting proxies. That's worth more to me."

"You could have explained all this in detail before you started." Nadine reached for her zipper.

Jake's eyes tracked the zipper. "I know it's complicated but you could just trust me."

"That never worked for me before."

"It always worked for you before. Or it should have, if you had taken my advice, rather than trying to do things your own way."

Nadine glared at Jake. "Fine, Stewart. How long can you run this scam?"

"It's not a scam, it's a legitimate financial maneuver. All I did was secure fixed-price contracts for a necessary product that was in a temporary constrained supply situation."

Nadine rolled her eyes. "I'll play your game. How long will this 'constrained supply situation' last?"

"Now that the prices are skyrocketing, everybody is panicking and trying to get more fuel. The regular producers are already gearing up. Some of the corps have switched their ships from regular product runs to fuel skimming and processing. Those that have the capability, at least. One of the ground producers is substituting fuel bladders for their heavy lift capacity."

"So game over?"

"Nope." Jake shook his head. "It takes time to collect and process fuel for the ships that can do it. And lifting fuel from the surface is stupidly expensive. It needs specially modified containers. They'll only lift a limited amount, and only if the price stays high. As the price drops so will their production. Other players are hoarding fuel now, to see how far it will go. As soon as velocity drops, they'll unload their supplies onto the market."

"Velocity drops?"

"As soon as the price rise slows. The price is still rising, but not as fast. If it falters, they'll drop and try to flood the market. In fact, your good friend Mr. Pletcher is already doing that. He's started releasing supplies, and he's making a killing. I'll give it to him, he has a great sense of timing. I've already started unwinding my positions."

"Meaning?"

"I'm cashing out the biggest contracts or the highest priced ones to reduce my exposure. The people who promised to buy at the lowest contracts, I'm liquidating them now. Those people were on the hook for the biggest losses, so they're happy to get out." Nadine looked puzzled so Jake continued. "If you agreed to sell me fuel for one hundred twenty credits a ton, and the price is now—" Jake checked his screen. "Now three hundred forty-two, then you're going to be out a fortune. You'll take any deal to get out of that contract. But if you agreed to sell it to me at two-fifty, you have more room to maneuver, so you might wait."

"Do you make money on all of these?"

"Nope." Jake shook his head. "As more supplies go online, I'll be left holding the bag on a few contracts. But I staggered it. I offered to buy massive amounts at medium prices - one hundred fifty to two hundred fifty. But after that I only offered on small amounts, that was only to drive the price up. I've made contracts for ten times the amount of available fuel in the system for between one-fifty and two-fifty. I'm already clearing those out from the bottom up. I've got one contract at three hundred seventy-five credits, but that's only for fifty tons. I can take a hit on that."

"How did anybody believe you could buy ten times the available fuel?"

Jake shrugged. "Ten times the uncommitted fuel. Some refineries have long-term contracts with the Militia or corps, that fuel is accounted for. There's a surprisingly small amount of excess fuel capacity in the system. That's what I was playing with. Even a small mismatch between supply and demand can create big price swings. Without fuel, people have to idle ships or leave them stranded. It might only be ten percent of your fleet, but that might be a critical part."

"What if this continues forever?"

"It won't." Jake put another display on the screen. "The Militia could idle their least efficient ships and use the efficient ones more often. That would increase operational wear, but they could do it. Corporations could sideline some routes, the less profitable ones. Save the expensive fuel for the most profitable runs. Cut frequency on others." Jake shrugged. "This can't go on, something is going to happen."

Nadine continued to plot their leisurely path through the system. Piloting to maximize fuel savings and minimize communication delay was new to her, but she took it as a challenge. *Pretend that Jake told me I can't do it, that always motivates me.*

Jake didn't react to the occasional 'Ha' and 'In your face, Stewart!' muttered from the plotting console. He was familiar enough with Nadine's moods to not pay attention to her jibes. *I've become too predictable to him. He can use my own personality against me, like the admiral used to.* Nadine's eyes misted at that thought. *Stupid Admiral. Always telling me what I couldn't do. Made me so angry that I went and did it anyway.*

"Jake, I'm altering course. Stand by for maneuvering."

"What?" Jake's head jerked up. He had a half dozen spreadsheets open on his screen. "Sure. What station are we heading for?"

"None." Nadine popped the course plot up on his screen. "I've figured it out. We keep steering for stations, but that's wrong. We need to steer for clusters of ships. We don't need to maneuver to talk to stations. We know their routes, they can come to us. Ships we have to chase."

Jake expanded the course plot. "We're not steering for ships. You're taking us into empty sections of the orbits."

"Empty now." Nadine expanded his display. "Watch the time hack." She ran the time forward. "The station orbits are predictable. And they have boosters and repeaters too. They clank around their orbit. But the ships buzz like a herd of beefalo fleas. They're all trying to do what we do, save fuel. I figure out what the least time course *between* high traffic stations is for several ships, and I put us in the middle."

"Excellent solution Nadine. Organized. Well-planned. Prudent. You've become a cautious, prudent and respectable pilot."

Nadine's eyes narrowed. "Cautious, prudent and respectable. No need to call me nasty names, Stewart. That's not nice."

"Sorry. Then how did you think of that solution?"

"Easy." Nadine grinned. "What's the most fun thing we could pretend to be?"

"Um." Jake shook his head. "Corporate ship on a long trading mission with limited resources."

"Stewart, Stewart, Stewart." Nadine shook her head. "You can take the most exciting idea in the quadrant and convert it into the most boring corporate policy in a sentence or two."

"It's a skill I have. But if we're not thinking like a corporate ship…why are you doing this?"

"You're good at trading and spreadsheets. I'm good at crashing starships and stabbing people. Nobody here to stab, so—"

"No crashing! We don't need to crash into anybody."

"We won't be crashing into anybody. Not right away. Look, Stewart. I trust you."

"Why does you saying that make me very, very suspicious?"

"It's true. I've been thinking. Anytime you give me advice, it's good advice. At least about financial and trading stuff. I still don't understand this trading thing. I'm not sure how you're making money, not exactly, and I'm not sure how it's going to help us get the person, or persons, who killed the admiral and Dashi. But you've got a scheme, so I'm going to go along. The best thing I can do is get you where you need to go, and stab people when I get there."

"You promised no more stabbing!"

"I promised I'd ask first. Anyways, I'm helping now. I've got my own plan."

"Your own plan? Dare I ask?"

"Other than some crazed cargo-trader who hates disjointed messages, who tries to put their ship as close as possible to clusters of other ships?"

Jake shrugged. "Space dentists?"

"Nope." Nadine's grin widened. "Somebody who wants to attack as many ships as possible in the shortest period of time. I've plotted all my courses like I want to attack those ships."

"Nadine, you're not saying…"

"Yep." Nadine beamed. "Space Pirate Nadine! Arrrraugh!"

Chapter 27

"Avast me hearties!" Nadine waved her sword at the video pickup. "Heave to and stand by to be boarded!"

"Nadine, for Jove's sake." Jake pulled his harness tighter. Nadine had insisted he strap-in at his station in the control room. "Stop playing games."

"The channel pickup is turned off." Nadine waved her sword. "Nobody can hear me."

"Where did you get a sword?"

Nadine flourished it in front of him. "You like it? It came as a set, last time I bought my knives. Close quarter defense on a ship. It's too small for most men, so I got a deal on it."

"More like a dirk then?"

"I don't know a Dirk. Does he sell swords? Hang on." Nadine fired the thrusters to adjust her course. "And I matched it with these ear-rings. It really fills out the outfit, doesn't it?"

"You don't need a sword."

"Every pirate needs a sword. A pirate sword."

Jake argued with her while they maneuvered into a new orbit. Now their path would take them between two transfer stations. Any ships dropping from the farther or lifting from the nearer would pass in easy commo range. *Have to admit she's getting better at these least-fuel courses. And I do need to talk to all these folks.*

Jake tired of the argument after five minutes. "Fine. Dress how you want. Why don't you get an eye patch and a parrot to go with it?"

"An eye-patch? What a great idea." Nadine tapped her console to kill the thrusters. "Where would I get a parrot? I need a parrot."

"I've created a monster." Jake brought up his own commo link. "Trading Vessel *Chemung*. This is Jake Stewart. I'd like to talk to the cargo-master or the Captain, if they're available, concerning some contracts we have…"

Two hours later they were drifting out of range of that particular group of ships. Jake brought up his screen, leaned back, and crossed his arms. Nadine came back from the control room and sat at the lounge table. "I see you're finished gabbing. Next maneuver is in—" she checked the screen display in the lounge—"Fifty-three minutes. You have time to eat a tray, or to stare moodily at the displays. But not both, unless you hurry."

"Thanks Nadine. I'll be ready." Jake didn't uncross his arms, and his eyes kept roving between the screens.

"What's wrong, Jakey?"

Jake pointed at one display. "Look there."

"I see a bunch of numbers."

"The price of seven-day contracts is rising."

"Great news!" Nadine grinned. "We're rich."

"No, that's a problem. We have to enter the market to buy those. They shouldn't be going up, they should be going down. That's going to cost me a lot more than I expected."

"Bad news!" Nadine looked sad. "We're poor."

"We're not poor. But..." Jake frowned. "Who's doing it? Who figured it out this fast?"

Nadine leaned over and ruffled his hair. "You'll figure it out Jakey. Check this out. What do you think?" Nadine tilted to one side and preened.

"I don't think—Jove save us. What is that? What's on your eye? Are you okay?"

"Okay? I'm amazing?" Nadine preened again. "Don't I look stellar?"

"Nadine." Jake closed his eyes and counted to ten. "Why are you wearing an eyepatch?"

Nadine tilted her head. A black fabric eyepatch with a skull and crossbones logo on it covered her left eye. "All the best looking pirates wear them. Isn't it great?"

"We're not pirates."

"See, when I board enemy ships, when I leap from the deck into the hold, it's dark down there, and my eyes won't have time to adjust. But by keeping one of them shaded from the bright sun, I'll be able to whip off my eyepatch and I'll already be adapted to the dark. Then I can stab them with my sword." Nadine flourished her sword.

"Nadine..." Jake closed his eyes and counted to ten again. "We're in space. We're not going to be jumping onto the deck of a sailing ship and stabbing people."

"We could need it though. If I'm somewhere and the lights go out, it will be an advantage. Besides, I don't want to stab the wrong person by accident."

"Nadine. You've never cared who you stabbed before. You've stabbed me, and shot me before."

"Yes, but that was on purpose, because I was mad at you. It wasn't an accident."

"Nadine, it looks—"

"Careful, Stewart." Nadine flourished the sword. "I'm feeling the mad thing approaching again."

Jake held up his hands. "It looks wonderful, I meant to say. But in other news, we have a problem. Somebody is buying up my contracts before I can close them out."

"You said that would happen."

"Not this quickly. And not this many. Somebody figured it out."

"Well that's—" Nadine's comm buzzed, and she looked at her screen. "That's an incoming call for me."

"Who is it?" Jake asked.

"Your friend and mine, Vince Pletcher." Nadine raised an eyebrow. "Said he wants to talk about some contracts." Her eyebrows went higher. "Your contracts."

Chapter 28

Jake pulled his harness tight and aligned himself with the camera pickup. He remembered to comb his hair away from his face, then twist it under his ship cap before bringing the channel live. "Always a pleasure to hear from you, Mr. Pletcher. How may the crew of *Accounting Error* be of service to you?"

Vince Pletcher's face appeared on Jake's screen. "Thanks for taking the time to speak to me, Mr. Stewart."

"Vinnie!" Nadine's head popped over the top of Jake's camera, upside down. She and Jake had celebrated her newfound agreement with his plan by cutting the engines and coasting to their next comm spot. They had both floated into the lounge when the radio bonged Pletcher's call. "How's it hanging big guy? Long time no talk!"

"Uh, hello Nadine." Vince leaned closer to his camera. "What is that you're wearing? Are you hurt?"

"I'm not hurt" Nadine pulled the patch away from her head and snapped it back. "Ow. Wasn't hurt. It's an eye patch."

"I can see that. And that's a very distinguished icon on it. Skull and Crossbones?"

"Yep." Nadine nodded. "I'm a pirate. Pirates have eye-patches." She rotated over the console, then reached under the lounge table. "And swords." She yanked her holdout sword from its hiding place.

Jake ducked sideways. "Watch it!"

"Relax, Stewart. I know what I'm doing. Do you like my sword, Vinnie?"

"It totally suits you. Matches the earrings. Tough yet feminine."

Nadine beamed. "See Jakey? There's a man who knows how to compliment a girl. Say, Vinnie. Do you know where I could get a parrot?"

"A parrot." Vince shook his head. "No. I can get you an owl, though. Would you like an owl?"

"Does it sit on my shoulder and say 'aaaarrrhhhh' and 'walk the plank' and 'shiver me timbers'?"

"I'm not sure. I've never tried to get it to talk. Want to come over and test it out? I have this great dinner—"

Jake broke in. "We don't have time to eat right now."

"I wasn't asking you. Just Nadine," Pletcher said. "But we could try it out. If you don't have time for dinner, I have this wine…"

"Nadine doesn't like wine. She likes vodka, or tequila."

"I like Vinnie's wine." Nadine smiled. "He has the best wine. Muuuuch better than yours Jake."

Jake looked offended. Nadine stuck her tongue out at him, then turned back to the camera. "But we're kind of on a schedule here. Maybe next time Vinnie. What did you want to talk about?"

"I need to talk to Jake—Mr. Stewart I mean, about some contracts."

"Boring." Nadine shook her head. "I'll leave you boys to play. Jake, don't stay up too late balancing payments, or whatever you do. Bye Vinnie."

"Bye Nadine."

Nadine pulled her head back from the camera. Jake shook his head and sat silently.

Vince stared back at him on the camera.

Jake broke the silence. "Nadine can be a trial, sometimes."

"I'll bet she's worth it."

Jake nodded slowly. "Barely." He took a breath. "What can I do for you, Mr. Pletcher."

"Call me Vince."

"Vince, what can I do for you?"

"You owe me a lot of money."

"Is that so." Jake stroked his chin. *Should have figured he'd be the one to catch on first. He must have picked up the extra agreements. I have to be careful. If I don't play this right, I'm in deep tabbo excrement. And the Flandre isn't here yet. That's a problem.* Jake had been counting on the arrival of more materials from Magyar. His trading program was in disarray without them. He would survive, but only if he played his cards very, very carefully. "I don't remember borrowing any money from you."

"You didn't."

"Then how do I…."

"I have a bunch of your contracts. Your fuel contracts. I bought them on the secondary market. If you want to close them out, you owe me a bucket-load of cash."

"Indeed." Jake nodded. "Depending on how many you have, several bucket loads. Luckily I have plenty of money. But I'd need to know how many."

Vince brought up the contract numbers and delivery specs and displayed them for Jake.

"Well played Mr. Pletcher, well played." Jake nodded. "I wondered who was smart enough to pick up the extra contracts." He shrugged. "I pay my debts, where would you like it delivered?"

"Delivered?" Vince cocked his head. "I don't want delivery. I want to be paid out."

"Doesn't matter what you want," Jake said. "The contract's for fuel delivery. I have fuel, I'll deliver it to you. I believe that several delivery locations are specified. All stations. And I have several days to arrange delivery on all of those contracts. I assure you that I have adequate fuel reserves to meet those amounts. Let me know where you want it sent."

Vince grinned. "You're bluffing. You don't have that much fuel."

Jake kept his face blank. "If I don't, I'll buy it." *Don't lose your nerve, Stewart. Pretend you don't care how this works out. If he wants fuel, drown him in it. Financial manipulations are one thing, having to deal with reality is another. I bet he hasn't considered that.* Jake could meet the delivery requirement if he had to, but at a cost.

"Then you'll lose a fortune."

"I will, I will." Jake smiled. "But not to you. And you won't make as much as you planned. Oh, you'll be able to take advantage of the last price jump, but as soon as you start unloading quantity, and everybody realizes I've exited the market, prices will plummet. You'll be stuck with all this fuel. Storage costs, transportation. Insurance. Security. The works. You'll lose a fortune." *As will I. But I'll bet he can't take the chance.*

"But you'll lose more that way than if you just bought me out."

"Will I?" Jake smiled. "Perhaps. But perhaps not."

Vince crossed his arms. "Maybe I should sell these contracts to somebody else then."

"Who would buy them?"

"TGI. Jose. Well, Jose is TGI now. And he'd buy them. Or the Militia would buy them."

Jake shrugged again. "Why don't you sell them to Jose then?"

Vince shook his head. "Jose doesn't like me."

"I don't like you either," Jake said. "And yet you're talking to me. Why?"

"Because I want to be on the winning team." Vince stared at Jake. "You always win. I admit, I've had my doubts. But I've been watching you. You always win on your own terms. I'm not sure what you're up to. But I want to be on your side."

Jake nodded. "What's your offer then? Price plus twenty percent?"

"For the contracts I have, my costs plus ten. No extreme profit."

"That's generous. Too generous. There must be an 'and'."

"Checking out all these contracts, look here." Vince brought up another point on the screen. "Jake Stewart Enterprises contracts for delivery…blah-blah-blah. But this point here. 'All proxies relating to the next Free Trader Council Meeting'. 'Proxies relating to Senate votes, agreements on support in the Senate'. You're buying political support, not money."

"What if I am?" Jake asked.

"I'll give you my vote in the Senate, those of some others in my faction—" Vince named several other Senators—"These proxies I got, all of those. I'll use them in your support. And in return, you use them in support of me."

"Support you in what?"

"It's all commercial." Vince detailed his plans. Ownership in several companies. Stations. Tariff exclusions. Priority access to lifting space.

"All business as you can see," Vince said. "On my side it's all about money. The politics I leave to you."

"Why?" Jake asked. "Why leave the politics to me?"

"I want to be rich. You want to be famous. And." Vince pursed his lips. "You're after who killed Dashi. I don't want to be on the wrong side of that. Anybody you decide is on the wrong side of you ends up dead, broke, or both. I only want to build some ships and do some trading. Here's the list."

Jake stared at the list. "You'll have to bring Chaudhari and his people onside to do this. And that Sergeant, Russell, too. What about him? Are you square with him?"

"He wants to meet you. I can arrange it. Bring him up to orbit, some quiet station. You pick one. I'll meet you there, bring him. We can go over things in depth. And both of you owe me a favor."

"That works. Has to be soon."

"You pick a place. Give me two shifts to talk to Russell. I'll tell you where he is. You have a landing boat on that beast up there?"

Jake nodded. "I do. How will you talk him into it?"

"Leave that to me." Vince nodded. "I know what he wants."

"Fine. You explained why you didn't side with Jose. But why me? But why didn't you sell all this to Shutt? The Militia has ships, they can help you."

"I'm scared of her. She's crazy. You're not crazy. I'm safer with you."

"She would have done business."

"She would have shot me. She likes shooting people. I'll bet she's shooting somebody right now."

Chapter 29.

Sergeant Russell shook his head. "I'm not going into Landing right now. Too dangerous for me."

Chaudhari's voice came over the encrypted radio, delivered that morning by the barge crew. "Dangerous? How is it dangerous?"

"Shutt's upset with me. She's sent me some pointed messages telling me to come into town."

"You mean orders?"

"You could call them that. I don't."

"I'll bet she does. Scott, you can't disobey orders."

Sergeant Russell stared out his window. He'd moved into one of the old offices on the second floor of the factory, and now he understood the phrase 'corner office' and why it was desirable for executives. He could watch the loading crew down at the dock, and at the same time the mules moving up and down the pathway to the tidal bluffs. From the other window he could watch the workers tending the robots that swarmed over the fields of super-potatoes, carrots, the apple trees and the other crops

And if he sited a machine gun here, he could mow down anybody attacking the factory from either of two directions. Possibly not needed these days, but thinking that way was habit, and the situation was unsettled right now. The Militia had taught him that habits like that kept him and his troops alive.

"They're not really orders, they're more like suggestions."

"Jove's knees. She's a major. She's got the whole force of the Militia behind her."

"And I'm a Sergeant, and I've got powerful friends. Senators, Factory owners, Traders. Besides, I've got more people to take care of here every day. I can't take the time to run off to Landing. Certainly not to orbit. And they don't get what I have to do here. The spit-and-polish Militia is a long way away from some rural factory."

When the war of the corps had happened, they'd cut off everything east of the cut in the Monorail. Most of the workers had fled their homes and factories, and hoofed it into Landing. But not all.

Now the housing area was nearly full—new workers came in every single day, from farther east, and some had even hiked out from the city at the suggestion of friends working for him. He had a fully functioning operation out here, self-sufficient in food. With his barges and a few sailing ships, trade could bypass the shattered monorail and head directly to him. He'd sent working parties out east to take over the corporate farms there and get them back into production. The crews were enthusiastic. Finally somebody cared enough to give them a job. And the fact that every worker got a single share in their company and was able to vote on initiatives made a big difference.

"Shutt has concerns too. And one of them is you. She's got the entire Militia to take care of. She'll do the same for you."

"If I go to Landing, she'll take care of me in a more permanent way."

"Scott." Chaudhari sounded worried. "If you keep disobeying orders, she'll have to do something. Send out a squad at least."

"She's welcome to try. I've got plenty of troops here. Guns, ammunition. And they'll listen to me before anybody she sends."

"What if she sends more?"

"We'll grind them up. She'd have to send a full company of ground troops, and where is she going to find them? Even if she had the troops, she can't risk that, regardless."

"Why not?"

"She's not the only one with troops in the city. She can't afford to strip the garrison, not with the other factions breathing down her skinsuit collar."

Chaudhari was silent. The three largest competing factions on Delta—TGI and it's associated Corps, the Militia, and the Free Traders and their allies—kept groups of armed troops in Landing to keep an eye on each other. If Shutt cut her presence back to do something outside of the town, whoever she left behind might be overwhelmed by her enemies.

"She could order an orbital strike."

"Not gonna happen." Russell shook his head even though he knew Chaudhari couldn't see him. "Maybe two years ago she could get away with it. Maybe even six months ago. Not now.

Everybody knows how fragile things are. Anything that cuts down our ability to feed ourselves or make things, nobody's going to agree to do that. Even if she finds an officer or two to do it, the crew's won't let them. They'll mutiny first."

"You're risking a lot on the good nature and sober thought of Militia troopers."

"I'm not risking a plucked bean on that. I'm risking it purely on their self interest. No farms, no food for them. That's something I can count on."

"Plucked bean?"

"I've been listening to the pickers. They talk funny."

"Fine, if you won't come into Landing, then how do I get you to meet with this Stewart guy?"

"Tell him to come here."

"Pletcher wants to meet too."

"Tell him to come here as well. Tell them both to come."

"It's too far."

"They have a spaceship. They can go anywhere."

"Stewart explained it to me. They can go up and down, but not across. Drop down and pick up a group, then take off and meet at a station. We talk on the station, we're safe from the Militia. The Militia won't shoot down a station. But a single small shuttle owned by a rich guy. Who's going to care? And the longer they hop into and out of orbit, the easier the targeting is…"

"Right, right." Russell shook his head. "Hold on this channel. Give me a minute." He stepped away from the radio and out onto his balcony. Below, a line of mules plodded down the hill to the dock, each loaded with a section of rough cut wooden strakes. A tall man in an all-blue uniform walked beside them. "Roi?"

The tall man shaded his eyes and looked up. "Yes?"

"I've got Chaudhari here on the radio. If you have a moment, could you come up and talk to us?"

"Of course." Roi strolled uphill.

"And tell Sweet Pea to ask Kim to come up when she has time."

Sweet Pea was one of the mules. Roi looked down at the mule, back up at Russell, shook his head, and continued up.

Less than two minutes later, Roi was standing next to Russell on the balcony.

Russell proffered a metal case. "Cigarette?"

"You know I don't use those vile things."

"I do."

"Then why do you keep asking me if I want one?"

"Makes me appear polite at no cost to myself."

"It's all for appearances."

"And appearances count for more than reality. Which is why you have to appear to be following the banishment order, even when you aren't."

"And you have to appear to follow Militia directives when you've turned into your own private warlord out here.

Russell inhaled and held the smoke. It tasted of burnt potato. Every cigarette tasted worse than the last, something wrong with the machines in the city. He glared at Roi. *He's smarter than he looks. And if he has figured it out, so can others. I'd hoped to cruise under everyone's radar for the next while, but if Roi knows, then so does everybody. I'm out of time. Perhaps I better meet with this Stewart guy after all. Maybe we can help each other.*

"I'm not a warlord. I haven't been in any wars."

Roi shrugged. "You control a disputed region by force of arms, you have personally loyal troops, and your own economy. You collect taxes, and exercise executive control of the area. I don't recall voting for any of that."

"That's because you don't live here. You're supposed to be out in the ocean tasting the water or something like that."

"Mapping currents, and charting the world ocean. It's valuable work, Delta was never properly surveyed."

"Valuable work, huh? Then how come you jumped at a chance to be here?"

"It is valuable. It's not interesting. What do you want?"

"How's the boat building going?"

"Very well, as I told you this morning, and yesterday, and every day before that. With proper supplies, we can make a barge a week, and load them with food and provisions, as well as goods for shipment. What we don't have is motors. As I've told you. Repeatedly."

That Stewart guy has a reputation for finding solutions to technical problems like this. I'll bet he can help. "I might know a guy who can fix your motor problems. I have to meet up with him. But not in Landing. Somewhere else."

"Why not here?"

"It has to be somewhere that…others can get to quickly. And secretly. You used to run a secret base on the south continent, can we meet there?"

Roi looked down at the dock. A new barge was taking shape on the ways. Their current motorized one was tied up. And his pride, a sailing schooner was anchored under some trees. Not exactly invisible from aerial reconnaissance, but hidden well enough unless somebody knew where to look and for what. "How quickly do we have to meet them?"

"A day at the most."

"South continent is too far. Where are the others?"

"Me, here. A few in Landing. The other will be coming from orbit."

Roi nodded. "A secret meeting. With the other factions, of course. Which ones."

"None of your—"

"I must look at the weather, and know the capabilities of their ships, how good their navigation is, and the capabilities of their shuttle. To start with, if it lands on the ocean, will it float or sink?"

Scott had no idea. "Chaudhari is on the comm in there. It's encrypted. Talk to him, find out what you need. Tell him what he needs. Set it up, no later than tomorrow night."

Roi nodded and stepped into the office. Russell continued smoking and staring at the ships.

"Sergeant?" Kim One appeared behind him. "Sweet Pea said you were looking for me."

Kim One claimed she had a mystic connection with her mule, and that they communicated telepathically. Russell thought she was two rounds short of a magazine, but she kept…knowing things. Things that she couldn't have seen, but which happened when her mule was nearby. It creeped him out.

"I'm going away for a few days. You'll be in charge. Keep the barges moving. Handle anything that comes up with the factory. Sign up new people. You know the drill."

"Yes, Sergeant. Sergeant?"

"What?"

"You're not going into Landing are you?"

"What if I was?"

"Shutt will kill you. She wants to be Empress. She killed Dashi, and the admiral. She tricked you into killing Marianne. She wants control of the Militia, and you're going to be in her way. She needs to get rid of you."

"Did Sweet Pea tell you that?"

"Of course not." Kim shook her head. "How would she know that?"

"I thought—"

"My cousin in Landing keeps me in the picture. Everybody there knows. If you go to Landing, she'll get you."

"Not if I get her first."

"If you do that, you'll split the Senate. Some still view her as the legitimate leader of the Militia. You can't mess with that."

"I guess not. Well, what should I do? What would Sweet Pea do?"

"Sweet Pea would concentrate on strengthening your position here, but meet with the other factions to hear what they say. Somewhere safe. But secretly so that you can disavow anything they say."

"That's Sweet Pea's advice, is it?"

"Yes."

Russell shook his head. "Now I'm taking advice from a mule."

"Does it matter, if it's good advice?"

Russell finished his cigarette and put the butt on his desk. Tobacco was scarce enough he couldn't dump even dregs. "Maybe Sweet Pea should be the new emperor. Would you like that?"

Kim shook her head. "Too much work. And people would never accept her."

"Glad you understand that."

"She doesn't want to be in charge, but she's fine with giving advice."

"Great. Thanks."

"You could make her a senator. She'd like that."

"Mules can't be senators."

"There was an earth Emperor who made his horse a senator."

"Didn't know that. But there're no vacancies right now."

"Oh Sergeant." Kim laughed.

"What?"

"One way or another, after you go to meet these people, in Landing or elsewhere, there will be a vacancy." She smiled. "Either you'll kill somebody, or somebody will kill you and Chaudhari, unless you get them first."

Chapter 30

"We're in the middle of nowhere." Sergeant Russell pointed at the ocean surrounding them. "No islands, no land, no other ships. How will they ever find us?" They were aboard Roi's modified sailboat, *Deuxième Chance,* a two-masted wooden hulled boat. Roi called it a ketch since the forward mast was taller, and the aft mast ahead of the rudder post. Russell called it a sure way to a watery death.

Roi spun the boat's wheel left, taking the rising wave on the quarter.

The boat lurched, and Chaudhari grabbed at the wire next to the wheel—the stanchion Roi had called it. "And I hate sailing. I'm going to get sick, again."

Roi ignored them, shading his eyes to stare ahead.

"Roi, answer me, or I swear to Jove I'll go puke in your spare shoes." Chaudhari said. He swallowed a mouthful of saliva. "Or at least drool in them."

Roi continued to stare at the bow. "My shoes are in my berth. Do you want to go below and hunt for them? The motion is worse down there. You won't even last beyond the end of the ladder before you puke. And you're so unsteady you'll end up falling down and wallowing in it."

Chaudhari glared at him, then opened his mouth to speak. Another swell lifted the boat high, held it there, then dipped it down. The boat swung left, the stern accelerating. Chaudhari's face paled, and he staggered to the side and vomited noisily over the side.

"Hold him please, Russell." Roi spun the wheel hard right, held it, then eased it back to center. "I have some delicate maneuvering here.

Russell grabbed Chaudhari's collar. "How come he's so sick and I'm not bothered. I get seasick too."

Roi shrugged. "Everybody gets seasick when they first get on a boat, but the motion is different for different people. There will be some sort of weather that makes you sick that he doesn't mind. But it happens to everyone, eventually."

"Maybe I'm immune."

"Maybe you are." Roi turned the wheel a quarter turn, waited for the bow to swing slightly to their left, then looked over his shoulder.

Russell pointed. "The ocean is…what do you call it… lumpy? In front of us." They raced ahead of the swells rolling down from behind them, from the south-east. Ahead, the regular period shortened, and every third or fourth one foamed upwards.

"Confused. Breaking." Roi continued to stare backwards. He ignored the waves breaking in front of him.

"Why is that?"

"The water in this whole area is shallow. The waves bounce off the bottom and interfere with each other."

"How shallow?"

"We could anchor here if we wanted."

"We could?" Russell hauled Chaudhari back from the rail. "Feel better?"

"No."

"Go lie down below—"

"Not below. I'll lie down at the back of the cockpit, up here."

"If the waves come over the deck, you'll get soaked."

"Cold water. Sounds great." A green-faced Chaudhari crawled to the back of the cockpit and lay down.

Russell gripped the rail with both hands as he leaned over the side. "Doesn't look shallow."

"Shallow isn't the same as clear. There is barely twenty feet below us. But it's so turbulent we can't see the bottom."

"Okay." Russell pointed ahead. "Those waves are breaking."

Roi nodded. "Yes, that's a reef." He returned to gazing back over his shoulder.

"We're headed right for it."

"Yes. Yes we are."

"What happens if we hit the reef?"

"The boat will smash to bits, fill with water, and we'll drown."

"Okay." Russell grabbed the rails and tried to stay upright.

Roi risked a glance at Russell. "You don't look worried."

"I'm not."

"Even when we're headed directly for a boat-killing reef."

Russell shrugged again. "I don't know much about boats. But I know you. And I know that you're not going to crash us into those rocks, or whatever they are."

"You think I care about you, or for that matter about life that much?"

"You don't care about me at all. And I think you're disgusted with life."

Roi swung the wheel hard left, then right, then hard left again, stopping a spin.

"They why shouldn't I kill us both?"

Russell rapped the wooden cabin in front of the helm. "You love this boat. You wouldn't kill the boat just to kill us."

Roi laughed. "D'accord. This is true. She deserves better than the two of us give her."

Russell held onto the rail with one hand and shaded his eyes against the sun with the other. The waves crashed against the unseen reef ahead of him. It bothered him that the violence of the waves contrasted with the warm sun and pleasant temperatures. Shipwrecks were supposed to happen in the dark, in a cold rain, not at noon with the smell of salt in the air.

A narrow gap of water showed ahead. The waves crashed in piles of spray on either side, but in the middle the waves continued through without foaming white.

"What's that spot there in the middle, the green part?"

"Salvation," Roi said. "Salvation. Hang on."

He adjusted the wheel again, his eyes never leaving the waves behind. He turned the boat left for five seconds, then swung right. The boat lifted again, slewed sideways, until he pivoted it to the right.

Russell tapped Roi's shoulder. "This reef thing is ahead of us."

"I know this."

"Shouldn't you be looking where we're going?"

"I know where the gap is. And how wide it is. Wide enough for us to go through, if we are pointing correctly. But if those waves behind cause us to broach, we'll lose the ability to steer. So I steer by the waves behind."

"Broach?"

"Turn sideways."

Russell blinked. Now Roi's sideways steering made sense. They had left the factory that morning in the dark, on the outgoing tide. The tide dragged them far offshore, and once there, Roi had turned them to head northwest. Now they were heading roughly in the direction of Landing, the wind behind pushing them along at a fair clip. It had been an easy sail, with the wind behind them, until the reef appeared, stretching to either side of them.

"What do I need to do?"

"We cannot be too slow." Roi said. "Put your hand on the throttle. When I tell you, give us as much speed as you can."

The waves were moving faster than the ship, and they banged the stern back and forth. If it got banged too far to one side, the waves would wash over the ship and push them down. This was much more dangerous than he thought.

Russell squirmed in beside him to grasp the throttle lever. It was metal. Cold and wet. He barely had enough room to touch it, so he twisted until he was laying down, one hand stretched, facing sideways. White glinted in the sun, and he looked back over the stern.

The biggest wave he had ever seen was overtaking them. Watching the giant green and white wall bear down on him, Russel shivered. *Where did that come from? It will knock the boat over, cover us in green and drown everyone.* "Roi," he yelled. "The entire ocean is coming behind us."

Roi continued to make adjustments. He turned the wheel two inches. "Rogue wave, maybe too big for us. Hold on and get ready to shove that lever when I say so."

"Why not now?"

"Because we have to ride a wave in from beginning to end. If we get to the reef too soon we'll dig in and pitch-pole, too late and we'll bottom out and break our back. Wait for my order."

"I hate not being in charge." Russell kept his eyes on the wave behind him, and his hand on the lever in front. "And what does pitch-pole mean? Is it good?"

Roi's head swiveled back to check the giant wave overtaking them, then swiveled to gauge the distance to the passage in the reef. "Steady. Steady." He adjusted the bow, pointing it directly at the gap. "Steady."

The boat rose on a medium-sized wave. Russell had a clear view of the giant wave right behind it. Time slowed. The sloop settled down, then lifted up by the stern. Even with the stern angled up behind them, the following wave still towered over them. They rode the wave up higher, but still the next wave overhung them. The first wave raced through to the bow, and the stern dropped as it raced away. Russell stretched his head up, up, up. He had to roll on his back to see the crest behind them. He looked forward. The breaking waves were two dozen feet on either side. A flat gap line of gray-green foam showed the channel.

"NOW" Roi yelled, hands twitching sideways on the wheel. "Gun it!"

Russell shoved the throttle hard and kept shoving until it slammed into the stops. Black smoke blew out of the exhaust pipe, then they surged forward. The waves behind them slowed. *We're driving almost as fast as the wave now.* The bow was only feet from the breakers.

The boat twitched left, and Roi spun the wheel full right to compensate. "Hang on, we might swamp!"

"Swamp?" Russell yelled. "Swamp sounds bad."

Despite the wheel, their boat slid to left, and again, as it rode the giant wave behind them. The water rushed under the boat. The rudder couldn't bite, it needed water flowing past it.

They lifted higher, and higher, until they were above the crests. The sun was bright and hot, the deck was dry except for the odd minor splash. Past the breakers, inside the reef, the water was flat, and crystal green.

"Come on my girl, come on!" Roi held the wheel hard over. "My sweet girl! Come on!"

"Roi, do you want some privacy with Miss *Deuxième Chance*—"

They drifted farther left, and now they rolled, the wave was catching up, they were going to broach.

"My sweet girl. Don't let me down!" Roi yelled.

Russell could see the channel clear ahead. The waves to either side of the bow crashed over the edge of the reef.

The boat tilted farther, then the rudder bit. The bow swung right, slowly at first, then faster and faster. The right side—*what did that idiot call it? The starboard?*—ducked under the water, but they kept spinning right. Russell lost his grip on the throttle and slid backwards. The stern slewed sideways, and the waves smashed on both sides, blasting them with gray spray from both sides. The wave's support vanished, and they dropped down, down. SLAM! They cracked into the bottom, spray flew on both sides.

Russell gripped the railing as waves splashed over him. *Better to jump now, or wait until we roll over? I don't even have a life jacket on? We should be in pieces now. Always thought I'd be hung, not drowned.* Russell gripped the rail. *Stay on board until the last minute. Wait until the boat breaks up. I can grab a piece of wood or something.*

The waves receded. Water ran off the railing, the deckhouse, his hair. The Dragon appeared, red-yellow under a blue sky. They coasted into the middle of a circle of placid blue-green water, only minor ripples marring the flat surface. Behind them the line of waves continued to boom onto the rocks at regular intervals.

"Welcome to our lagoon, Sergeant." Roi looked at the sky. "Still early. We'll anchor and wait for the others to come to us. The reef protects us, it's shallow enough we can anchor, and everyone overhead will think we're fishing in the middle of the world ocean. We can dry out while we wait." Roi shook his head. "Good thing that the waves weren't big. An anchorage like this." He waved his hand at the placid waters. "Would be hard to get into if the weather was even the slightest bit bad. Why," he leaned closer to Scott. "It might even be exciting."

Chapter 31

"On course, ETA eight hours, fourteen minutes to rendezvous." Nadine punched another setting into her board. "*Accounting Error* confirms course. Going dark." Lights went out, and the motors running the air system ran down. "Prepare for the stink, and the cold. Going to get close in here. Hope you enjoy it."

Jake and Nadine had crowded into Jake's private shuttle, and separated from *Accounting Error*. Once on course, Jake had insisted on shutting everything down, except battery operated life support. Once the main power was down, air scrubbers that froze noxious gases out wouldn't work. The shuttle would soon smell like old feet.

"It's necessary." Jake played with the co-pilot's console. "Thank you for agreeing to take the pilot's chair."

"About time you recognized my brilliance, Stewart." For seat-of-the-pants maneuvering, Nadine was much better than Jake, and they both knew it. "And I'm looking forward to getting us down with a minimal fuel profile. You're not the only one who can do calculations. But you're lucky you didn't kill me during loading."

She and Jake had loaded up a dozen crates of metals onto the shuttle. Nadine had cursed the whole time. They were in zero-G, so no weight. But plenty of mass, and they were hard to maneuver, and several of the crates had nearly gotten away from them.

"You were the one who tried to catch them, Nadine. I told you to let them go."

"And miss all the fun? Then I'd have nothing to complain about."

"I'm hoping we'll have nothing to complain about here." Jake brought up a system display on his console. "No traffic close by."

Nadine craned her head to see what he was looking at. "Where are you getting those readings? You shut everything down, including sensors."

"Everything that radiates shut down. Your control links, the radar, everything like that broadcasts something, even if it's heat. Here, I'm receiving the telemetry from *Accounting Error*, we're not emitting anything. I'll copy it to you locally, so there's no excess power output."

Nadine displayed the traffic pattern on her console. "Jake, if somebody intercepts that directed beam, they can backtrack our course."

"It's not a narrow beam. It's broadcasting over most of the hemisphere, so no way to tell where it's supposed to go."

"That's what you loaded up on *Accounting Error*. But what if somebody calls the ship and we don't answer?"

"Before we left, I started an encrypted conversation with Skimmer. There's a constant stream of back-and-forth traffic between him and *Accounting Error*. Our channel will show as busy all the time."

"Skimmer can do that?"

"Absolutely not." Jake shook his head. "Or at least I don't think so. I didn't ask him—he's asleep. But it doesn't matter because I have his codes. I loaded a program on his personal comm and slaved it to his station antenna. I'm sending garbage traffic that looks like encryption, and his comm is re-encrypting it and sending it back to me, with variable delays built in." Jake shrugged. "I hope somebody spends good computer time trying to decode that."

"You're even more devious than I imagined, Stewart." Nadine laughed. "I like that in a man."

Jake prepared to doze for the next eight hours. He'd had very little sleep these last few days, wheeling and dealing. He'd had to handle all the contracts personally, even when someone called in the middle of his night. This was his first time off line in days.

And I can use the rest. Jake stretched preparatory to falling asleep. *If everything goes as I planned, I can unload the last of my contracts at a profit, and I'll have most of the Free Traders and the independents on my side. I need another day, and not have Pletcher blow the whistle on me.* His last thought before falling asleep was that maybe he should send Nadine to talk to Pletcher. She could convince him to do anything.

"Jake. Jake, wake up."

Jake sat up and rubbed his eyes. "Re-entry?"

"Nope."

"Oh." Jake yawned and stretched. "Not much of a rest. I feel like I've only been asleep for fifteen minutes."

"Twenty-two minutes. We're still hours out. I need you to do something for me."

"You woke me up to do something? What?"

Nadine handed him her personal comm. "Check my math."

"Check your...what?" Jake sat up straight. "You don't do math."

"These are three orbits. Ones is ours. The other two cross it."

"Orbits cross, Nadine. What's special about these."

"These two cross at the same time."

Jake took the comm from her and started checking her assumptions. "They do cross. Almost same place and time. But why do you think this is serious enough to wake me up?"

"Where they cross, that's where, and when, we'll have to start atmospheric maneuvering to land in that asstole."

"It's not pronounced that way, Nadine."

"You mean ass—"

"Never mind." Jake played with his screen. "Yes, if we have to go to that atoll, that's where you'll start maneuvering."

"They'll see us." Nadine played with her display. "Those two dropped from a Militia Station seven and nineteen minutes ago, respectively. Exactly timed to meet us. Want to bet they're cutters with boarding parties?"

"No bet. Can you avoid them?"

"Not easily. Not without them seeing us. And there's one other problem."

"Which is?"

Nadine pointed at the display. "I don't have good telemetry on that one there, it's outside of *Accounting Error's* scan area. I think it's dropping as well, and it will be in the same vicinity soon. You know what that means?"

"What does it mean?"

"We're boxed in." Nadine zoomed in on her display, showing three orbits crossing almost at a point. "Unless we do something, they'll catch up. The Militia is coming to destroy us."

Chapter 32

Balthazar's sailing ship had arrived. Chaudhari and Russell watched it sail serenely through the pass on the far side of the lagoon.

"They look indecently clean," Chaudhari said. "I'll bet their captain didn't make them puke everywhere."

After entering the atoll, as Roi called it, they had turned south and motored into a corner. There Roi tucked them into a cove made by the curving of the reef. The rolling swell crashed over the rocks less than fifty feet away, but they floated in a clear pool of water, the sandy bottom visible below them.

"I didn't puke on anything," Russell said.

"That's because you're his favorite." Chaudhari glared at Roi. "You didn't have Captain Keen here put you into the worst possible waves."

"We were only in the big waves for sixty seconds. And everybody was too busy with not getting smashed on the rocks to worry about getting sick. Or should have been. Plus you were sick before we got here."

"He arranged it this way, just to make me uncomfortable."

"How would he do that? The waves come from hundreds of miles away, from storm fronts or something, and the wind comes from the land up north, way far away."

"He set it up."

"Don't you know how weather works?

Chaudhari shook his head. "Weather? No. I'm an orbital guy, remember. And why should I? What use is knowing that."

Russell opened his mouth, then closed it. He shook his head. "And you're a Senator."

"Yup. World's going to hell, isn't it?"

"Already has." Russell dug for a cigarette. *Total hell. Not enough cigarettes, the boss is an idiot who's trying to kill me for doing my job, and I've got ten times as many people counting on me as before. Never thought I'd be nostalgic for running my old squad.*

Roi came back from the bow. "We're ready for them. I am going to take a nap while you conduct your business."

"Are you done gybing the chain stay, or whatever you were doing."

"Attaching the anchor snubber, and yes, I am." Roi watched the other boat sail across the lagoon. "He made good time, considering the winds. But he didn't have to deal with the swell as we did."

"He didn't bounce or anything when he sailed in. The water there is much flatter than here."

"Smoother." Roi nodded. "Given the wind direction, and the state of the tide, that channel would be easy for him to sail in. Placid, almost."

"Why didn't we sail in that way?" Chaudhari asked.

Roi shrugged. "The winds were against us, and Commandant Russell said we were on a schedule so I took the direct route. We could have sailed in from that side, but it would have added another hour to our journey."

Chaudhari's eyes widened. "An hour? We went through that watery hell-scape to save an hour."

"Yes." Roi nodded. "Or perhaps only forty-five minutes. Hard to tell." He grinned. "But it was fun, no?"

Balthazar and his brothers guided their schooner next to the *Deuxième Chance*. They yelled incomprehensible questions and orders back and forth with Roi. Russell couldn't figure out the details, but ten minutes later the two ships were securely tied together. Now Balthazar's schooner, *Magus*, was the one anchored to the bottom, and Roi's *Deuxième Chance* was lashed to it. And the boats were arranged nose to tail.

"Why are you backwards?" Russell asked as he stepped aboard *Magus*.

"From our point of view you're backwards," Pletcher said, shaking his hand. "Bal said something about keeping the riggings separate. Put them together this way and the masts won't bump into each other."

Russell looked up. The ropes and pieces of metal swayed back and forth, but Balthazar and Roi had arranged things so they didn't jangle together. "Say what you like about that renegade Roi, he knows a thing or two about boats."

"Whatever."

"You don't think so?"

Pletcher shrugged. "I don't worry about those things. When I find somebody who knows their stuff, and seems competent about it, I let them do it, and I don't interfere."

"Good plan. Too bad the Militia doesn't work that way." Russell reached into his pocket to pull out a cigarette, then cursed. The waves washing over them during their entry had soaked them.

"Looking for one of these?" Pletcher extended a box of cigarettes. "I found some in my office."

"Fallen off a truck?" Russell took one and lit it.

"More likely a boat, but something like that."

Russell lit one and took a long drag. "Ah. That's better than sex sometimes. Thank you. Thank you, Senator."

"I was wondering when you'd remember."

"I'm not impressed with Senators," Russell said. "I've sort of got one of my own." He waved at Chaudhari, who stood with Roi and Balthazar. They pointed at the anchor chain and discussed something nautical. A thought struck him. "And you're a senator yourself and you have a couple of senators of your own. And plenty of money. Why didn't you just buy Chaudhari, too?"

"Why buy when I can rent?" Pletcher asked. "I couldn't organize the votes properly to get another full senator. But by supporting one of the Militia's finest, I get support when I need it, and in return I have to help you out from time to time." He shrugged. "Helping you has helped me along so far."

Russell took another long drag on his cigarette, then sighed. "What do you want?"

"Me?" Pletcher grinned. "To make money. To be left alone. To be left alone to make money."

"Don't you want to be Speaker of the Senate? Or Emperor. Or the King of Port Siam?"

"Never." Pletcher shook his head. "I've got a company to run, ships to organize, roads to build. That's fun and exciting. Sitting in a chair in a robe while people argue over taxation structure, that's nothing I want to do. So very boring."

"You're going to sit quietly down here, keep your head down and get rich?"

"That's the plan. You have a better one?"

"Nope." Russell took another drag on the cigarette. "Not really."

"What about you?" Pletcher asked. "Going to take over the Militia?"

"Nope."

"How about killing Shutt?"

Russell glared at him. "Why would I do that?"

"Because if you don't, everybody says she'll kill you. She's gone nuts. She killed the admiral, you know."

Russell shook his head. "No proof."

"I heard it directly from somebody at your headquarters. They were in the room two minutes after he died. She's crazy. She thinks she's the only one who can run the Militia, and she'll take out anybody who might get in her way."

"You're so excited about who's going to be in charge of the Militia, why don't you take control?"

"A civilian? They'll never accept me." Pletcher shook his head. "But what about a hero of the war of the corps? Someone renowned for stepping up and taking care of his troops, giving them a place to live and to work. A real warrior type. They'd accept him."

"You mean me?"

Pletcher craned his head. "Any other Militia guys around here?"

"Senator Chaudhari?"

They both laughed. Russell's laugh turned into a cough. He pounded himself on the chest. "Orbital guys wouldn't accept me. I don't have enough space stink on me."

"You could get it. Spend more time up there."

"I do that, and the Free Traders will ram my ship and blow me up, first opportunity. Or board and throw me out an airlock without a suit. They're still upset about Marianne dying."

"You did shoot her in the chest." Pletcher nodded. "Shot her in cold blood."

"They were supposed to be frangibles. She wasn't supposed to die."

Pletcher shrugged. "But she did. And it was your fault."

Russell started cursing and went on for several minutes. Pletcher stood placidly by. After Russell ran down, Pletcher checked his comm. "Five minutes, forty-three seconds. You didn't repeat yourself either. I've heard about your cursing streaks, but I wouldn't have believed it if I hadn't seen it."

"I'm screwed either way, aren't I?"

"Unless you find somebody else to run the Free Traders who doesn't want to kill you, and somebody to run the Militia you can take orders from without wanting to kill them."

"I'm okay with wanting to kill them, I've felt that way about all my bosses. It's become a habit with me." Russell took another drag, and cursed. His cigarette was done. "You have another of these?"

Pletcher gave him the box. "Keep it. I've got a half dozen boxes inside, you can have them, too. What are you going to do?"

"How about make you the next emperor of the known galaxy? Head of the Militia, leader of the Free Traders, Chairman of the board of Trans Galactic Insurance. It would look good on you."

Pletcher laughed. "It might be worth it, just to have you come into my office and salute me every day. But it wouldn't work. I can't run a Militia, nor the Free Traders council. I can make some inroads at the corps and the independents for a while. But that will take time, and time is something you don't have."

"Why all this concern for me?"

"I have no concern for you at all. Don't really care if you live or die. But you won't go quietly, whatever happens, and this is a small moon. No way you are going to go gentle into that good night. I'm worried about collateral damage. We need to find some non-violent way to settle our disagreements in a hurry, or we'll all be in trouble."

"So what do we do then?"

A sonic boom roared in the distance. Then another. "Ask a smart guy." Pletcher raised his eyes to the sky. "I think I hear him coming now."

Chapter 33

"Chased by a dozen armed ships into the depth of a planetary gravity well, the intrepid Nadine, pilot extraordinaire, depends on her skill, cunning, and razor sharp reflexes to save the day. Ducking and weaving, her insane piloting skills befuddle all her pursuers. Watch, amazed as she out-pilots the best the Militia has, taking them for the ride of their lives." Nadine raised a clenched fist above her head. "You'll never take me alive." She turned to Jake. "What do you think?"

Jake yawned. He'd come up to the control room and strapped in to watch the pursuing ships. "Sorry, just woke up."

"I give this amazing speech, and all you can do is yawn?"

"Well, I mean… never take me alive? Isn't that kind of… hackneyed?"

"You have anything better?"

"No. No. That's fine. But, ummm, twelve ships? I only count three…"

"They're bound to have more available. I'm sure there are others waiting. They must have more on duty. At least a dozen."

"Could be," Jake said. "But they normally only have two rapid-reaction ships crewed in orbit. Even a few years ago when they had lots of ships. Now, I doubt if they could get a half-dozen done in a day. And not all of those are armed… I'm sure one of them is, but not sure which one."

"But one of them is armed. It must be."

"Sure, sure." Jake nodded. "And well, you can't say the best of the Militia, because with the cuts, and the war, and the problems, they lost a lot of good pilots. And ships. The ships are barely out of dry dock, the pilots barely trained."

"You don't know that."

"No, but it's the way to bet. Also…"

"What?"

"We're talking right now, you're not flying. You have the auto-pilot on."

Nadine crossed her arms and glared at Jake. "Fine, Stewart, fine. How about this?" She raised her hand in a fist. "Chased by the dregs of the Militia, the barely competent Jake Stewart snoozes his life away while his autopilot keeps them from thumping into the decrepit ships chasing him, ships that are too slow and broken to avoid smashing into him."

She lowered her hand. "Is that the inspirational talk you want?"

"It has the virtue of being true.."

"Jove's knees." Nadine disconnected the autopilot, then gave the controls a slight side-to-side wag, testing how the shuttle responded. "Hang on, while I figure out how to get us out of this."

"I need a minute to think." Jake looked at the screen. Most times, Delta had plenty of orbital traffic launching, landing, docking and undocking. Looking at all the motion on the screens, it was hard to tell who was going where. But Nadine's analysis was sound. The Militia was chasing them.

"Listen, Admiral, this isn't your thing. I'll take care of the tactical situation, and you… add some numbers or count something."

"I'm not an admiral."

"Yes you are. Dashi make you an Admiral, remember? When we first found *Accounting Error*? Back when we called it the Jump Ship?"

Jake nodded. "He did." A few adventures back, when Dashi had sent him to investigate nearby systems, he'd given him a commission as an admiral of the Delta Militia. It was temporary, but it had never been rescinded.

Nadine adjusted their trim. "And until you report back to Dashi, you're a temporary plenty-hairy type."

"Plenty hairy?"

"Remember, you explained it to me once. You're plenty-hairy, so you get to make decisions by yourself, without asking headquarters. It's a title ambassadors get."

"Plenipotentiary?"

"Yeah, that was it." Nadine adjusted the ship. "Plenty-hairy. We're not in the atmo yet, but we'll have to make some decisions. That's your job." Nadine looked to Jake. "Tell me what you want to happen, and I'll make it work. You figure out what, and I'll do the how."

"I get to decide what happens then? That's new, you've never let me decide before."

"That's what I'm telling you Stewart. You decide what, and I decide how."

"Fine." Jake played with his screen, zooming the planetary display in. *Things are coming to a head. I need to know where the others stand. But I can't afford to get locked up by the Militia. Or worse, shot up.* "Given where we're going…" He muttered to himself. "Right, I've got it."

"Care to share?"

"Yes. My decision is," Jake smiled. "We're going to crash."

"That's not a cutter." Chaudhari followed the distant spot through binoculars. "It's a regular shuttle. One of the heavy lift ones. And it's dropping, heading for Landing."

"We were supposed to be alone out here." Russell shaded his eyes. He couldn't see the actual shuttle, but the contrail blazed across the sky. "That's why we picked it. No orbital traffic overhead."

"I thought so too," Pletcher said. "Somewhere close to the city, easy for everyone to get to, but not on the regular flight paths, so that we wouldn't be accidentally observed."

Russell shook his head. "Can they see us? Will they look?"

"They will look," Roi said. "From that high, the only ships for miles, we will stand like the nose on your face. At that altitude they can see the ocean all the way to Landing."

Russell furrowed his brow. "Stand like the nose on your face?"

"Yes." Roi tapped his nose. "This. Here."

"I know what a nose is." Russell turned and yelled to the bow. "We're blown. We need to get out of here. How soon can we gybe the anchor?"

Pletcher coughed. "Umm, we might not be blown. They'll see us, sure, if they choose to look. But they won't suspect us of anything strange. "

"We're the only ship in view from up there," Russell said. "The only nose on a face, like Roi says."

"D'accord." Roi nodded. "We must go."

"Bal," Vince yelled to his captain. "Did you call your fishing friends, tell them that thing we talked about?"

Balthazar was also looking at the shuttle through binoculars. "Yes. Like we agreed."

"How many friends?"

"Twenty-seven. All throughout the area."

"That's enough then." Vince turned back to Russell. "We're safe. Balthazar and I arranged for a whack of other boats to set sail yesterday and today. More than twenty fishing boats put to sea last night, and they're spread all along the coast, up and down, and out to sea as well. Roi's right, from that altitude they can see all the way to Landing, and all they can see is boats and boats, all of them out fishing."

"We don't look like we're fishing."

"If you look close enough, sure. But we don't look like we're not fishing, and we could be on our way to the fishing grounds."

"Two boats? Tied together?"

Pletcher shrugged. "Can't help that, but are they going to take a close look at every single boat they see from up there? From that high we're a smudge on the ocean."

Roi frowned. "It is not safe to stay, we must go. If we are found—"

"If we are found, nothing more happens to you, you're still exiled," Russell said. "I might get shot, and Senator Pletcher here might get put in jail, or fined, or something, but nothing worse will happen to you, so relax. How much longer until smart guy gets here?"

"Two hours." Pletcher checked his comm. "Less than two hours. We can't get far away in that time."

"We stay." Russell said. The contrail disappeared over the horizon. "Too many things going on. We need to talk and make a plan. A good plan."

"That's a horrible plan, Jakey." Nadine pivoted the shuttle ninety degrees, and accelerated perpendicular to their course. "I'm not a fan of dying."

"You told me the decision was up to me." The main engine pushed Jake back into his seat. "So I decided. We're going to die."

"Just hop out the airlock then."

"Not just me, we both need to die."

"I didn't sign up for this."

"Nadine." The main engines cut out, and they floated for a moment. "What was that for?"

"Changing our re-reentry aspect. I want to come in gentle, watch what they do."

"Nope." Jake shook his head. "We have to come in hard, fast, and burn up. Not just die. But die gloriously in a shower of flames and fire, streaking across the sky like a meteor, burning up all the way down until we disappear in an explosion of flame." He grinned at Nadine.

She glared back. "Fire?"

"And flame." He grinned wider.

"Burning across the sky?"

"Like a meteor. We're going to have a death that they will talk about for years and years and years. It will be glorious."

Nadine glared at him. He kept grinning at her. She scrunched up her face and narrowed her eyes, then grabbed the controls. "You know the problem with you, Stewart."

Jake lost his grin. "I'm sure you're going to tell me. What?"

"You do know how to impress a girl. You've got words." She fired the thrusters, pivoted the ship, and slammed the main engines on full. They both slammed into their seat. "You've got words," Nadine said, pressed almost flat. "But your timing truly sucks."

Chapter 34

"Where did they all come from?" Nadine kicked the thruster pedal and the shuttle pivoted left. She held course for six seconds, then kicked right for two, then back left.

Jake lurched sideways with each kick, but he kept focused on the display on his screen. "They're not all chasing us. That shuttle is going in for a landing. And the two up above aren't going to be a problem, unless they drop hard."

"Not a problem to this orbit, no," Nadine said. "But somebody has read a tactics manual. They're the high guard. Highest in the gravity well. If we start to climb, they can slow and drop on us like a falcon on a beefalo. While we're climbing, we'll need to keep a steady course, and they'll get to take pot shots at us the whole time we do it."

"Assuming they're armed," Jake said.

"Put them on the main screen." Nadine tapped her controls and the piloting display shrank and switched the side screen. She kicked the thruster pedals again.

"On Screen."

They pivoted right and left on a random pattern. Their course serpentined on Jake's screen. *Her turns are nearly random…she's flying like they do have weapons. This keeps them from getting a good shot. Like we're in deep space and they're using kinetics. Where did she learn that?*

"They're deploying like they're armed," Nadine said. "The high one, Bogey-Alpha, is climbing to keep us in sensor view. The other up there with him, Beta, she's trying to mimic our base course and keep us in range. The lower one, she's getting telemetry from the high ones. But they're too far—there!"

Jake's sensor screen flared. "Heat plume. Do they have a ventral laser?"

"Either that or an extra engine on their belly, which will burn off the first time they hit atmo with any speed, so my money is on a laser." Nadine pivoted them again. "Right now they're too far to make a difference with it. This much atmosphere between them and us, that laser just plumes. I'll bet they hit us, but we didn't even notice. What are the trailing two doing?"

Jake changed the focus of his display. "Nothing special. Trailing. Keeping close, but nothing radical." He checked a screen. "One of them looks way lower than us. Why is he all the way down there?"

"If I climb, I'm a sitting duck for the top guys. If I drop, I have to slow down, and the two behind are close enough to get a shot. That close it will be a good shot, that can cause damage. Anything onboard goes bang at this low altitude will crash us."

Jake played with his screen. "I can't tell if they have working lasers. Fifty years ago all the Militia cutters did. Now it's maybe half."

"But which half is following us?"

"Exactly." Jake played with his screen. "I might be able to get a remote scan from *Accounting Error*, but she's far away, and we'll be behind the moon at some point. Can you keep this orbit?"

"For how long?"

"Till I get a good scan?"

Nadine shook her head and kicked them left again. "No, we're on a clock. Right now we're all on different orbits, but things won't stay this way forever. The high guys will fall behind eventually, and the low guys will overrun us. But for now, they've got us boxed in. If we stay on this orbit, that lower guy catches up and takes a shot up at us. If we climb, the high guy has us. And there's gotta be a fifth one somewhere—they'll have a spare running in the same orbit, to back up whichever way we break."

"Marvelous," Jake said.

"Doctrine is to climb, and force the trailing ships to commit, then climb rapidly and take on the high ships. Only way to safety is up."

"Doctrine? Where did you learn tactical doctrine?"

"Grandfather taught me."

Even in his stress, Jake focused on the word. "Grandfather?"

"He wanted me to join the Militia. Like my mom."

"Your mother was in the Militia?"

"Yes. She died."

"How did she—"

"Don't want to talk about it. Not now."

Jake put several things together in his head. "Was your grandfather involved."

"It was his fault."

"How—"

"Not now, Jake." Nadine focused on the screen. "But good news. He made me study books of tactics when I was younger. And he quizzed me on them. I've never had to use them, not until now. Up until now it's always been one on one and that means the craziest person usually wins."

"That matches your history, yes." Jake nodded. "But why the focus on doctrine and tactics right now? We're not armed, so it's not as if it can help you."

"Not me. Them. Why do you think I'm going so slow? No crazy turns, no spinning. Just a slow descent, with enough random movement to keep them focused on me. And enough variation to keep them reacting, not enough to confuse them, but enough to keep them from thinking."

Jake followed her course plot. "You're watching how they react to your different moves."

"Yes. Somebody back there fancies themselves an Imperial tactician, old-empire style. The leader of that gaggle is trying to do a standard envelopment. They're pretending they're chasing down a rebel corvette with a destroyer squadron. They figure they'll have us in the bag in an hour, tops." Nadine cut the engine back, and they floated against their restraints. "That's what I want them to think, so that if something happens, they won't react quickly enough."

"You're going to disabuse them of this notion?"

"Disabuse? No. I'm going to screw with them, that's what I'm going to do. Have the computer calculate a landing vector to where your friends are waiting."

"No need." Jake displayed the course on the screen. "I've had it loaded and updating since we got in. We can start serious deceleration any time. Once around the planet and we'll glide in nicely. They don't know that, of course, but—"

"We're not going once around the planet. Is everything important locked down for maneuvering?"

Jake checked his board. "All green for maneuvering."

"Good." Nadine grinned, then held a gentle turn. It was the first time that she hadn't been twisting for the last hour. "Operation disabuse commences in thirty seconds."

A fiery plume lanced across the sky. An ionized shock wave pulsed ahead of the shuttle, glowing white hot from the friction of air shoved aside. The plume burned white, then red, then yellow as oxygen and hydrogen molecules, freed from atomic bonds by heat, recombined in a burst of fire, the yellow plasma stretching behind for miles. Observers on the ground would see the glowing ball blast past in silence, then be knocked over by the powerful trailing sonic blast.

At least Jake assumed that's what was happening, because every sensor on his board was down, shut off to prevent destruction during the violent maneuvers. He slammed into his seat harder than he'd ever slammed in his life. Nadine had pivoted them one-hundred eighty degrees, and blasted the main engine at full power. *My eyeballs are being pushed into my brain. And I can feel my organs squishing into each other.* Jake had been on some crazy maneuvers with crazy pilots when he was on his home station, but nothing like this. He already had tunnel vision, and his eyesight progressively grayed out. *It must be six-G. How did she even get the engines to fire that hot? And how are we going to recover? We can't even move a finger.*

He didn't even try. Even if he got a hand up, there was no way he'd reach his board, and when he stopped pushing, it would slap back so hard he'd break bones.

The acceleration dropped. Half at least. Three G's, sustainable, and controllable.

She put in a timed recovery. No way she stopped that manually.

Jake croaked. "Lives of dead emperors, Nadine—"

"Not now, Jakey. I'm busy." Amazingly, Jake felt the ship pivot again. *She's turning now? At this accel? I told her we had to crash, but I meant theoretically.*

"Hang on. We need to do this for another fifteen seconds."

"We can't—"

"Shut up, Stewart. I'm busy here."

The acceleration pushed back and sideways. His insides churned. *Was that his liver? No, liver was on his right side, this pain was his left side…*

For a horrible moment, Jake wondered if Nadine's maneuvering had squished his liver under his ribs and out the other side.

Their acceleration dropped again. Jake took a deep breath. Then another. They were the best breaths he'd ever had in his life.

"Nadine, we're—"

BAM. The ship bounced. Jake slammed into his chair, then floated out. Nadine's hands flew, and the ship coasted for a moment.

"What are you doing? What was that? Did we crash?"

"We didn't crash. We bounced off the atmosphere. We're hiding. I'm busy piloting here. Can you see the high guard? Use something passive."

"I have no sensors at all. Everything shut down to avoid burn out. Infra-red is useless, nothing on the radar receiver."

"Get something back online. Telescope at least. Tell me where the high ones are."

Jake muttered curses, but overrode the warnings and focused the telescope straight up. The computer refused to engage, so Jake overrode another setting and told it to extrapolate. It chewed on it for a moment and refreshed the screen. "High altitude orbits are blank. So are the trailing ones. Insufficient sensor data."

"Good. We can't see them through the heat plume, which means they can't see us through the heat plume."

"We can't see anything." Jake wiped his brow. "And it's hot in here."

"Had to shut off all the life support, sorry. Including the heat dumping.

"What are we doing?"

"Riding the shock wave, sort of. All this heat, we're hiding below it. And we slowed so much their tracking algorithms won't look in the right place. They'll think we're waste heat, or that something burned up during re-entry."

"We nearly burned up."

"But we didn't, so bite me. We hit at a shallow angle, that's why we bounced. That gave us free altitude back, even with the deceleration.

Jake shook his head, and pain jolted through his neck. *Ouch. Forgot she's still dropping at 3G. Stay still, Stewart.* "What now?"

"Hopefully the higher ones are confused enough they'll keep looking in the wrong place. Eventually we'll pass out of range, or they'll lose us against the ground clutter. We've slowed enough that the lower ones are over running us."

"Can't they climb and engage, us, like, well, I don't know. Can they shoot?"

"Sure." Nadine grinned at him, her mouth squashed wide by the acceleration. "But that's not doctrine, so whatever tactical genius is controlling them won't order it. Now we worry about the ones behind us. They can see us, but we don't care."

"Why don't we care?"

"We're landing. This orbit. As soon as possible. I eyeballed it. They can't follow us down—they're not shuttles. They'll burn up. But we can land. We make sure they're safely over the horizon before we do, so they can't tell if it was successful or not."

"You can do that."

"A great pilot like me?" Nadine grinned her squashed grin. "Trust me, Stewart. What could possibly go wrong?"

Chapter 35

"Whoever picked this rendezvous is a moron." Russell stepped from the bridge of *Deuxième Chance*, onto the deck, crossed his arms and stared up into the sky. He'd finished stowing the boxes of cigarettes Pletcher had given him. "Nothing but non-stop orbital traffic overhead. I'm surprised that one of them doesn't land on the back deck and ask what we're up to."

Pletcher shaded his eyes. "I recall you telling me to meet you here."

"I let Roi pick."

"So he's the moron."

"Nope. I am, for picking him, then not giving him correct instructions." Russell looked at the placid lagoon. "He gave me what I asked for. Somewhere in the ocean that was easy for all of us to get to, where Stewart's shuttle could land."

Pletcher gestured at the empty anchorage. "It's private. There's nobody here. And no reason for any other boats to come here."

Roi had chosen the atoll for the meeting - a triangular reef, miles on each side, out in the middle of the world ocean. It was midway between Landing and the factory, an easy day's sail from both. The reefs formed a right triangle, the hypotenuse running north south, a shorter side running east west across the top, and a longer side running from the northeast point to the southeast. Navigable channels cut into the reef from the west and east sides. Roi and Balthazar had sailed them to the southern area of the lagoon. Reefs protected them from the swells on two sides, running another mile south until they met.

Russell nodded. "According to Roi, water's shallow enough to anchor, and we're not bouncing in those waves." *Or at least not what he calls bouncing, those bounces on the way in were exciting enough. I better make sure that I don't end up in charge of more stuff, otherwise I'll be behind a desk permanently.*

"Hope that Stewart has a pilot good enough to land inside here."

"I hope that he's got a pilot who can avoid all those Militia cutters up there."

Pletcher shaded his eyes. "Another contrail up there. That makes, what, five, six shuttles?"

Russell counted on his fingers. "The first was a shuttle, then those two cutters that passed three minutes ago, and those two we can barely see up there. I think they're cutters too."

"At least they're high up," Pletcher said. "Won't get a good look at us."

"Only takes one." Russell shielded his eyes against the glare. *Did Shutt send these to track me down? Who knew we were here? Where's the leak? I trust Chad, but not Pletcher's people. Or Stewart. Somebody sent those ships. Who?*

"Who knew we were meeting here?" Russell asked.

"Worried I set you up?" Pletcher asked.

"The thought did cross my mind."

"Well, uncross it. It doesn't make sense for me to do it. Much easier to rat you out from a distance and then not show up. Why stand next to you while somebody lobs a kinetic strike?" Pletcher raised his eyebrows. "They're not exactly precision weapons, I'm told."

"They're not."

"And," Chaudhari interrupted, climbing on board next to Russell. "These days harder to convince somebody to drop one. Drop it from up high, who knows what they would hit. Come in too low and your cutter burns up. They can't re-enter easily. Much easier to send somebody to shoot you in the head."

"Good point." Russell squared off against Pletcher. "Wasn't you then. Must be one of your people."

Pletcher shrugged. "Or yours."

"I trust mine completely."

"And mine are all untrustworthy blabbermouths." Pletcher nodded at his ship. "Smugglers are renowned for running their mouths off, right?"

Russell laughed. "Fine. Nobody here. Who then?"

"No idea. There's another one." Pletcher pointed to a bright light in the east.

Russell stepped to the side of *Deuxième Chance* for a better view. "Coming in hot too."

"How do you know?"

"That's a big plume for a shuttle. When they come into Landing, they kind of meander when they come down. They have to come down slow, otherwise they break up when they hit the water. I watched them land for years. Hardly any plume at all."

"Could it be bigger than a shuttle?"

"Not unless they come down in pieces." Russell shaded his eyes again. *It's sunny, warm, I can smell the ocean, and we're not bouncing. This sailing thing can be fun some days. Restful, except for all this Militia…*

"How big is this thing Stewart is coming down in?"

Russell shaded his eyes. "I don't know. Chad?"

Chaudhari watched the bright light. "No idea. He didn't say. I told him the co-ordinates and he said he'd be here."

Russell dug for another cigarette. "Those other ships might not be here for him, they might be here for us."

Pletcher continued to shade his eyes as he stared at the light in the distance. "*Cui bono?*"

"Who gets boned? We do."

"No. Who benefits. Who's interested in taking all three of us off at one go."

"Shutt is peeved with me right now," Russell said. "She might want to stick a knife in my stomach. But she'd want to do it personal, up close like. But collateral damage wouldn't bother her if it was the only way to get me."

"I'm too valuable a resource to her to be a direct target," Pletcher said. "There're things she needs that I get for her. Like fuel and ammunition, she needs those."

Russell laughed. "Too valuable a resource? Well la ti da, Mr. Too Valuable to Kill. You know, she doesn't have to act logically."

"I'm in her office all the time. If she wanted me dead, she could beat me bloody with her office chair and nobody on her staff would complain. If I wasn't valuable I'd be dead already."

"Point. Not you or me then."

"But why would Shutt kill Stewart? Does she have a hate on for him?"

"Don't know." Russell said.

"You know." Chaudhari pointed at the light. "Shouldn't that be moving sideways, as it passes?"

"What do you mean?"

Roi stepped up. "That light. The angle is constant."

"So?"

"Constant angle, decreasing range, that means that they are coming directly at us."

"They're supposed to overfly us, and land beyond. I know that much about shuttle landings - overfly the position, not crash into it." Russell looked at the light in the distance. "They will pass over, right?"

The four men stared east. Chaudhari put binoculars to his eyes. "No change in aspect."

Pletcher brought up his comm and centered the light in the camera. "Not moving sideways here."

Roi snapped a waterproof plastic box open and extracted a triangular metal object. It had a circular bottom and a swinging arm, and an eyepiece with two mirrors. He peered through the eyepiece and adjusted the arm. "Angular distance is constant."

Russell stretched his arm and used his thumb to block the burning plume. He stood silently, then stretched his other arm out, and touched his two thumbs together.

The three others waited while Russell closed his left eye and glared at his thumbs. Then he switched to his right.

"Scott?" Chaudhari asked.

"What, Chad?"

"What do you think?"

"Me? What do I think." Russell dropped his hands and stared at his left thumb. "It's weird. The left thumb nail always grows faster than the right one."

Pletcher coughed. "Are you right-handed? That would explain it."

"No. Left." Russell grunted. "I'll have to cut them separately."

"Good to know." Pletcher nodded. "Want to update us on the ship? Instead of talking about your fingernail hygiene?"

Russell fumbled for the cigarette, stared at it, sighed, and returned it to his pocket. "Pletcher, Chad, that ship is coming right here. For one of us. Any ideas who set us up, so we can drown them in the few minutes we have left before that shuttle comes screaming down and pulverizes us?"

Both Chaudhari and Pletcher shook their heads.

"Too bad. I wanted to go out shooting." Russell checked that his holster was unfastened. "Right. Troops! Stations for air attack. Captain Roi, Captain Balthazar. Get us moving, get these ships out of here."

"Nadine," Jake said. "We're too low and too fast. We can't land at this speed. You need to bleed off more speed."

"Sorry, Jakey." Nadine adjusted their course slightly left. "That will take too long. I need to stay high until the last group goes over the horizon. Don't want them getting a shot, or know exactly where we landed." Nadine nodded her shoulder at Jake's board. The higher ships were scattering. Jake recognized them as changing orbits to get the best sensor sweep over the largest area. As Nadine had predicted, from their perspective she and Jake were hiding in the ground clutter. And her rapid dropping and retro-firing had slowed her so much the lower orbiting ships were now almost over the horizon.

"He'll be gone in thirty seconds. But if we go any lower, we'll break into bits."

"How many bits?"

"Ever dropped a glass down a flight of stairs?"

"Nope. Have you?"

"Yes."

"A glass? Real glass? Super expensive thing to drop on a station? You must have looked like—"

"Nadine. Never. Mind. The. Glass. Slow. Down."

"No." Nadine didn't spare him a glance. Her eyes flicked from one screen to the next. "We need to outrace the last one.

Of the trailing ships, one had misjudged and dropped too low. Its new orbit had brought it under them, ahead, and past the terminator. Only one ship still had them in decent view, but was pulling ahead, fast. It was trying to climb and making a bad job of it.

"He'll see us no matter what."

"He'll run out of fuel if he keeps pushing his engines like that, or he'll chicken out, or the accel will get him. His sensors will be masked any second now."

"You don't know that. Anything can happen."

"Life," Nadine said, adjusting their course again, "Is full of these little gambles. The second he pivots, we're going lower, and faster, and get in among those boats."

Jake looked at their speed over ground, external temperature, and the sensors tagging the trailing ship. "You better do it soon."

Russell was impressed with how quickly the boats got moving. Roi and Balthazar yelled orders, lines were untied then re-tied, anchor chains spun, sails were hoisted. Two minutes later they had un-moored and were making way through the lagoon, captains at the helms directing the crews. It looked great. Which is why he was surprised that the two ships sailed only six feet apart.

"Tell it to me again. Why the tide means we have to stay only a large fart smell apart?"

Balthazar pointed. "Look down. See the dark spots."

Russell peered over the rail. The bottom looked a lot closer than a minute ago. There were dark patches on the white sand. Weeds? Rocks? He didn't know. Either way, they looked dangerous.

Balthazar grunted. "Nearly low water. Channel inside the lagoon is only twenty feet wide, or less. We get any farther apart, one of us runs aground."

"You sure?"

"Try it if you like, or ask Roi if he's willing."

The boat shuddered, something ground along the bottom. Roi turned the wheel hard right. "You two—Pletcher, Chaudhari. Get below and check for leaks. Seal them up best you can. Do it now." Roi swung the bow away from Bal's boat..

Russell grabbed the stanchion—the vertical pole holding the metal lines that surrounded the deck. They were called lifelines, he now knew. *Listen to me. I'm getting so nautical, I'll probably crap live fish from now on.* "Roi, move us away from Bal."

Roi gave Russell a look. He'd seen this look before. It said 'Stupid land-lubber person. If I do what you say, we will all drown, or possibly dirty our clothes. Do as I, the superior sailing person, says.'

"No." Roi shook his head. "We are nearly aground right now."

Russell pointed behind them. The flare from the landing shuttle, or cutter, or whatever it was, was brightening. Fast. "Better aground than burned up."

"Better able to maneuver, at the least, if that shuttle hits the water. The wave it will put up will swamp us if we can't ride it."

"We can't ride it if we're in pieces."

"We'll be drowned if it washes over us. If we're not afloat it will swamp us, if it hits broadside."

Russell reached for his holster. "You tell me that—Whoa!" The boat shuddered, and nearly stopped. They spun to the left, and Russell fell forward over the right-hand rail. He grabbed the lifeline as he pivoted over it. Their stern swung sideways and bounced into Bal's boat. Paint ground off and Bal surged forward. Russell grasped the lifeline with both hands.

"Hang on, we need to power out." Roi gunned the motor.

"Roi," Russell yelled. "This stupid stanchion is bending. I'm going in." The vertical metal pole that held the lifeline was kinking in the middle, and Russell was sliding farther overboard.

"You're too fat for it. Crawl back and grab the shrouds."

"I am not fat. And the what? What in Jove's name is a shroud?"

Roi watched the water forward, steering by the color. He gestured with one hand. "Metal ropes holding the masts up. Grab one of those."

Russell moved hand over hand to the stern. He caught one of the braided metal cables. *The shrouds. I hate boats. Even when they're trying to kill you, they make you learn new words.* "Got it."

"Hang on, I'll get the guys to haul you in."

Russell cursed in several languages he knew, and a couple he didn't. Kicking his feet didn't help, but then Pletcher and Chaudhari grabbed his arms and hauled him up and over the rail. The boat twisted sideways as they pulled him over, and all three of them fell in a heap.

"I hate boats." Russell grabbed the shrouds—now his new word of the day—and pulled himself up. Balthazar's boat had forged ahead, open water showing between them. Roi was constantly shifting the wheel from side to side, whatever he saw ahead he didn't like it. "And it took the three of you long enough. Are we taking on water? Sinking?"

"Taking on water, yes." Pletcher pulled himself up. "Sinking, no. Cracked a pipe on the side. Chad stuffed a towel into it. Still dripping but not a ton. We can pump it out."

"Well, get on the pumps then," Russell said. "Even I know that the water belongs outside the boat, not inside. Let's get started, Chad."

Chaudhari rolled over onto his back. He pointed. "I don't think pumping is the worst of our problems right now."

Russell jerked his head back and stared astern. A blinding ball of fire raced down on a collision course.

"I'll ease down next to them." Nadine edged the controls up. "We need to be on the deck now. The water will kill our thermal plume. If I get us right next to one of those ships, we're invisible from orbit, and they can tow us away."

The camera display focused on the two sailboats, then blanked. The belly and bow cameras had retracted behind armored thermal barriers. The magnetics kept the shuttle from melting, but anything poked outside of them would liquefy in the re-entry heat.

"They don't look like the tugs we're used to. What if they can't haul us away?"

"Then we float around here until those Militia Cutters drop rocks on us from a great height."

"Maybe we could call the Militia…"

"And ask them why they are trying to kill us up here? And could they pretty please sail out to our location and kill us there instead?" Nadine adjusted them down a notch, then back into their glide path.

Jake tapped his screen. "What was that?"

"What was what?"

"On the screen. I saw something. Give me the dorsal forward camera again."

"Stewart, we're on glide. And going way faster than we should be. Can't do it. But good news, this will be one outstanding landing from one amazing pilot when we're done.

People will talk about this forever in the history of shuttle landings."

Jake played with his screen. No cameras. *Could he use recordings?* He located the camera setting screen. They could save the feed, but he hadn't bothered to turn it on and send them to permanent storage. They fed the emergency flight recorder, didn't they? Not saved forever, but surely a few minutes.. *There. Uh oh.*

"Nadine, we have a problem."

"We surely do. The passengers keep talking and bothering the captain while she's trying to do a tricky landing. They should stop that, otherwise the captain is going to execute another one of her stupendously impressive landings, and afterwards kick the ever-loving crap out of them. The passengers should be very, very careful that they don't make her that mad. Best they shut up."

"The passengers are worried that the captain hasn't been paying proper attention to the landing area, because the passengers just looked at the landing area, and they see the tide has exposed a big line of rocks, right across the landing area the captain has picked. And the passengers are wondering if she can make a fifteen-degree side correction before we smash into said jagged rocks and break into bits."

Nadine's head jerked sideways. "You serious?"

"Of course, Nadine."

She gulped. "We can't move that far sideways, we'll break up. At this speed, any major turn will tear us apart."

"Well, if we can't turn, then what's your plan to avoid smashing into bits?"

"Hard to explain. Hang on." Nadine squared her shoulders. "I'll have to show you."

Chapter 36

"Roi, get us out of here," Russell yelled. "They're coming in hard, and we're right in the way."

"Can't." Roi twisted the helm again. *Deuxième Chance* heeled to one side. "Not enough water yet."

Russell grabbed his holster. "I'll shoot him."

Pletcher grabbed his hand. "No."

"Why not? This is his fault. He picked this place."

"If you shoot him, who's going to drive?" Pletcher released his hand. "Not me. Do you know how to steer out of a lagoon? You'll run us aground."

Russell slammed his revolver back into his holster. "Did I mention I hate boats?" He turned. The blazing light from the landing shuttle burned his eyes. "Ow."

Chaudhari, sitting on the deck shaded his eyes. "It's like staring into a sunrise."

"I hate sunrises." Russell said. "I hate boats, sunrises, meetings, and captains."

"Well," Chaudhari said. "Good chance in a few moments you won't have to see any of those again."

"Nadine, those rocks will tear us up."

"I know."

"You have to turn."

"Can't. I'm going to land."

"Nadine they're right in front of us. You can't land on them."

"I know. Shut up and hang on."

"I meant—"

"SHUT UP STEWART. I'M BUSY."

Jake shut up.

Nadine dropped the nose and felt the speed bleed off as the shuttle tilted. *Which way? Have to decide now.* The two boats were close enough you could count the masts, and the sails on each. Waves broke over a line of reefs across her bow. Too wide to avoid. *Didn't see those before. I can't get around them without the ship breaking up. I'll have to go straight over and into those sail boats.*

The two ships were dead ahead. The larger one dragged a white wake behind it and steered right. It's aspect lengthened as it crossed her bow. *Crossing to the starboard side, But not fast enough. I'll crash into it if I swing even the tiniest bit right.* The smaller ship sat to the left of her base course. It spun in place, like it was stuck on something. If it was moving away from her, she couldn't tell. *If I go left, I'll hit Small ship. If I go right Big ship will probably hit me. Have to go straight. Then I might hit both. Will there be enough space between them?*

"Nadine. Overfly the two, pass them and land later."

"Can't. Gravity has us. We'll be down before the reef…"

"Stop going down—"

"Hang on." Nadine pushed the throttles to max. They tipped and angled in.

"They're going to hit us." Chaudhari yelled. "Everybody overboard."

Russell gripped the rail. "They'll hit the rocks first and break up."

"Then the pieces will hit us."

With no warning, the approaching shuttle's thrusters flamed, and its bow flared up.

"Incoming!" Russell yelled, dropping to the deck.

The shuttle slammed into the ocean surface twenty meters short of the reef. A giant plume of water exploded in all directions, obscuring the crash.

Chaudhari's mouth gaped open. "That was—"

BOOM. The noise rolled over them, drowning conversation. Then the shuttle appeared flying upward from the waves. It had hit at an angle, and bounced.

Everything was quiet. The shuttles engines had flamed out. The shock wave stunned their ears, blasting away all other sounds. The shuttle sailed up and over the reef, a glowing red phantom shrouded with steam and blue water. It sailed up, up, up, and then down.

Russell sat entranced as it drifted down. *It's so quiet. Like when the guns stop firing. Is it real? It's like a giant, serene bird, gliding down.*

The underside of the giant bird caught the metal cable running from the top of the mast to the stern of the boat. The

Deuxième Chance rolled sideways as the shuttle pushed it down. The crew rolled with it, sliding to the edge of the deck. Then the cable snapped in two. The shuttle flew on, and the severed cable rocketed to the deck. Combat reactions saved Russell. He rolled onto his face and covered his head. The cable twanged, the whip-crack noise of a spinning cable cracked in his ear, and his left arm stung with fire. He lay still, as the boat rolled upright.

KER-SPLASH. Russell kept his head down. He didn't know that sound, so it wasn't good. Now the boat rolled right, and a wave of water surged up over him. He scrabbled for purchase on the deck as he slid. He banged into the shrouds. They gut-punched him, and he gasped for air, but only got a mouthful of salt water.

The boat rolled right, then left, then settled on an even keel. Russell wheezed a lung full of salt water and air, gasped, then coughed hard to clear his throat.

Chaudhari grabbed him and sat him up. "Scott, you okay? Were you hit?"

Russell gasped again, spewed some water and wheezed. "Air. Need air."

Chaudhari rolled him on his side, and let him spit water out and suck air in. "Lean over. Spit."

Russell wheezed away. "What happened?"

"Shuttle's up ahead, floating. We're aground. Roi is yelling a lot."

Russell rolled over, took another breath and sat up. Roi was staring over the bow, cursing in Francais.

Pletcher stuck his head up from below. "Crack's busted open. Water's pouring in. We're sinking."

Roi finished cursing and came back to the helm. "Hit a coral head. There's a hole in the bow, bigger than my head. I'll try to fix it, but I don't think I can make it. Get everything on deck that we need to save. Anyone hurt?"

"Just my dignity." Russell stood up. "What's up with the shuttle? Is it sinking?"

"Over there." Chaudhari pointed. "We spun sideways. It's there. Low in the water, but still there."

"What in Jove's name happened?" Russell said. "Why did they come in so fast?"

"No time for that right now." Roi popped open a locker and tossed bags out. "We need to abandon ship, and save what we can. Weapons, ammunition, personal items, we need to get it all up on the deck and move it to the other ship before the water gets to it."

"This isn't over. But let's get that sorted out. Chad, any injuries? And what's the damage?"

Chaudhari stuck his head down a hatch and conversed with Pletcher. He looked to Russell and shook his head. "Nothing serious, Vince says. Some clothing damaged, some personal items are soaked. Rations are fine, those trays and ration bars are indestructible. The ship's in trouble, the waters rising, but it's all wood, we can build another. We need to move the new ammunition before the salt gets to it, that's about it."

"Right, let's get on that."

"Scott…"

"What?" Russell looked at him. "What now?"

"The water from the bow came in quick. Some got into your bag, before he could lift it. There was some damage."

"Damage? My clothes I don't care about. Wait, you mean…"

"Yes." Chaudhari nodded. "The sea water destroyed all your cigarettes."

"We're okay. We're okay." Jake wiped his brow. The shuttle bobbed in the gentle swell. "I need to take a minute—" FOOMP. WHOOSH. "Um. Nadine. Did you open the hatch?"

"Emergency release. We need to get out." Nadine unbuckled her harness and slid from her seat. "I don't want to drown."

Jake held out his arm "We're inside a ship that's safe in space, with an internal oxygen supply. Sit down. You're not going to drown."

"But the water will fill up the ship…"

"The bulkheads will hold. And we float. Or we did, until you flooded the passenger compartment with water." The shuttle's bow display dipped as seawater flooded the forward passenger lock and unbalanced them. "Don't move. I have to flood another compartment to fix the list, so it goes down on an even keel."

"You're going to drown the shuttle?"

"It's called scuttling, not drowning." Jake ran the shutdown sequence on the board. "You scuttle a ship, you drown a person."

"We're holding it underwater until it's out of air, that's a drowning. We're murdering this shuttle."

"Calm down, we're not." Jake finished shutting down his board. "Are you sure that none of those Militia cutters can get an exact location on where we went down?"

"I was sure the first time you asked me, I was sure the second time you asked me, and I'm sure the third time you asked me, Stewart. That's why I did all that amazing piloting before. I found the one time that all those ships would be out of range over the horizon. It will be hours before they can get a good look at this spot again. Days for the medium altitude ones. The high one will be lucky if it's orbit brings it back in a week."

"Right." Jake fitted his skin suit helmet. "Well, with that hatch open, we're going to sink, no matter what. So we've got no choice now. These sailboats won't be able to pull us off the bottom without special equipment We need to get out of here and head to Landing now. This meeting has got way more important."

"At least the Militia can't find us."

"Hang tight a moment. I'm ready to flood the cargo hold."

"You sure that's a good idea? Salt water is bad for metal…"

"Cargo hold is vacuum rated. It will still rust, but not fast. All I need are a few days to figure out who is trying to kill us, and who isn't. Then we can get back here and dry it out. You told me you can launch from a standing start?"

"If I have enough fuel." Nadine checked her board. "Which we have none right now."

"We can get fuel in Landing and get it shipped out here. Meanwhile, I'm pumping every tank I can find full of seawater." Jake hit a final sequence and his board and Nadine's died. "Bridge, engineering, and the computer section will be dry. Reactor will be in standby, but that's easy to bring back to full power. Cargo hold will flood, every fuel or water tank will flood. Should give us negative buoyancy."

"I'd rather sit here while the fuel builds up…"

"Too long. You ready?"

"I hate leaving the ship, Stewart."

"A minute ago you couldn't get out fast enough. That's why you blew that hatch."

"Landings are stressful." Nadine tilted her head. "I might have made a tiny mistake doing that."

"Big of you, saying that. You should be proud of your newfound openness."

Nadine scowled. "It's annoying, such a great landing here. To screw it up with one little thing…"

"Cheer up, Nadine." Jake popped the dorsal hatch. "There're all sorts of people angry with us outside and in Landing. I'm sure you'll get to stab at least some of them."

"We are in deep tabbo do-do." Russell watched Jake Stewart and his friend Nadine climb over the bulwark of Balthazar's ship. They had floated over from their now-submerged shuttle, and Bal's people helped them aboard. "Shutt wants to kill me. That's why all those shuttles. And anybody who gets in her way of being in charge of this stinking little moon. Including this Stewart guy and company. We're short of everything, civilization is collapsing, and more importantly—" Russell grimaced. "I'm out of cigarettes."

"Mustn't forget the cigarettes," Chaudhari said.

"Agreed. Need to keep our priorities straight. Hello, Mr. Stewart. Trying to kill me again?"

Jake walked down the deck and shook Russell's hand. "Good to see you again too, Sergeant Russell."

"What in Jove's name is up with you two? That's the worst landing I've ever seen. You trying to kill all of us?"

Jake explained about the Militia chasing them, the laser firing, the extra ships. Nadine chimed in about what a great job she did during the landing and what a great pilot she was. Jake explained about the sunken shuttle problem and suggested they could get out of the area while they figured out how to get the shuttle operational. Russell cursed, but agreed.

They exchanged greetings with all the others. Nadine mostly shook hands, except with Pletcher, who she hugged and asked if he had more wine. He said yes, so she hugged him again.

"Can we get on our way to Landing now?" Jake asked. "Nadine's certain that the Militia can't get our exact location, but they can do a general search."

"You sure you want to go there?" Russell asked. "Given the recent…"

"Unpleasantness, as everyone calls it?" Jake nodded. "Yes. I don't have a choice anymore, Nadine can't launch us as things are. We need to get fuel and a crane somewhere. And somebody's tried to kill me. Twice in the last few days. I'm going to deal with that. And somebody killed Mr. Dashi. That will not go unpunished."

"Wasn't me," Pletcher said. "I barely knew the guy. Thought he was doing a great job."

"Wasn't me." Russell shrugged. "I met him. He seemed competent. He did a good enough job. I didn't hate him any more than the others."

Jake nodded. "But you didn't prefer the Militia to be in charge, Sergeant Russell?"

"If I did." Russell raised an eyebrow. "That would have been in the person of the admiral, not me. I liked the admiral. Hey!" He turned to Nadine. "Wasn't he your grandfather?"

The group dissolved into condolences for Nadine. She nodded and accepted them, but kept a poker face.

"Well, there we are." Russell said.

"I didn't kill him either," Chaudhari said.

"What did you say, Chad?" Russell asked.

"I didn't kill Dashi either."

"Nobody thinks you did, Chad."

"Okay, good. I just wanted that on record, you know."

"On record."

"Well, I didn't want to be left out. You know."

Everyone stared at Chaudhari in silence. Finally Jake spoke. "Good to know."

Russell turned back to Jake. "Right, so our meeting was supposed to discuss 'recent events of mutual interest' as you mentioned, Stewart. We've got time to kill while we sail to Landing. What do you want to say?"

"Well." Jake nodded. "The circumstances have gotten more complex than when we first spoke." Jake explained about all the shuttles and cutters that had shadowed them and taken a pot shot. "Clearly somebody is trying to kill Nadine and I. And they have a spy in one of your organizations, that's how they knew we would be here."

"I'm not happy about that," Russell said. "But I do agree. What do you want?"

"Take us to Landing. Nadine and I. And hide us for a little while I sort things out."

Russell shrugged. "You mentioned that before, and we're kind of on our way there now. Your shuttle sunk our sailboat."

"Only because we were forced down."

"Either way, you kind of damaged us." Russell reached into his pocket, then cursed when he remembered he had no cigarettes. "Which makes this your fault. Why should I help you?"

"What's your other option?" Jake asked.

"Take you to Landing and turn you over to the authorities."

Jake grinned. "And who are they? Shutt? If she sees you, she'll shoot you. If you go to Jose instead, he'll thank you, then tell Shutt where you are. And then she'll shoot you."

Russell reached for the non-existent cigarettes again, and cursed, again. "Fine. What do you suggest?"

"Come with me to Landing."

"And do what?"

"Kill some people." Jake grinned. "But only ones who deserve it."

Chapter 37

"You're rubbing your hands." Chaudhari tilted his head. "You're so excited to be going to Landing to shoot people, you can't hold it in." He and Russell stood at the bow of their boat, talking and watching the land approach.

"I am not excited about going to Landing." Russell watched the sun set over the water. "I'm just glad to be getting off these stupid boats."

"And getting to shoot people."

"Okay, fine…that does kind of make me happy. But you know me. That's kind of my thing."

"Who are we going to kill?"

"No idea." Russell shrugged. "But that Stewart kid is right, given all that's going on, somebody's bound to take a shot at me. When somebody does, we fire back. Bida-boo, bida-bing."

"Bida-boo, bida-bing? What in Jove's name does that mean?"

"No idea. But that's how that kid Stewart said it."

Russell, Chaudhari, Pletcher, Jake and Nadine went to the bow of Balthazar's boat for privacy. Roi sat with them for a while, quizzing Jake and the others on where they needed to be and when, so that he could help Balthazar navigate there. After that he confessed himself bored and retired to spell Balthazar at the helm. As captain, Bal had his hands full for the last twenty-four hours sailing the ship, and he welcomed an opportunity to catch a few hours of sleep. After discussing with Roi the locations where they would be meeting the land crew, he went for a nap.

Jake laid out his plans while they sat in the bow. "I'm looking for some sort of alliance. Sergeant Russell, one way or another you're going to have to take control of the Militia. The troops respect you, your own people admire you—your former squad will do anything for you. That's the reason that you've been so successful out east. You taking over all the ground operations of the Militia and the larger stations will be acceptable to everybody."

Russell shook his head. "The orbital people won't like it."

"They like Shutt even less. She started out fine, way back when, but power corrupts. She's become a grasping careerist, and she's obsessed with being a senator and running the whole moon. They can't stand her now."

"That's one thing you can count on with me." Russell grimaced. "I don't want to run a moon. I can run a Militia unit. And a couple of factories, maybe. But not a senate, not a city, and certainly not a moon or a planet."

"What about a company?" A rogue wave splashed over the bow and Jake ducked. "Would you like to be a chairman?"

"Not that either." Russell shook his head. "Definitely not that. Spreadsheets all day? Those people who look at numbers all day long are complete weasels."

Jake laughed. "Well, speaking on behalf of the weasels, I'm glad you feel that way. Means we all have one less thing to worry about when you're in charge of the Militia. I expect you'll be taking control of things there. I'm sure you can deal with any resistance there."

Russell gave Jake a sour look. "You mean Shutt. That's who you want me to shoot?"

"There is some expectation—"

"Look, I can't just walk in there and shoot Shutt," Russell unsnapped then re-snapped his holster. "That's not how things work. This is a military organization, not a street gang. We have rules. People follow orders in the Militia, that's how things get done."

"Even if they're…"

"Stupid orders? Especially if they're stupid orders. Mission comes first. Troopers never have the whole picture, and I can think of a half a dozen times I put myself stupidly in danger because I had to follow some stupid orders. And it all worked out in the end. I won't shoot her. Not first. If she starts a gunfight, I'll finish it. But I won't start it. I'm not taking over the Militia. Find somebody else."

"Well, well." Jake nodded. "She's too smart to start one, so I guess we'll have to hope that something else happens."

Russell pointed at Jake. "If you want her dead so much, why don't you shoot her? Sounds like the Militia has it in for you. Tried to kill you twice so far."

"It does appear that is what happened. The first time somebody was trying to kill Nadine and I, the second time we're not sure. Of course we're not a hundred percent sure that it was the Militia doing it, we only had the unsupported words of two killers."

"Who else could it be?" Russel asked. "All those ships? Those were Militia ships."

"That was the Militia. But I don't think they were trying to kill us. Herd us might be a better word."

"They shot at you."

"From a great height, with a weak laser, and the rest of the time they only chased us. Didn't even call to threaten us." Jake turned to the bow. "Nadine?"

Nadine had been watching the remnants of the sunset. Unusually, she'd been sick over the bow earlier. She blamed stress. The primaries light dimmed in the west, but in the east the Dragon was already rising, changing the light from orange yellow to red. "What is it Jakey?"

"If you were trying to shoot us down and kill us, would you have done it that way?"

Nadine shook her head. "Put the best armed ship as close as possible and have it sneak up and smack us, would have been my plan. Get close, take a pot shot, and don't give us a second chance. And you're right. I was too busy at the time to notice, but in retrospect, for an interception, that was a little odd."

"Odd or not, the first one you described sounded like a real attempt," Russell said. "When they boarded your ship."

"It did. It was." Jake shrugged. "But I'm hearing you're not willing to become the head of the Militia if Shutt is killed? Even if somebody else does it.?"

"Nope. She stays. And I won't shoot her unless she tries it on me. Assassination is no way to run a military."

"Well, we can all agree on that. Shutt stays until she is removed by proper process. Very well." Jake sighed. "Mr. Pletcher, you're more attuned to the commercial side of things. What do the corps think of this violence?"

"Violence is bad for business," Pletcher said. "Raises costs, makes things uncertain. We want structure. We need structure."

"You'll support anybody who provides structure, then?"

Pletcher shook his head. "No, not anybody, not any structure. And I'm not 'all the corps' either, so other people have other ideas. But if we get back to the trading environment we had before the war of the corps, nobody is going to ask too many questions about how it happened."

"You make your money as a smuggler…"

"If there weren't so many stupid rules, and stupid people with guns blowing things up, I'd make it out in the open. Smuggling is the only way to earn a profit right now."

"That's why you support Jose, because he provides structure?"

"Look Stewart," Pletcher glared at him. "I've got a business to run. I didn't ask for this mess, I'm trying to survive the best I can. If I can make a little money while I'm doing it, great. But I'm not a crusader, just a businessman. And looking at you, don't you spend all your time running off to other star systems, stealing starships, and manipulating markets? If anything, you're much worse than Jose."

"A solid hit." Russell said. "Jose has provided stability, of a sort, while you've been away."

"I agree," Jake said. "In many respects I am like you—I'm doing the same thing you did, doing my best work within the rules. That's how I've made my money. But I haven't tried to have anybody killed."

"That we know of," Pletcher said. "And Jose hasn't killed anybody either, that we can prove."

"What about having Russell shoot Marianne?" Jake asked. "Couldn't that have been his plan? Russell kills her, by accident, and in a rage the other Free Traders attack him and take him off the board."

Russell furrowed his brow.

"After all," Jake said. "Things might have worked out this way. Russell killed Marianne, angering the Free Traders. Shutt kills the admiral, putting her in charge of the Militia. When you go back to talk to Shutt, there's a gunfight. Either she kills you, in which case the Militia are going to be scared of her, or you kill her, creating a backlash. And what do you think your squad would do? If they were with you, think they'd let you be shot out of hand? It would be pure chaos."

"Nope." Chaudhari shook his head. "We'd all blast away right there."

"I'm touched." Russell said, tapping his chest. "Right here. Strong emotions." He belched. "No wait, it was gas. But thanks for planning on avenging me."

"Wasn't just you," Chaudhari said. "If she can shoot you for no reason, she can shoot us. It's pure self-interest."

"Knew I could count on you, Chad."

"Don't mention it."

"I won't. But both Shutt and I get shot, who runs the Militia then?" Russell asked.

Chaudhari frowned. "Kim's mule?"

"I've taken orders from people stupider than that mule." Russell shrugged. "Also not my problem if I'm dead."

"What if you're not dead?" Jake asked. "What if you lived? Then the Free Traders are gunning for you, and eventually they catch up and kill you, unless someone reins them in. Now all that's left is Jose and his friends in the Senate. The Militia is leaderless, so Jose can appoint anyone he wants, and you know it will be one of his people. The Free Traders are on the run and broken up already. After shooting you there won't be anything else they can agree on. He can keep using the Militia to squeeze them, or force them to take his choice of leaders if they want to stop the squeezing. Now he's got both organizations under control. And Mr. Pletcher here and his friends are going to keep quiet as long as this doesn't impact trade and commerce. Jose's been running TGI for Dashi for the last year, everybody knows that. Looks to me, in one swoop, if things go his way, Jose ends up in charge of TGI, the Militia, and the Free Traders. Plus a majority in the new Senate." Jake exhaled. "That's the longest I've ever talked to you four without being interrupted."

Russell, Chaudhari, Nadine, and Pletcher exchanged glances.

"Well Jakey," Nadine said. "What happens next?"

Jake turned to look at the sky. "The sun is almost gone. I'm not used to sunsets, so much time in orbit. They're pretty."

"Jake," Nadine said. "What do we do now?"

Jake grinned. "All hail emperor Jose the first!"

The ensuing debate did not go well. Jake argued for supporting Jose. Nobody was happy, and eventually they all split up to different parts of the boat.

"I don't want Jose to be the next Emperor," Chaudhari said.

"Do you even know what the Emperor does?" Russell asked. He and Chaudhari had returned to the stern. Chaudhari refused to go down below, he said it made him sicker. Russell made fun of him, but he was secretly glad—the motion made him ill as well.

"He makes laws and stuff."

"And stuff?"

Chaudhari tried to stick his nose in the air. Then dropped it to retch over the side. He came back up and wiped his mouth. "This isn't something I concern myself with."

"If not him, who? And stay close to the side, you're green."

Chaudhari gulped air, then leaned over the side again. "Now that I think about it, I don't care what he does. Or who he supports. Whatever. I'll take anybody who doesn't start another war, and can feed us. Think Jose can do that?"

"He did before," Russell said.

"What about Shutt?"

"If she leaves me alone, then I'll support him. That will be my price to Jose. Keep Shutt off me and I'll support you as emperor. We need somebody. He's adequate."

"Emperor Jose the adequate." Chaudhari vomited over the rail.

Pletcher hung out at the helm, asking Roi how things worked.

"We can use the satellites when they are visible." Roi pointed to a screen. It read 'No signal'. "But not many are left, often times we lose signal for hours, occasionally days. That's why I have this." He held up his sextant and explained to Pletcher the method for determining position. It was a long explanation. "There you see? So long as I have a good watch to tell the time, I can calculate where we are by the stars."

"Lots of math." Pletcher said.

Roi shrugged. "At sea, you have time to do math. Excuse me, hold the wheel for a moment, thus." He demonstrated and had Pletcher try. "Good. I must use the radio. I have to inform Balthazar's people when we are coming and where. They will need to know to help us unload. I'll be back in a few minutes." Roi went below and busied himself with the radio while Pletcher steered. Ten minutes later he came up and checked their track.

"You did well, Mr. Pletcher. A straight course. We will make a sailor out of you yet."

"Thanks." Pletcher nodded. "Jose will become the next Emperor. What do you think?"

Roi shrugged again. "Somebody has to do it. It won't be me. Or you."

"I guess not. Don't you want a Militia person in charge?"

"Who? Sergeant Russell? He is a peasant. His type should not be in charge."

"Major Shutt then?"

"No." Roi shook his head. "I want nothing good to happen to her. She helped kill my brother officers, during the Militia Rebellion. And she helped organize my banishment. I do not like her, and I owe her nothing."

"I guess Jose is the best choice, then." Pletcher said. "Need somebody."

After a long nap, Nadine came up from below. The motion made her queasy. They had entered the river and were approaching Landing. She chatted with the others then sat with Jake at the bow. "How far are we?"

"Nearly at the dock, a few miles downstream of Landing."

"The others say you've decided to support Jose as Emperor."

"He's already running TGI. The Free Traders are scared of him. The Emperor has to be somebody the Militia support. Russell will support him."

"Shutt won't."

"That's how he'll keep her in line. Threaten to let Russell take her on. Another civil war in the Militia, and she could lose. Russell's position is stronger than he knows. He's safe from both Shutt and Jose."

"Free Traders won't support him."

"But the corps will. Pletcher is right. Everybody is exhausted right now, they want this to end. The Free Traders don't have a real leader now. They think only spacers understand them, and they're correct. They need somebody with a lot of space in them to make it work."

"What about who killed Dashi? And my grandfather."

Jake looked at her. "We might have to let them go."

"Jake! You promised."

Jake shook his head. "Times have changed. And so have my plans. I have to be flexible. You can't kill them."

"I don't care about your plans. You can't let Shutt get away with killing grandfather."

"You don't know that she did that for sure."

"Everybody says she did!" Nadine raised her eyebrows. "Everybody. Including you."

Jake shrugged. "We don't have real proof. Only accusations."

"You're the one who explained it all to me. You're the one who convinced us."

Jake shrugged again. "Sometimes you can't get what you want. Jose is right. Pletcher is right. Stability is more important than revenge."

Nadine's voice rose. "It's not revenge. It's justice. You can't let people get away with murder."

"Sometimes you have to do that. Do you still have all your knives?"

"What?" Nadine narrowed her eyes. "Yes. Want me to stick you with them."

"And you've got those two revolvers?"

"Of course."

"The other one in your back holster?"

"I always do. Jake, why are you asking?"

"Any other weapons?"

Nadine's eyes drifted to her boots. In the past she'd kept a disassembled gauss pistol hidden in her heels as a holdout.

"Why are you asking Stewart?"

"Nadine, I want you to promise that you won't kill Shutt. If you won't, I'll have you disarmed."

"I won't promise you anything, Stewart."

"Nadine." Jake took a deep breath. "I absolutely forbid you to kill Shutt."

"Forbid? you're forbidding me? YOU?" Nadine's voice got even louder.

"I'm through talking about this Nadine. No shooting. I forbid it."

"Forbid this." Nadine stepped forward and smacked him, hard.

Chaudhari and Russell leaned over the back rail, watching the show at the bow.

Russell took the cigarette out of his mouth. "Did he just say 'forbid'?"

Chaudhari nodded. "Seems like."

"Why would he tell her that? That kid is way stupider than everybody says he is."

The yelling continued. Chaudhari looked out at the shore looming out of the dark. "Maybe somebody should tell them to be quiet, we're almost there."

CRACK. Nadine had punched Jake in the face. He staggered, but continued to yell back.

"Be my guest." Russell took another drag on his cigarette. "I'm sure she'll take it well. But don't worry."

"Why not?"

"This can't go much longer. At some point she'll—"

Nadine grabbed Jake and heaved him bodily over the rail. He slammed into the river with a splash. Nadine leaned over the rail and continued shaking her fist at him.

Chaudhari watched a splashing Jake float by. "Looks like she won."

"Indeed." Russell grabbed a lifebuoy from the rail and flung it at Jake's struggling figure. "She usually does. Crap!"

High-intensity headlights flashed on from the shore, pinning *Magus* in their beams. Russell covered his eyes. "What now?"

Lines of bullets stitched splashes across the water in front of and behind the boats. A bullhorn boomed out. "Those were warning shots. You're surrounded. Give up now and nobody gets hurt. Fire back and we'll turn you into shredded Beefalo."

Russell and Chaudhari dropped to the deck. "Did you see where it came from?"

"Three different places," Russell said. "At least three. Heavy weapons too. Probably the last few machine guns."

"We can run."

"Already in range. And the steering guy—"

"Helmsman."

"Whatever. I hate boats. The steering guy is up top there, he'll be the first to go. This boat is made of wood and plastic, there's no where to hide. If we do anything dumb, they'll mow us down like green troops at their first battle."

"What do you want us to do?"

"The smart thing, like usual." Russell stood and raised his hands over his head. "We surrender."

Chapter 38

Roi docked them with help from Pletcher. Russell and Chaudhari had headed to the bow and jumped onto Nadine when she threatened to shoot everybody who came near. She fought like a drunken tabbo until four of Jose's people—because it was Jose's people who were arresting them—came onboard and piled on, holding her down.

"Hello again, Sergeant Russell." Jose greeted them. "You can put your hands down."

"Not worried about us attacking you?" Russell asked, dropping his hands.

"An acceptable risk," Jose said. "I'm counting on your good sense. I was never in the Militia, but even I know that automatic weapons fired from a prepared position will beat handguns fired from a rocking boat." Jose gestured behind him. Dozens of figures, all armed, were visible in the headlights of the trucks lining the dock. "I suppose you could get a shot or two off, and possibly hit me, but then my people would destroy you. You're not the type of person who likes those odds. Will you behave?"

"I will," Russell said. "Both Chad and I. And our people."

"Good." Jose nodded. "You may keep your hand weapons then."

"Really?" Russell said. "Why?"

"A gesture of trust." Jose smiled. "My fight isn't with you. Nor with you, Mr. Pletcher, even though I had to temporarily arrest your people here. I'm letting them all go right now. A small number of them had weapons, and, unfortunately, I can't let them keep those. They'll all be disarmed, then released. And I'll need any personal weapons you're carrying surrendered to me."

Pletcher shook his head. "I don't have any. But why do Russell's people get to keep their weapons and not mine?"

"Weapons of violence are a monopoly of the state," Jose said. "And only the State's representatives can have them. Major Russell is a government official, so he can be armed."

"Sergeant Russell."

Jose smiled wider. "The new deputy commander of the Militia can't be a sergeant. Traditionally, they're a major. And

I'm fond of tradition. Now, with both you, Senator Pletcher, and you, Senator Chaudhari, here in Landing, we have a full quorum for the Senate, so I've convinced the acting speaker to call a meeting tomorrow. We'll discuss several matters. One of them is promoting Senator Shutt to Colonel. She'll be the new official head of the Militia, and Sergeant—sorry, Major—Russell will be her new deputy. Congratulations, Major Russell."

Russell and Chaudhari exchanged glances. Russell shook his head. "Won't work. She hates me. I don't like her much either. What's stopping me taking a shot at her to get her out of my hair?" *Or she might arrange an unfortunate weapon misfire during our next meeting. Is that why he's letting me keep my weapons? He wants another faction fight inside the Militia—divide and conquer. I hate politics.*

"No you won't. You believe in the Militia. You believe in rules. You're not going to shoot a properly appointed superior officer. You said so yourself, not more than an hour ago."

"How in hades name did you know that?" Russell asked.

"Same way I knew where you were landing, and when." Jose pointed. "Roi told me. He's been a spy for me from the beginning."

Jose had to send a rowboat for Jake. His skinsuit imparted buoyancy, so he was in no danger of sinking, but like all Belters Jake couldn't swim and had no idea how to get back to shore. Once he was dragged out and dried off, Jose put him in a ground car with a guard. Russell and Chaudhari were allowed to keep their weapons, but they were driven to Militia Headquarters under guard. Once there, they were strongly discouraged from leaving, and their communicators were confiscated. They were treated politely, but not allowed to leave their rooms or to have visitors.

Jose's people had already arrested two of Pletcher's loading crew who had warrants out. TGI security confiscated all the goods on board the ships, including a dozen crates of ammunition, various forged metal items, and a pallet of food trays.

"Seizing contraband helps defray our expenses," Jose had said.

"Barefaced theft," Pletcher had said.

Nadine remained tied up while being sent to a doctor. Everyone agreed that it was for the best, except perhaps her.

"Jake, we need to talk," Jose said.

"We do." Jake stared out the window of the ground car as they drove into Landing. There was no debris on city streets, and people thronged the stores, but the shells of destroyed buildings surrounded the monorail station and the fusion plant, relics of the 'past unpleasantness'. "Can you just jump to the end of the discussion where you offer me a deal, and skip the parts in between. I've had a long day. Nadine's piloting can be very tiresome. What are you offering me?"

"Not being shot?" Jose smiled.

"You can't shoot me. Not now that I'm in your custody. Too many people would know. I've got too many friends. They'll tell everyone and it will ruin your facade. You can't be Dashi's heir if you shoot Dashi's agents. If you wanted to do it, you should have blown up the ship or done something deniable before now. Like when you had those two fake Militia guys try to kill Nadine and I."

"I don't know what you're talking about."

Jake laughed. "Of course not. Did you have to kill Dashi?"

"What makes you think I killed him?"

"You're the one who benefited the most."

"I'm not saying I did. But don't you think it was necessary? His fantasy of re-establishing the empire? With a single moon, in the back of beyond, and only a few jump capable ships. And I'll be wanting those turned over to me."

Jake took a few moments to control his emotions. This was too important to screw up. "*Accounting Error's* computers are encrypted and it's driving out of the system," Jake said. "You can't have her, and there is nothing you can do to me that will make me turn over those codes."

"I could torture you."

"And you'd have to kill me afterwards, same problem as before. Nope. I keep my ships."

"Fine." Jose glared. "I want you to support me as Emperor. I'll take over from Dashi. I'm going to announce it in the Senate tomorrow. We're publishing Dashi's will then as well. There's plenty in it for you, so I'd like you to be there, and indicate your support for me."

"I'm not a Senator. I can't speak there."

"Before you left, Dashi made you a plenipotentiary, on a diplomatic mission. You're supposed to report to the Senate on your return."

"So?"

"So report. Give a report tomorrow, then endorse me for Emperor. Name me as Dashi's heir."

"What about the Militia, TGI, and the Free Traders?" Jake asked. "You'll need their support. What happens to them?"

"You already figured it out," Jose said. "Like you told Roi and the others. Shutt keeps the Militia. Russell keeps her in line as her deputy. If she looks at me crossways, I'll get him to shoot her and take over. The Free Traders are having an election as we speak. They're hopelessly divided, they'll appoint some nonentity without widespread support if they appoint anybody at all. They don't want to get on my bad side. And I've been acting director of TGI for weeks. We only need a stockholder's meeting to make me the new chairman."

"Okay." Jake nodded. "Okay."

Jose sat silently for a moment. "That's it. Okay?"

Jake shrugged. "Sure. Why not? What happens here doesn't matter much to me, because I won't be here. I'm going to take my ship and go exploring. Back to Magyar to help the people I met there, maybe take up residence. I won't be here to bother you."

"What if I don't let you take your ship?"

"That's what's on offer Jose. Think of it as buying my silence with exile. I'll leave whatever I have in this system here. I've made good money doing my trading. I'll head out to the stars. Nadine will want to come along with me once you let her know. And it makes sense. It's a good deal for you. You'll have too much to do here, and you don't need another potential enemy here."

"If you keep your ship, you go right away."

"Only if the succession is settled." Jake turned to stare at Jose. "If you get the head of the Militia to support you for Emperor, and whoever is the head of the Free Traders guild supports you, and if you become the chairman of TGI and get support of the other corps, then I'll get up and give my report as an ambassador, walk out of the Senate house, get on my ship, and go. I won't be first, though, because I want it to be unanimous. But if you have managed to collect that sort of support, then you should be the Emperor. That's what Dashi would have wanted - if somebody has that much support, then he should be in charge. And I'm committed to following Dashi's legacy."

"I didn't think it would be this easy." Jose cocked his head. "You're not thinking of trying to shoot me later or something like that."

"Jose," Jake said. "Dashi was like a father to me. If I could prove that you killed him, I'd tear you apart with my bare hands. But I don't have proof, and if it was him, he'd never act without proof. I swear on his soul. I won't shoot you. Or attack you, or any-type-of-violence-you. I won't order somebody to do it, or pay them, or command them. Nothing like that. But I won't defend you. I'll point out that Dashi would have wanted the person with the most widespread support to become Emperor. If you meet that criteria, then you should be in charge. That's what he would have wanted."

Jose sat silently for a moment, then extended his hands. "For Dashi."

"For Dashi." Jake agreed, and shook.

Chapter 39

The next day started late. Jose had kept Jake at TGI headquarters overnight, another "you're not a prisoner but don't try to leave" type of guest. Jake didn't complain, simply went to bed and got a good night's sleep. In the morning he lingered over breakfast, surprising the breakfast staff with a request for glasses of Basic, rather than coffee.

"Stewart, you are a complete and utter dirtbag." Nadine slid onto a bench across from him. "Have I ever told you that?"

"Too many times to count, Nadine." Jake looked at her swollen face. "You have two black eyes. How did you get *two* black eyes?"

"I got hit in the face twice, that's how." Nadine glared at him. "I have a cracked rib, and my left big toe is broken, the doctor says." Jose had provided a doctor. The doctor had run a battery of tests and given her a long list of things not to do. Most of which she ignored.

"How do you break a big toe in a fight?" Jake asked. "That seems unusual."

"Kicking somebody barefoot."

"I guess that makes sense." Jake pointed at his plate. "Do you want my eggs? They're fresh, and I never got a taste for fresh eggs. I like the dried ones on the trays."

"That's all you can say, 'do you want eggs'? I had the crap kicked out of me yesterday and that's all you can say?"

Jake chewed. "You could have stopped anytime."

She took a sip of his drink. "Blech. Basic. Have anything else?"

"Want me to order you some vodka?"

A shadow passed across her face. "No. Stupid doctor says I can't have any vodka."

"Too bad. Why didn't you stop fighting?"

"Why do you think? Didn't you know I was angry?"

"I believe that's why you threw me in the river. Which prevented me from helping you out during the ensuing altercation."

"Okay." Nadine grimaced. "I guess my timing wasn't the best on that."

"Not really. But I'm sure you gave as good as you got. What did the others look like?"

Nadine smiled. "Like they were hit by the freight monorail and dragged for a mile. They deserved it."

"I'm sure they did."

Nadine glared at him again, then took his plate. She ate his eggs while she talked. "I forgive you for not helping me, because you were distracted."

"By distracted you mean trying not to drown."

"Don't be a big baby. You weren't going to drown. Float away maybe. But listen Stewart, telling me you forbid stuff. That's a bad idea."

"It is."

"You know how I react when people tell me I can't do something."

"Yes. I do."

"That's why you shouldn't do it. Because you know the way I react."

"I do know Nadine, I do. I've been speaking to Jose…" Jake explained his talk with Jose, but he left out a few important details. He didn't want her upset, yet.

"That's what you want? Jose to be Emperor."

"He seems qualified."

"I don't think—"

"Nadine, I'm the one sitting here eating a nice breakfast, and you're the one who was beaten within an inch of your life. Who has a better grasp of the situation?"

Nadine glowered at him and finished the rest of the eggs.

"We need to—Aha. Show time." A group of TGI security people had entered the breakfast room and were heading over. The leader introduced himself and said he was there to escort them to the Senate chamber—the re-purposed Imperial Agriculture building.

The leader joked with Jake. "Don't worry about a thing, Mr. Stewart, we're here on orders of the TGI council to protect you. More as bodyguards than anything. There's always rumors of violence from the Free Traders, and who knows what the

Militia are up to these days? But we'll make sure you get to the Senate house okay."

"Thanks," Jake said. "I hear your folks and Ms. Nadine had a bit of a dust up last night during the confusion. I hope there are no hard feelings."

The leader glowered at Nadine. "None at all. None at all." He was clearly lying. He motioned to the others, and they formed a group to 'escort' Jake and Nadine to the car.

Nadine trailed behind Jake, two guards behind her. He chatted with the TGI crew, joking about a rumor that he was going to stand for election as deputy-chairman of TGI. They asked what he'd do with his new raise.

Nadine glared at his back. *He doesn't need the money, why would he bother running in a corporate election right now? And I'm still mad at him for goading me into that fight. He knew with my temper what telling me something was 'forbidden' would do.*

She watched Jake saunter to the ground car. Relaxed, cheerful, smiling. Completely at ease. *He knows that. He certainly knows that. Which means he did it on purpose. Why?*

Jake turned over his shoulder and gave her one of his grave smiles.

You're up to something Stewart. What is it this time?

The ground car deposited them at the door of the Agriculture building. Again, Jake's not-guards formed a group around Nadine and him and ushered him up the stairs. A mixed group of Militia, Free Traders, and TGI people surrounded the doorway.

"Shipmaster Stewart. Congratulations!" one of the Free Trader Guards called.

Jake waved. "Free Trades to everyone!" The Free Traders in the crowd cheered and waved back.

Nadine followed behind him. "What was that about?"

"I did some trading deals with them, remember? All that fuel. They're happy I let their captains off the hook."

"I don't remember you doing that. And they seem excessively happy."

"You were asleep. Or piloting. And I don't tell you everything I'm doing."

"Don't you trust me?"

"I trust you completely to be yourself at all times, Nadine. Completely yourself."

"Thanks." Nadine walked behind him for a few more steps. "Wait, is that a compliment?"

"It's what you make it." Jake, Nadine and their escorts stopped at the door to the Senate chambers. A mixed guard of three groups waited there. Standing near them was Roi.

"Mr. Roi." Jake said. "Good to see you. I'm glad you're okay. You've been treated well?"

"Very well, thank you," Roi said "I'm looking forward to hearing you speak."

"Thank you. We'll see you inside." Jake walked to the door, but was blocked by the guards.

The senior guard was a Militia Lieutenant that Nadine didn't recognize. "No weapons on the Senate Floor. And we'll need to see ID."

Their TGI escort shook his head. "I'm supposed to escort Mr. Stewart inside."

The armed Free Trader guard shook his head. "Shipmaster Stewart doesn't need to show ID, we all know who he is."

"Well, I don't." The Militia guard squared off with his TGI escort, demanding proof he was who he said he was, and the Free Trader added to the bickering. Things might have gotten ugly, but Jake raised his hand. "I have an ID chip given to me by the late Emperor Dashi, may he rest in peace." He pulled a chip from his pocket and extended it. "Will that be sufficient?"

The Militia lieutenant stuck out his hand. "Gimmee."

Jake gave him the chip. The ID authorization took a long time, requiring a fingerprint and retinal scan from both Jake and the Lieutenant. Then it required a call back to the main computer system. Jake sighed while he waited. "Will this take much longer?"

"Just you wait, buddy." The lieutenant said. "I'll need to— oh." He stared at his screen, then stamped to attention and saluted. "Sir. Very sorry sir. Welcome to the Senate Chambers."

"Thank you lieutenant." Jake didn't even try to return the salute. "Ms. Nadine is my aide-de-camp. She'll be accompanying me."

The lieutenant swung to face Nadine and saluted. "Ma'am."

Nadine looked to Jake. "What?"

One of the TGI spoke up. "We have to search them for weapons…"

Nadine glared at him. "Anybody here tries to search me, is going to have first a broken finger, then a broken jaw."

"Searching won't be necessary," Jake said. "We've been in… protective custody with TGI staff for twenty-four hours, and we were searched when we arrived. I'm not carrying any weapons. And if you can tell me where Ms. Nadine has hers concealed, I'd be very interested."

All eyes swiveled over to Nadine. She was wearing her custom skin-suit, which was both skin tight and stylish. There wasn't any room to hide much of anything.

"Good enough for me," the Free Trader guard said. He pulled the heavy door open. "Welcome to the Senate, Shipmaster. Free Trades."

"Free Trades," Jake agreed. "Nadine, you're with me." Jake paused in the doorway. "Once we're in, who else can come in?"

The Militia guard shook his head. "Our orders are that once you're in, seal and bar the door. Nobody from outside gets in, and the doors stay shut until the Senators open them from inside."

Jake turned to the Free Traders, who nodded. The TGI guards shrugged. Jake thanked them all, then entered.

Nadine followed him through. "Jake, what did that ID say."

"I used the plenty-hairy one that Dashi gave me. The one that said I was an ambassador. Remember?"

"I guess. But what does it have to do with the Militia."

"Hush Nadine. Things are happening. Follow my lead. "

The Senate chamber was square, with three rows of chairs facing a dais. At the back of the room was a set of open bleachers—metal frames with wooden bench seats. Togate men and women stood in groups on the main floor, talking. Every eye had swiveled to them as they entered. Jose broke off from his group and strode over.

Nadine glared at Jake's back. "Hush? You want me to Hush?"

"Nadine—"

Nadine leaned over, grabbed his earlobe and hauled him down to her mouth. "Oh don't worry Jakey. I'll hush. For now.

I'll even follow your lead. For now. But after, after all this, we are going to have a very, very long chat."

"Jose is coming." Jake muttered. Nadine let go of his ear.

Jose stopped in front of them. "Jake, are you ready to give your report?"

"Of course," Jake said. "I've got detailed reports on the sales of various products, including the ores and heavy metals, a complete plan on construction of new assets, a financial plan for increasing tax revenues by instituting a new tariff methodology…"

Jake droned on for a few minutes then stopped. "None of you are listening to me, are you?"

"Not even for a moment," Jose said. "We all know you. None of this will make sense to anybody except you. You remember our conversation from last night?"

"Yes," Jake said. "You read Dashi's will. Then you'll make a short speech about the needs of the Empire, and you'll ask the head of the Free Traders, the Chairman of TGI, and the head of the Militia to support you. After they do, then I'll endorse you as Emperor, and give my report."

"And leave immediately for your ship?"

"You keep your promises, I'll keep mine."

Jose clapped Jake on the shoulder, and strode off, calling to the senators.

Nadine was aghast. "Jake, you're running away."

"Think of it as a tactical maneuver, Nadine." Jake looked at her. "Are you going to come with me?"

"Jake, I, I." Nadine swallowed. "You're just giving in. Giving up."

"I'm not giving up," Jake said. "I need to gain some time, as I just said."

"I, I—"

Jake touched her arm. "Hush. Jose is calling things to order. Sit down. Relax. Take a load off your feet. You're going to have to trust me completely, for once." Jake gave her a significant look. "Take your shoes off, If you want."

"If you say 'hush' one more time I'm going to—"

But Jake ignored her and marched off to a rostrum on the side. An usher guided Nadine to a seat. She sat at the back of the room and fumed. Legally, she was in a visitors gallery at the edge of the senate floor. Practically, she was on a set of bleachers not unlike what you sat in to watch a roller-ball show. Every move she made was visible. *But he said to take my shoes off. He knows I have my gauss pistol in my shoes. He doesn't want the crowd to see it, but he wants me to have it ready. Trust him? Hah!* But she kicked her boots off and let them sit on the floor without anybody noticing. But removing and assembling the pieces would draw notice. *Sit tight. Stewart knows what he's doing. I hope.*

Jose called the Senate house to order, and the acting speaker, a TGI executive who Nadine didn't recognize handled several housekeeping items before the main agenda.

"The late Emperor Dashi's will has been in limbo for some time. Even though it was filed with the agricultural computer— I mean the Imperial mainframe—we've been unable to access all of it due to encryption protocols. Those protocols were lifted this morning, and it's available to present. Senators, shall we commence with the reading of the will at this time?"

There was a quick vote, and all agreed. A screen next to the dais lit and a picture of the late Mr. Dashi appeared. He began to speak.

Nadine tried to listen to the words, but she'd never liked speeches. She normally considered it a win if she didn't fall asleep. Dashi's figure droned on and her eyes started to glaze over. She shook her head to stay awake and concentrated on his words from beyond the grave.

"All of my work has been to re-establish the empire. After my death I hope you will consider continuing—"

A figure slid into the seat next to her, on the aisle. She ignored it until he spoke softly.

It was Roi. "The man could make a good speech, I'll give him that."

Nadine turned to him. "You're a spy for Jose."

Roi shrugged. "Somebody had to do it. All I had to do was answer some questions when he asked. Besides, Jose is supposed to become the new Emperor. Why not work for him?"

"You're a weasel."

"I did what I had to do." Roi watched the show. "What I was told to do."

"I should shoot you," Nadine said.

"Yes, you could, but I'm not sure you'll have enough bullets in whatever gun you've got hidden in your boots. You'll need some for later. Besides, it looks like it will take a while to put it together."

Nadine's mouth dropped. "You know I have a gun?"

"Of course I do. Mr. Stewart told me."

"You never said anything to Jose?"

"He never asked. And it's better that one of us is armed."

"And why's that?"

Roi gestured with his head. "Because there are armed Militia troopers sneaking into the side doors. I expect gunplay shortly."

Nadine gaped. While everyone was entranced by Dashi's talk from beyond the grave, Militia soldiers were swarming in through the side doors.

Chapter 40

Russell was grumpy. First, he wasn't happy that his watery attempt at subterfuge in meeting Jake Stewart had been uncovered. *Should have stuck with shooting people, Scott. No head for politics.* Second, he was annoyed that since he wasn't a Senator, he had to sit in the back with the others. Chaudhari had smirked at him as he strode onto the main part of the floor.

And third, he wasn't allowed to smoke.

A shiver ran down his spine, an old combat reflex. Something had changed. His eyes scanned the room. While everybody concentrated on Dashi's speech, doors on both sides swung silently open and squads of armed Militia slid in. *Revolvers and shotguns. I didn't hear them come in, no shooting, so they must have been inside waiting. Shutt snuck them in last night. Are they going to shoot me? No, I'm in a Militia uniform, and besides, they're all staring at Shutt.* Russell settled on his seat. He surreptitiously unsnapped his holster. *I'll wait and see what happens.*

Dashi's recorded voice continued. "Therefore, I give you my final will and testament, disposing of all my assets, including my corporate shares, for which this is my warrant. An inventory is attached in detail, encrypted with my personal cipher. I have made arrangements with a trusted member of my staff to have the decryption brought forward before this is presented." The figure on the screen looked up. "I will assume that whoever is listening to this speech will inform the Senate of its contents, or perhaps they may present it directly to them. And I ask one more thing of the Senate, that all the temporary assignments of rank and privilege in effect at my death, be made permanent. These are people I trusted in life, and I ask you to trust them after my death.

"Hear hear!" A voice called from the senate floor.

"Vote, vote," called another.

Pletcher stood up on the Senate floor. "I motion that we do as Dashi says. All in favor?"

"AYE" the crowd roared.

"I ask the acting speaker to record the vote—uh, who are these people?" Pletcher noticed the crowd of Militia in the wings. Voices surged as the Senators noticed the extra armed troops.

Shutt stood. "Everyone pay attention! As the saying goes, I have taken the opportunity to secure the corridors. For too long, we on Delta have been hostages to the corporate interests that have ruined our...."

Russell sat without expression. It wasn't the first time he'd had to listen to a dumb-ass superior pontificate. *Any minute now she'll be talking about our 'glorious past' and 'heirs to an Imperial tradition'. I don't care, I'll put up with whatever as long as nobody tries to shoot me. I need a way to increase food production, and I'll need more of those iron ingots. I'll bet Pletcher can get me more aluminum too, if I could figure out a way to machine it...*

Russell drifted off in a haze of production numbers and plans for a new drill press. He almost didn't catch the last part of her speech.

"Therefore," Shutt said. "I have no choice but to take on this patriotic task. I proclaim myself the new emperor."

"Jove in a bucket of Basic," Nadine said. "I did not see that coming. She wants to be the Emperor?"

Next to her, Roi shrugged. "Doesn't matter what she wants, it's what the Senate wants."

"She has a lot more guns than the Senate does, right now," Nadine said.

"Which is why you should be putting yours together right now," Roi said. "You might want it soon."

Nadine darted a look at him. *What does he know?* She looked to Jake. He sat serenely behind the rostrum at the side. His features were untroubled, and he gazed at the Senate chamber as if he was playing with his favorite fuel consumption modeling. She caught his eye. He nodded, then looked to his shoes and raised a questioning eyebrow.

I have no idea what that crazy boy is up to. Better be prepared. She grabbed a boot to pry her heels open and pull out the pieces of her gauss gun.

Jose faced Shutt on the Senate floor. "You can't become the Emperor. Certainly not by shooting anybody. I have the support, you don't. TGI is behind me, the Free Traders won't support you, and the Militia won't accept you shooting me to take power. Don't even bother, Clarisse."

Shutt laughed. "You think so, Jose? You think the Militia will stand against me? I'm one of them. The only person left who could possibly disagree with me is Sergeant Russell. And he's promised not to shoot me."

"You can't count on that, Clarisse."

"Yes, I can. You already asked him, and he already answered. As long as I leave him alone, he'll leave me alone. He's already promised you that. Isn't that right, Sergeant?"

All eyes in the Senate swiveled to stare at Russell. Nadine's mouth gaped open. *How in Hades does she know that?*

Jose looked equally confused. "How in Hades do you know that?"

Shutt grinned. "Roi told me. He heard you and Jose talking earlier."

Now every eye swung to Roi. He looked at the crowd. "I was well paid. Major Shutt made me an offer I couldn't refuse."

Eyes swiveled back to Shutt. She smiled. "The Militia is behind me, Jose. Sergeant Russell and all the others. Your plot to have him challenge me won't work. He can't afford to take control, it will destroy the Militia. And the Free Traders want him dead, but they won't cross me. If he puts himself in charge, he'll have to deal with them alone." Her grin widened. "Face it Jose, I'm going to be proclaimed the new emperor."

Jose glanced around the senate chamber. Half of the senators were nodding, and not just the Militia ones that she controlled. The independents, some of the Free Traders, even one of his TGI people.

"You have control of the Militia, but the corps will never support you, Clarisse. They don't trust you. You know nothing about corporations—"

"I don't, but I don't have to. Bring him out," she yelled to the Militia guards at the wall. Ten seconds later, a bemused Senator Pletcher was hustled in from the side rooms. "Meet the future chairman of TGI."

Nadine wrenched one heel from her boot and pried the combined barrel/railgun piece out. It took only a moment to fit the handle to it. She dropped that boot and reached for the other, digging at the heel to get the battery and capacitor unit.

The heel was stuck, and she couldn't pry it out farther. She looked to the Senate floor. Jose confronted Shutt. Pletcher stood with his arms folded, waiting to see how it played out. The other senators stood mouth agape and eyes wide.

Shutt raised her voice. "Fellow Senators. I am the only logical choice for the new Emperor. The Militia supports, me, and when Senator Pletcher is installed, then so will TGI."

"TGI will never support you, not as long as I'm running it," Jose yelled.

The room quieted. A voice coughed from the sidelines. "Excuse me, could I speak."

All eyes swung to the side of the room. Jake strode out from behind the lectern. "This will only take a minute, then I can get on with my report. Jose, what makes you believe that you are in charge of TGI?"

Jose blinked. "I'm the acting chairman. I've been running things for months."

"You're only chairman until the next meeting. Dashi's will being promulgated will release his personal shares to his heirs. I'm one of them, many of those shares go to me. We need an election to make the chairman official."

Jose shrugged. "You're late to that party, Jake. The majority of the shares are vested in whoever is the acting chairman. To allow them to govern effectively, it's designed to give them an absolute majority on the board. Regardless, Clarisse here can't appoint Pletcher to be the chairman. The chairman has to be elected. And I'm not voting for him, nor is anyone else, and there's nothing she can do about it."

"What about appointing him vice-chairman?"

"Why in Hades names would I do that?" Jose said. "And regardless, the vice chairman is always the person who has the second most shares voted in the election. You know that Jake."

"I do, but I wanted it brought out in public." Jake nodded. He waved his comm unit to the crowd. "In fact, with the emails I have just received, it appears Dashi has gifted me with a substantial inheritance. I am now the second largest stockholder in TGI, after the reigning chairman. Which makes me the vice chairman."

Shutt laughed. "Well congrats, trader boy. But that doesn't matter, you'll be working for me, once I become Empress."

"We need a vote for that," Jake said. "Only the Senate can choose Dashi's heir."

"Well they won't be choosing Jose, you know why."

"Why is that?"

"Because." Shutt grinned. "The admiral told me, before he died. Jose was the last one to handle the wine before Dashi died. He saw him slip something into it. Jose killed Dashi. He poisoned the Emperor."

Chapter 41

The crowd in the Senate gasped at Shutt's admission. Nadine's jaw dropped. "That can't be true. He wouldn't say that."

"Quiet everybody." Russell yelled. "Major, what did he say? Exactly. Did he specifically say that Jose did it?" The crowd noise increased and Russell yelled louder. "Let her speak. Let her speak." He raised his hands over his head and made quieting motions.

Jake caught Nadine's eye, and looked to her feet, where pieces of boots tumbled in disarray. He nodded once, then turned back to the senate crowd.

"Let her speak," Russell repeated.

The crowd quieted, and all eyes locked on Shutt. Nadine shook herself out of her funk and tried to pry her remaining heel open. Russell looked down at her and frowned, then ignored her in favor of the ongoing drama. Even Roi spared her a glance, then resolutely turned away.

Shutt stood and addressed the Senate. "That's what he told me, the admiral. When I had my last meeting with him, he told me that he was feeling ill, and that he was sure he wasn't going to recover from being poisoned. He told me that he'd seen Jose fiddling with the drinks before he and Dashi drank. It was those drinks that poisoned Dashi, it was those drinks that killed him, and it was those drinks that Jose gave him. Jose did it. Jose killed him."

"You lie. YOU LIE." Jose yelled. "I didn't kill him. You did! I poured the drinks, yes, but I didn't poison him. He was like a father to me. You brought them to him. You did it."

"Why would I poison Dashi? It wouldn't help me? I was a junior officer in the Militia, not Dashi's assistant. It's you who would benefit. You would take over TGI and now you're trying to be Emperor!" Shutt reached into the folds of her toga, and pulled out her service revolver. "This will not stand, Jose. There is no way we're going to let the killer of Dashi lead us!"

"You're the one who is trying to be Emperor." Jose yelled. "Killing the head of the Militia, usurping the job."

Nadine gave up trying to pry her heel open. She stuck her boot under the edge of the bleacher rail and levered it sideways. The heel bent, then popped open, spilling its contents. She snagged the battery, but the capacitor bounced out. She grabbed for it, but it bounced, and dropped over the edge. She cursed, clambered over Roi and Russell, and dropped beside the bleachers, searching for the capacitor.

"Enough of this." Shutt waved her revolver. "Militia, arrest him, and take him away."

Jose pulled out a square object from under his robe. Shutt yelled a challenge, then brought up her revolver. BANG. She fired once, hitting him in the chest. His body jerked. She fired again. BANG. And a third time, BANG, advancing all the while. All three hit, jerking him sideways. He fell. The square object hit the floor, bounced, and rolled to the side. Shutt advanced until she stood over the body, pointed the revolver and pulled the trigger again. SPLIFF.

The revolver didn't bang, it sputtered. Smoke poured from around her hand with a puff. She yelled in pain and dropped the revolver. "Jove!"

The crowd stood still, mouths agape.

Nadine spied her capacitor under the bleachers. She dropped to all fours and wormed her way towards it, catching it at first grab. Then she rolled onto her back and screwed it onto the pistol.

Shutt stood silently in the middle of the circle of amazed faces. Nobody spoke. Russell stood, stepped down two rows to the Senate floor, and walked to Jose's body. He rolled him face up and checked for a pulse. "Nope. He's gone." He looked at Shutt. "Good shooting Clarisse. Three hits, single-handed in a stressful situation. Gotta hand it to you, you've got guts."

"He tried to kill me, you all saw that." Shutt bent over and retrieved her revolver. "It was self defense. He was reaching for a weapon."

"Well." Russell leaned down and picked up what Jose had dropped. "Not a weapon. High security comm." He peered more closely at it. "It's unlocked. There's a video." He tapped the comm, watched for five seconds, then grimaced.

Shutt cradled her arm, the revolver dangling. "It could have been a weapon. You all saw it. It was self defense. I didn't have any choice."

"Guess not." Russell said.

Nadine finished screwing the capacitor onto her gauss pistol and engaged the battery. A soft whine indicated the capacitor was charging.

"I had to do it," Shutt said.

"Of course you did," Russell said.

"Well." Shutt took a deep breath. "Well. Sergeant Russell, do you accept my authority?"

"Always have," Russell said. "Always have. I follow the duly elected leader of the Militia"

"Am I going to have problems with you?"

"Nope." Russell shook his head. "I'm not an assassin. I follow instructions. I'll take orders from whoever is in charge of the Militia."

"Good." Shutt took another deep breath. "Good, I need you to—"

Jake Stewart broke in. "Sergeant Russell. What's on the screen, that Jose wanted to show us?"

Russell held up the comm unit. "This? This comm unit. Nothing. Only video."

"A video of what?"

"Nothing special. Just the room camera in Admiral Edmund's room. Him and Shutt arguing. He makes some rude remarks. Shutt tells him he should have listened to her. Then she suffocates him with a pillow."

Everyone gasped.

"No, not—"

Russell held up the comm unit. "It's right here, Clarisse. I just watched it."

Nadine walked around the front of the bleachers. She lifted her gauss pistol up. The charger hadn't spun up yet, the light was still red, and the charging whine continued

"You killed him," Nadine said. "You killed my grandfather."

"I let him go easy," Shutt said. "He wasn't getting better."

The gauss pistol light switched from red to orange. Nadine pointed it at Shutt. "That's not what the doctors said after. They said he was getting better."

"They were wrong. He was going. He was in pain all the time."

"I got messages from him. Videos. He sounded fine. Everybody said he was fine. They said he was getting better." The light on Nadine's gauss gun changed from yellow to flashing orange. The flashes started slowly, then sped up.

"He was, oh Jove." Shutt brought her revolver up and pointed it at Nadine. "He needed to go. He was part of the old regime. Dashi had to go. He had to go. We're better off without both of them." She pulled back on the hammer, to cock the gun. It wouldn't move. She shook it, then yanked the hammer again. Nothing changed.

"Sorry about that Clarisse," Russell said. "We've still not got the hang of the ammunition production yet. You got a squib load. Only the primer fired, not the powder charge. Bullet's stuck halfway up the barrel. You'll need an extraction tool, or a hammer."

The light on Nadine's pistol changed from flashing orange to a bright green. The whine faded. "He was right about you." She aimed the pistol squarely between Shutt's eyes. "You are a shitbird." Then she pulled the trigger, once, twice, and a third time.

Chapter 42

"Did you have to shoot her three times?" Jake asked as the cleaning crews hauled the bodies away. Nadine's fusillade hadn't so much killed Shutt as chopped her up into small bits.

"Yes, I did. Shut up, Stewart." Nadine slumped on the chair staring at the bloody spot where Shutt's corpse had lain. "She deserved it."

After Nadine's explosive coda to the Senate session, pandemonium reigned. Russell had taken control of the Militia guards, and prevented them from shooting everybody out of hand. Some of them were still loyal to Shutt, but the revelation that she had killed the admiral confused them all. They pointed their weapons in random directions until Russell argued with them that they could always shoot everybody later, but in the meantime things needed to be cleaned up and they should stand down. Natural authority and a loud voice goes a long way with Militia.

After the doors were pushed open, the guards outside rushed in. The Free Trader guards took their direction from Jake for some reason, and so did the TGI guards after a quiet word from him. Dashi had been immensely popular, and the charge that Jose had killed him stunned everyone.

Russell walked back to the bleachers and climbed up onto them. He faced the crowd. "Okay, Senate people. What happens now? Who's in charge?"

Various names were yelled as the crowd argued. Then Jake stepped up to the lectern. "Sergeant Russell, I'm ready to give my report now."

Russell glared at him. "You think now is the time to talk about a trading mission."

"I can do that later," Jake said. "Right now, I have a few announcements that the Senators should hear."

Russell crossed his arms. "Do tell."

"Thank you, Sergeant Russell. Senators, Militia Members, Members of the TGI board, Free Traders, distinguished guests—"

Voices rose. Senators faced their neighbors and muttered urgent conversations.

"SHADDDUP." Nadine yelled. "Let him talk."

All the senators ignored her. She yelled again, barely overheard in the din.

Russell pulled out his revolver and fired it at the ceiling. Everybody froze.

"Thank you all." He pocketed his revolver. "Jake Stewart wants to talk. Everybody knows him as Dashi's troubleshooter. He wasn't here when it happened, so he can't have been involved in killing Dashi. He's worked with all the different factions. He hasn't shot anybody today. And Dashi trusted him. For that alone, we should let him talk." He holstered the revolver. "Besides, everybody who knows him knows we can't shut him up. Best get this over with."

The crowd stilled. Jake gulped, then spoke loudly. "Senators, this is an unfortunate day for all of us. But we've all seen it coming. For the last few years, the lack of resources caused by the abandonment has created conflict." Jake spoke for a few more minutes. The hazards of being abandoned by the empire. The loss of capabilities as tech too complicated to repair failed. Population growth without corresponding economic and agricultural creations. Difficulties with the economy. All things Dashi had fought against.

"As you all know, Dashi had a plan. That plan was to hold fast until we could reconnect with the empire. Bide our time until we could find ways to rejoin the main part of the galaxy. You all know that Ms. Nadine and I have been on a mission to other systems in the area. We didn't find the empire, but we found several other settlements and planets. Some larger, some small. All loyal to the empire and willing to co-operate. And trade. Trade that will benefit us all. We're not past the comet shower yet, but we have hope for a brighter future."

Jake expanded on the pending trade deals with the other discovered former Imperial colonies, especially Magyar, the planet he and Nadine had returned from.

"In conclusion," Jake said. "With the death of Dashi, Jose, Admiral Edmunds, Major Shutt, and the former chairwoman of the Free Traders council, most of the pre-war leaders are dead. We need a new leader who can command the respect of all factions. Especially the Militia, the Free Traders, and the various corps, particularly those supported or involved with Trans Galactic Insurance."

Jake returned to his seat and sat. One of the Senators stood. "Who then? Russell?"

"Not me," Russell said. "Never. I was born a Sergeant, and I'll die a Sergeant."

"Pletcher—"

"Nope." Pletcher shook his head. "Definite Nope. Too dangerous. Too many people getting killed. Too much stress, not enough money."

Roi stood and marched down to the Senate floor. "Perhaps we should hear from some of the leaders among us. From the Militia, the Free Traders, and TGI. A question, with all the deaths, who controls TGI now?"

People in the crowd looked at each other. The muttering started again.

Jake stood and coughed. "Um, Senators. As recorded in the minutes of the Senate, with Dashi's will promulgated, I received his shares, which made me the second largest shareholder in TGI, after the late Mr. Jose, who held his position by virtue of the chairman controlling numerous proxies. Which made me vice chairman. Therefore upon his death, the chairmanship accedes to me, along with all the voting shares. Which makes me the majority shareholder of Trans Galactic Insurance, as well as several associated companies. Therefore, I am the duly elected chairman of TGI, as recorded in the minutes. The recorded minutes."

Quiet responses rustled through the gathered senators. Nadine smiled and walked up to Russell. "Watch this. We're seeing the start of some of that weird Jake Stewart magic." She stepped up onto the bleacher next to Russell. "Hey, all you Free Traders! You called him 'Shipmaster' when he came in, how come."

Eyes flipped around, then settled on the small group of Free Trader senators. One stood. "The Captain's council had an election last night. Mr., sorry, Shipmaster Stewart had a whole bunch of vote proxies he traded for. Under our rules, you can Trade for votes as well as money. He'd collected enough to vote himself as head of both the Captain's guild and the Free Trader's council. It's unusual, but legitimate. We're okay with it.

If somebody is smart enough to buy enough votes, he's smart enough to run our trading. He's our new leader until somebody else votes him out." He shrugged. "Don't expect that to happen too quickly. Those fuel trades were slick. Very impressive."

"You voted him in as your leader and didn't tell anybody?" Nadine asked.

"That was Free Trader business, lady, and none of yours. We pick our own leaders our own way, and we don't give a damn what you dirtsiders say about it. No requirement to tell you anything."

Nadine nodded. "You'll all do what he says?"

"It doesn't work that way exactly, but you need a good reason to go against the Captain's council. I can't think of one right now." He sat.

Nadine crossed her arms. "Well Stewart. You've taken control of Trans Galactic Insurance, and the Free Traders. Only thing left is the Militia. How you going to pull that out of your skin suit?"

Russell snapped his fingers. "Dashi's will. He asked us to confirm all his appointments, of his trusted people. What did that make you? Didn't we set you up with an appointment when you went hunting for the empire?"

Eyes blinked across the chamber, then chins nodded. When Dashi sent Jake away on his voyage of exploration, he'd made him a plenipotentiary, an Imperial official. And an Admiral. Jake explained the details.

"Which makes me," Jake said, "As the senior surviving officer, commander of the Militia."

Russell shook his head. "Neat trick, but nobody is going to take orders from a kid with no military experience. Least of all me."

The crowd muttered, but Jake raised his hands. "Which is why, Sergeant Russell, I appoint you temporary commander of all troops on the surface of Delta. You will be the new ground commander. After all," Jake smiled, "you've already proved your loyalty to the government. I don't expect a coup from you."

"You won't get one either," Russell said. "But what about the orbital forces? They need a regular commander."

"And they'll get one. Colonel Roi, step forward."

Roi straightened, marched forward and saluted. "Sir?"

"I rescind your exile, and appoint you to the command of the Delta Militia orbital forces, with the rank of Rear Admiral, effective immediately."

The crowd gasped. Some clapped. Some glared.

"Stewart," Nadine said. "Have you lost your mind? After what he's done to you?"

Jake raised an eyebrow. "Given his faithful service, it seems like a just reward. It's what Dashi would have wanted."

"Faithful service? Faithful! He was a spy for Jose. Or Shutt. Or both. Neither. I don't care. He wasn't on your side. He was some sort of double agent at the least."

Jake shook his head. "You're wrong there, Nadine. He wasn't a spy for either of them. And he wasn't a double agent. He was a triple agent. He was working for me. Dashi sent him to exile, but agreed to bring him back after a decent period. In the meantime, he worked for Dashi. After Dashi died, he released the codes to me, and I've been in contact with him since we arrived."

All eyes swiveled to Roi. He nodded. "The exile was real, initially, but Mr. Dashi came to me later, and we made this arrangement. After Mr. Dashi's death, Mr. Stewart—sorry Admiral. Admiral Stewart contacted me when he arrived back in system. He had the right codes, and he knew all about the things I was doing. It was his suggestion I help out Sergeant Russell here, and later pass that information on to Mr. Jose. Helping him was the right thing to do."

"And it paid well," Russell muttered.

"What was that Sergeant?" Jake asked.

Russell braced. "Sir. Your fortitude and advanced planning certainly paid off."

"I believe so." Jake strode across the Senate floor, and advanced to the Emperor's chair, standing on the step just below it, and turned to face the crowd. "Senators. Others. I stand before you representing the forces of order, trade, and discovery. I pledge to follow the path that Dashi has laid out for us all. On behalf of the Militia, TGI and the Free Traders, I ask that you proclaim me emperor."

Nadine laughed. "Emperor Jake the first."

"Yes." Jake nodded to the hall. "Emperor Jake the first. *Sic transit gloria mundi.*"

Chapter 43

It wasn't that easy, of course. First, the senate had to debate. They talked and talked for most of the morning, but couldn't do it. Jake simply lounged on a chair next to the official Imperial chair, and waited them out. When they suggested breaking for lunch he stood.

"I remind you all that the senate remains in session until adjourned. And you can't adjourn until you pick a leader."

A voice in back called out. "Why not? Why can't we adjourn for lunch?"

"Because all the guards here work for me, and they're not letting anybody in or out until you decide. No supplies either."

"You'd starve us out?"

Jake shrugged. "I had a big breakfast. I can wait." He sat.

The debate went faster after that. The direct TGI senators wanted Jake. The Militia ones had questions, but they were too afraid of Jake to ask. They finally convinced Chaudhari to stand up and ask on their behalf.

"Some of my colleagues wonder if Sergeant Russell will be able to control the Militia properly, they worry about future rebellion."

Jake smiled. "Why not test it out? He's right over there. Walk over and tell him you're thinking of not obeying his orders. See what he does."

All the Militia senators shut up.

The Free Traders bickered, but the biggest problem was the unaligned corp leaders. Finally, one of them stood. "You can't run TGI."

"Why not?" Jake asked. "You don't think I'm competent?"

"Too competent. But also too busy. And you've got too many competing political problems to pay attention to. You'll hurt business. You won't have enough time to deal with our problems."

The Free Traders piped up. "We will have that problem as well. You being emperor is well and good, but we will need our own advocate at the table, and it can't be you."

"Good point." Jake nodded. "Then I'll appoint Mr. Pletcher as acting chairman of TGI. He can deal with your day-to-day issues. He's focused enough."

"You mean mercenary enough?"

"Po-ta-to, Po-tat-o," Jake said. "He'll certainly devote his attention to maximizing revenue, don't you agree?"

They did. They sat.

"What about us?" the Free Traders asked. "We need day-to-day operations as well. But not some slick trader type like Pletcher here, we're more hands on. And we like vigorous debate."

"I understand," Jake said. "Which is more important, the technical trading knowledge, or strength of personality?"

"Strong personality is much more important. If the numbers work, we can all figure that out ourselves, it's when there is competition for resources that we need somebody to make a choice and force us to stick with it."

"Then I see a solution. All I have to do is appoint somebody who knows their own mind." He pointed. "I appoint Ms. Nadine as my representative to the Traders Council. She will arbitrate any disputes."

Nadine stood up. "Jakey, I don't know anything about the Free Traders."

"Your grandmother was part Francais. She was a Free Trader."

"Yes…that's true. But I wouldn't know where to start."

"Hasn't stopped you before." Jake turned to the Free Trader Senator. "What do you think? She certainly knows her own mind."

"Yes, but she just said she can't do it. She's not up to the job."

Nadine bristled. "Listen, Trader boy, I said I don't know anything about you Free Traders, not that I couldn't do it. I can definitely do the job. It's whether I want to. And I've decided I want to."

"But you—"

"Shush!" Nadine pointed at him. "Just Shush. Jake appointed me, and I'll do it. Now be quiet, or I'll have to shoot me a few Trader Delegates."

Jake smiled. He was doing a lot of that today. "Yes. *Pour encourager les autres.*"

"Does that mean 'I like to shoot people'?"

"In a certain context, yes."

The Traders sat. Jake surveyed the room. "Anybody else? Good. Here's my suggestion. You appoint me, Jake Stewart, as Dashi's official heir, and as such the Emperor of the known Galaxy." He stared around the room. "And also, break for lunch after the vote. Could I have a motion to that effect?"

Jake got his empire, and the Senate got their lunch. Jake took over Dashi's old office and planned an industrial renaissance. The *Flandre* had finally arrived in the outer system, days outside the jump limit, but in system. Their main fuel processing plant had broken, and they'd had to use the secondary, tripling fuel processing time. He spent the better part of a day contracting construction projects. With all the factions currently united, they had a good chance of starting some long-term growth projects, and finishing them. These projects had been in abeyance. Long-term growth needed a functioning government, stable markets, and critical materials. Jake's machinations had provided the first two, and the arrival of the *Flandre* would fix up the third.

Crowds gathered outside, and he walked out onto the balcony and gave a speech. He talked about his love for Dashi and his determination to continue his work. He talked about a bright new day for Delta, reconnecting to the Galaxy at large, and the great future in front of them. The crowd cheered. Then he talked for twenty minutes about all the great opportunities in heavy metal trading, and the ways their supplies could be utilized, and how they could use zinc to build a future of prosperity.

Nobody understood any of it, and they cared even less. They cheered, then left him to his business, chattering happily.

Jake called all his representatives back to the office, made arrangements for a coronation, made various official appointments, and set out his plans for the next year.

Pletcher produced a bottle of expensive red wine, which he left for Jake and Nadine to celebrate with. "I'll leave you two alone, I've got a lot to do. Russell?"

Russell stood. "It's good to have direction again. Finally somebody in charge who can think farther than next week." He stood and turned to leave the room, then stopped. "I forgot. You're so self-effacing I forgot." He stamped to attention and saluted. "Sir."

Jake nodded him out. Pletcher stood and followed Russell out the door.

"What's zinc, anyways?" Russell asked in the hallway. "Do we eat it, or what?"

"No idea," Pletcher said. "But I'm buying tons, regardless."

Jake watched them go, then picked up the bottle. "I think this is from old earth."

"Probably," Nadine said. "Very expensive, if I know Pletcher. I'm surprised Vinnie gave it to you."

"Nobody rich enough left to sell it to," Jake said. "It works out well as a gift."

"Aren't you worried about him making too much money from TGI?"

"Nope. There are few ways in which a man can be more innocently employed than in getting money."

"Sounds like a quote."

"Yes."

"Did you have to reward Roi? He's such a weasel."

"True, but now he's my weasel. And is it really a reward? All he wanted to do was sail ships on the ocean, and now he's stuck behind a desk, forever. No ships for him."

"Jake Stewart. He always wins because he gives you want you want."

Jake smiled. "Might as well try the wine." He hunted for a corkscrew.

"Are you worried it's poisoned?" Nadine asked.

"Nope." Jake uncorked the wine. "All the people who wanted this job are dead. The ones working for me don't want it. The only thing they want less than this job is one of their rivals getting it. They're all united in keeping me alive. I'm safe."

"Aren't you upset coming to the… throne I guess is the right name. Aren't you worried about coming to the throne after all this violence?"

Jake poured two glasses of wine and pushed one over to Nadine. "I didn't do any violence. I didn't plan any rebellion. I sold people what they wanted and bought what they didn't. It's not my fault they didn't think clearly enough about the future."

"Well, you've got your dynasty now."

"A reign at least. A dynasty will take more work." Jake held up his glass. "Cheers."

"About that dynasty." Nadine stared at the full wine glass on the table, then slowly pushed it back at Jake. "I won't be drinking that."

"Why not? Its supposed to be excellent. It's certainly unique. This might be the last bottle in existence."

"Might be. I'll never know. Listen, Stewart. We have to talk."

Jake's eyes widened. He stuttered. "Taaalk? Talk about what?"

Nadine put a hand to her belly. "About dynasties."

Enjoying your time in Jump Space? Try my other series, Decline and Fall of the Galactic Empire. Want a free prequel in the Jump Space Universe? Get your free ebook. Liked the book and want to tell your friends? Leave a review here.

Books by Andrew Moriarty

Adventures of a Jump Space Accountant

Trans Galactic Insurance

Orbital Claims Adjustor

Third Moon Chemicals

A Corporate Coup

The Jump Ship

The Military Advisors

Revolt in the Palace

Decline and Fall of the Galactic Empire

Imperial Deserter

Imperial Smuggler

Imperial Mercenary

Imperial Hijacker

Imperial Privateer

Imperial Raider

Imperial Legionary

Join my mailing list and get a free ebook

Thanks for reading. I hope you enjoyed it. Word-of-mouth reviews are critical to independent authors. Please consider leaving a review on Amazon or Goodreads or wherever you purchased this book.

If you'd like to be notified of future releases, please join my mailing list. I send a few updates a year, and if you subscribe you get a free ebook copy of *Sigma Draconis IV*, a short novella in the Jake Stewart universe. You can also follow me on Amazon, or follow me on BookBub, or even follow me on Goodreads or Facebook!

Andrew Moriarty

ABOUT THE AUTHOR

Andrew Moriarty has been reading science fiction his whole life, and he always wondered about the stories he read. How did they ever pay the mortgage for that spaceship? Why doesn't it ever need to be refueled? What would happen if it broke, but the parts were backordered for weeks? And why doesn't anybody ever have to charge sales tax? Despairing on finding the answers to these questions, he decided to write a book about how spaceships would function in the real world. Ships need fuel, fuel costs money, and the accountants run everything.

He was born in Canada, and has lived in Toronto, Vancouver, Los Angeles, Germany, Park City, and Maastricht. Previously he worked as a telephone newspaper subscriptions salesman, a pizza delivery driver, a wedding disc jockey, and a technology trainer. Unfortunately, he also spent a great deal of time in the IT industry, designing networks and configuring routers and switches. Along the way, he picked up an ex-spy with a predilection for French Champagne, and a whippet with a murderous possessiveness for tennis balls. They live together in Brooklyn.

Please buy his books. Tennis balls are expensive.

Printed in Dunstable, United Kingdom

78453887R00150